# Full Circle

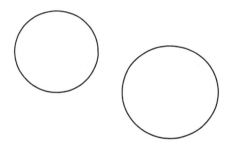

## Sheila Kinston Dean

Beatrice Joseph Publishing

Published by
BEATRICE JOSEPH PUBLISHING
P. O. Box 191383
Boston, MA 02119

Library of Congress Control Number 2003102526

ISBN 0–9729392–0–2

Printed in the United States of America

Edited by Kari Bodnarchuk

*To all those who helped me in any way—from reading my manuscripts and giving me valuable feedback, making referrals on my behalf, and encouraging me through enthusiastic support—to buying this book and spreading the word about it to friends and acquaintances, I thank you, and I love you one and all.*

*Sheila Kinston Dean*

*The author wishes to thank Rosemarie LoSasso and the Foundation for A Course In Miracles for permission to use quotes from the text.*

*This book is dedicated to my niece, Sejal.*

*May she create a life's work that fulfills her.*

*—Aunt Sheila*

*"The opposite of love is fear, but what is all-encompassing can have no opposite."*

—<u>A Course In Miracles</u>.

# One

---

*Boston, Massachusetts*

Terry pulled into the garage on Renaissance Street, across the street from Bay State Hospital. She always parked here instead of the hospital garage because the spaces were larger, with wider lanes that made maneuvering in and out so much easier. She also usually drove up to the roof, unless there was rain. It was just much brighter up there, and she knew that people from the surrounding office buildings could see everything. Some of these large, dark, parking garages made her a little uneasy.

The clock on her dashboard said 9:15. "Good," she thought. "By the time I've packed up my samples and sales materials, the doctors should be in." Not that that would make any difference—whether they were in

1

or not. Most of her targets here would not speak with pharmaceutical sales representatives, and the hospital policy prevented doctors from accepting samples. But the industry continued to flood the market with more and more sales representatives to call on fewer and fewer doctors, who, four by four, were closing their doors to reps. That was the industry's dirty little secret, or one of them anyway.

In the lobby of the hospital, Terry decided to go to the phone bank before going up the stairs to the Corridor—the hallway that joined different buildings of the hospital. She had not checked voice mail since Friday afternoon. Usually, after she got home on Fridays, she would spend two hours or more on administrative tasks. Then she would change for a date with the boyfriend of the month. She would come home around midnight or one o'clock, head to bed, and sleep until ten or eleven the next day. She would have breakfast or brunch, go to the gym for a workout, and either go on another date or do something with her friend Sanaya. On Sundays, she would do laundry and housework, or the shopping. Occasionally, she went to church. By Sunday evening, she barely had time to do the myriad reports that her manager requested, so checking voice mail got pushed to the next morning.

*"That's right. My name is Monday and my time is now. You can't put it off any longer!"* That's what was going on in Terry's head.

Terry felt a wave of anxiety wash over her as she picked up the phone and dialed the 1-800 number to access her voice mail. She felt this anxiety each time she checked her messages, and thought maybe she was just anxiety-prone. She changed her mind, however, when she heard colleague after colleague say they also felt this way. She wondered what the day-to-day stress was doing to her health. Whatever it was doing, she was certain it wasn't good.

"Shit!" Terry thought. She had three messages, the computer voice told her, and along with this information came the familiar pressure in her chest. The first message was a general one letting the field sales force know that it was the last day for ordering medical samples for distribution to the various clinics.

The next message was from her friend and colleague, Geena, who worked on the North Shore. She was wondering if Terry had any of the art deco pens that they'd received as a promotional giveaway. Geena had a customer who wanted some for his teenage daughter.

Then, the final message with the fake cheery voice:

*Good morning, Terry. I hope you had a great weekend. The reason for my call is that I would like to come spend the day working with you in the field tomorrow, Tuesday. So let me know where I can meet you at seven-thirty. I look forward to working with you.*

"FUCK!" Terry said out loud. "What an asshole. Why can't these guys give you some decent notice before coming to work with you?" Then she remembered what a former manager—a sincere person who had remained down-to-earth throughout his career—had told her. Not that he should have been anything but down-to-earth. Terry wondered why people thought they were a big deal when they were hired into pharmaceutical sales, and a REALLY BIG DEAL when they became district managers. After all, the work was pretty humiliating when you got down to it. And if you stayed at the field sales level for more than a year, it grew pretty boring as well.

Anyway, this former manager had told her that it was company policy for managers to sometimes call reps for *work withs* without even giving a full day's notice. It didn't take a rocket scientist to figure that one out—she had in no time at all.

Her day was ruined. Hell, just being out there had ruined it, but now it was totally fucked. She would have to try to get in a reasonable number of sales calls, then get to the car wash, since reps were graded on the cleanliness and orderliness of their cars during *work withs*. In addition, she would have to get to her storage locker before it closed at five thirty to make sure she had her supplies for the day in place.

"How the hell did I end up in this place?" she asked herself. The job had started with so much promise, but turned out to be a dead-ended, glass-ceilinged, doctrine-of-exclusioned bitch of an experience.

Terry took a deep breath, then dialed the voice mail access number again and left a message for her manager, saying she would meet him in the lobby of

Suffolk County Medical Center. At least there you had access to a majority of the doctors.

After leaving the message, Terry gathered herself as best she could and went up the stairs to the Corridor, which she took to the Internal Medicine office. She smiled graciously to the receptionists at each station, and handed them a stuffed toy with her product logo prominently displayed. She could see them warm up to her—gifts had the tendency to make people melt, which is why sales companies spent so much on them.

All of this was to no avail that day, however. At each office, the receptionist would come back and say that the doctor had no time to speak, and no, they do not take literature, nor do they sign for samples. This seemed to make the patients happy. Some of them had started to grumble about having to wait so long after their scheduled appointments to see the doctor. They did not take kindly to having a drug rep come in and take up even more of their doctor's time.

Terry continued down the Corridor to Dr. Jacobs' office. Dr. Jacobs would talk to her briefly on most occasions, but the nurse said that he would not be in for two more hours, and would she like to stop back by around eleven thirty? Terry said she would and left the office.

Next, Terry walked over to two of the medical buildings on Columbus Avenue. She spoke with several doctors about the new antibiotic she was promoting. The sales interactions went very well. The problem was that half of the doctors she spoke to were not on her target list, so those calls were actually strikes against her, even if they generated prescriptions. "A dollar is no longer a dollar is no longer a dollar," she thought.

Terry walked back to Bay State Hospital and Dr. Jacobs was in— "Hallelujah!" She spoke with him at length, which was good because it took her mind off of doomsday (the next day with her manager). Terry left the samples that Dr. Jacobs had signed for and walked out of the office.

By this time, Terry had lost what little appetite she'd had left. She skipped lunch, made as many more calls as she could fit in, and headed to the car wash.

It was while Terry was waiting in line at the car wash that she thought about Tyrone. An idea had begun to form in her head, and the thought of Tyrone seemed to be the catalyst to help her ideas crystallize. The line at the car wash was long—there had been snow the

7

previous day, but now it was sunny—so Terry had plenty of time to map out her action plan. The car wash was one of those automatic drive-thrus, and normally you spoke to the attendant only when you rounded the bend and drove into the building. That day, however, because the line was so long, one of the attendants was going to each car to find out if the driver wanted just the regular wash and dry, the super wash, or the premium wash.

Terry was so deep in reverie, that when the attendant rapped on her window, she almost jumped through the roof. *Jose* was the name on his shirt, and he laughed before apologizing for startling her. Terry rolled her window down and gave Jose the eight dollars for a super wash. Then, when he walked away, she took out her cell phone and called Tyrone. He picked up on the first ring, and she could hear the pleasure in his voice when he heard her. She told him that if he could use two hundred dollars, plus the chance to practice his drama skills, she had a job for him.

"Give me a sketch," Tyrone said to her, and they talked for fifteen minutes about the job.

Terry arrived home around five o'clock. Her home was a cozy brownstone on Claremont Street in the South End. It had three levels of living space, and Terry felt lucky to have it. When she had moved in seven years earlier, real estate prices hadn't skyrocketed yet.

She had been twenty-three years old then, and working as a hospital nurse. There was one patient—Mr. Benjamin—who had been very sick, and who had been in the hospital for about three weeks. Terry had felt sorry for him because he was an old man, with a slight frame that made him appear fragile, and nobody ever went to visit him. She would talk to him during her rounds, and found him to be extremely interesting and very quick-witted. He usually had a funny story to tell, unless he was in a great deal of pain. One day, when Terry went into his room, he was sitting up in bed, watching a sitcom and laughing heartily. She thought it would be a good time to ask a question that had been on her mind.

"Mr. Benjamin, do you have any relatives? Any children or grandchildren?" Terry watched a pained expression march across his face.

"I believe there are only two grandchildren, but I don't really know where they are," he said. "The last I heard, one was in Italy and the other in California."

"That's too bad," Terry answered. "I'd be willing to help you find them, if you want."

"Oh, no, no. I don't think that's necessary at all." He seemed tired all of a sudden, so Terry made sure he was comfortable and went to finish her rounds.

On the day he was to leave the hospital, Terry stopped by his room. She had bought him a pair of pajamas and matching robe, and had them gift-wrapped. When she gave him the box, his face lit up like a child's at Christmas. He opened it right away, and when he saw what was inside, Terry was certain that she could see tears forming. The set was not a blue light special—Terry had spent good money on it. "You shouldn't have spent your money on me," Mr. Benjamin kept saying, but Terry thought that he was pleased just the same.

"Where will you be going, Mr. Benjamin?" Terry asked.

"Home. I'm going home. I have a house in the South End. A visiting nurse will come check on me everyday, so I'll be okay." His speech was a little slow.

"Well, give me your address, so I can stop by from time to time with my nurse's bag."

"Okay, Terry, but there's one request I have to make before I'll let you into my home. Now you know I'm fond of you, but that hasn't stopped me from noticing how much you love needles. And I happen to think that's a little perverse. So I'm going to have to search your nurse's bag before I'll let you in."

"Deal. I promise, no needles. Just a minute and I'll be right back." Terry went out to the nurses' station and got a pad of paper and a pen.

"Okay, shoot," she said, and wrote down the address and phone number.

"Now, I'm going to write down my phone number and put it in this envelope with your instructions from the doctor. If you need some help with anything, call me." The medical assistant came in with the wheelchair. Terry gave Mr. Benjamin a hug, and they said their goodbyes.

Three weeks passed. Terry was working a night shift one weekend to earn extra money. The floor was pretty slow. Most of the staff were sitting in the lounge, but Terry felt that she needed to keep moving. She began to walk the floor and look in on the sicker patients. When she passed the room that Mr. Benjamin used to occupy, she stopped and wondered how he was doing. "Well, I'll just have to go see," she said to herself.

The next morning, a Sunday, she decided to look Mr. Benjamin up. As soon as her shift was over, she pulled out her address book and a map and found his street. The weather had started to get cold, and in New England, that meant gray skies, bare trees, and an overall dullness blanketing everything. Terry just wanted to go home to her little apartment where it was warm and she could curl up and veg for the rest of the day. But she was curious about Mr. Benjamin, and thought she could spare an hour or so detour.

Terry went into the locker room and took her overnight supplies out of her locker. She kept a toothbrush and toothpaste in here, some facial cleansing cloths, and a comb and oil for her hair. She did not straighten her hair, and she usually combed it to the center of her head and tied a silk scarf around it, or used one of those comb-like circular berets to secure it.

Terry stood in front of the mirror, and then decided that she would take a shower. It would refresh her for the detour. She grabbed one of the clean towels from the stack, turned the water on, undressed, and stepped in. The hot water beating against her skin felt so good that she stayed in longer than necessary. When she stepped out, she heard the toilet, which was on the other side of the locker room, flush. Then the smell came, that rotten, what-in-the-world-have-you-been-eating smell. A few seconds later, she heard the door to the locker room open and close. Whoever was responsible for the smell had probably just left.

"I'd be willing to bet that was Kristen the Bulimic," Terry thought. "She's probably taken enough laxatives to make her intestines squeak. Unfortunately, the sludge doesn't smell squeaky clean." Terry took the bottle of perfume that she kept just for these occasions out of her locker and sprayed the air. She put on her street clothes—a pair of tight-fitting jeans and a bulky sweater—and brushed her teeth. Then she felt refreshed and ready for her visit.

Terry took the stairs down to the garage, and walked the short distance to her car—a red Ford Mustang that had seen much better days. She had had it since she was eighteen, and even then it was five years old. Terry had recently started working the weekend night shifts to try to save money for a new car, but now her rent was going up, and that was going to eat up at least part of the overtime money. She hated driving an unreliable car, though, so she was determined to figure something out.

Mr. Benjamin's house was on a side street off of Tremont Street. The place looked a little run down, and there were a few n'er-do-wells standing on the corner, but on the whole, it was not bad. Terry parked in front. When she got out of the car, she got her coat from the trunk of the car and put it on. Then she walked up a few steps and rang the doorbell. She could hear a slow shuffling inside, and after a long period, she heard Mr. Benjamin's voice on the intercom asking who was there. When Terry answered, the door was opened almost immediately.

"Come in, come in," Mr. Benjamin said to her after they had embraced. Terry was struck by how fragile he seemed. His eyes were still alert, and he was still sharp-witted, but he moved so slowly. She was pleased to see that he was wearing the pajamas and robe she had given him. He led Terry through the foyer into the main living area and told her to sit down. Terry took off her coat—it was predictably warm in the house—and, once seated, allowed her eyes to adjust to the dimness. Then she began to look around. Both her eyes and mouth opened wide at the same time, and she stood up.

"Wow! Your home is so unusual and beautiful! May I look around?"

"Yes, by all means. Here, let me show you," and Terry followed him as he showed her the most exquisite items that Terry had ever laid eyes on—an oblong table made from a rare African wood and stone, a beautiful wall clock, first edition books in mint condition, a plush rug with beautiful patterns in vibrant colors, and an old trunk with intricate inlays. She followed him from room to room, each one containing stunning treasures. The house needed some cleaning and dusting, but even so, Terry could see that it had been well maintained. She guessed that Mr. Benjamin had been a spry old man, and had been able to keep things up until he took ill.

"You must have lived an interesting life to own so many rare items. Where were you born, and where did you grow up? I remember your saying you have grandchildren, so I assume you were married. These things look like they came from exotic places, so did you travel to get them?"

"I will answer your questions, young lady. Would you mind fixing us both a cup of tea first? And I believe there are some cookies in there."

The kitchen, which was off to the left as you walked into the house, was large enough to have an eat-in table and chairs, and still have ample walking-around room. There was a heavy, stainless steel teakettle on the stove, and Terry, not seeing a microwave anywhere, put some water in it and turned on the burner.

There were many items of beauty in this old-fashioned kitchen. Terry admired the pedestal table with four matching chairs and cabinetry of the same wood. They were obviously made by master craftsmen. She found a delicate, white porcelain tray containing two cups and a sugar bowl and creamer. Next to it on the counter was a matching canister, and when Terry looked in, sure enough, she found teabags. She yelled into the other room to Mr. Benjamin, asking if he wanted sugar and cream.

"No cream. Just lots of sugar," he replied.

Terry pulled open a few drawers before she found one containing the flatware. She took out a teaspoon, an antique, and spooned sugar into the cups. She added the teabags and hot water, put some chocolate chip cookies on a saucer, and walked back into the sitting room with the tray.

Mr. Benjamin was sitting on a brown leather sofa. The windows were covered with wooden blinds that looked fairly new. The floors were a wide planked hardwood with geometric inlays. Terry guessed that it was maple, but whatever the wood, it was in good condition. She could not detect any scratches. Before she sat down beside Mr.

Benjamin, Terry asked if she could open the blinds a bit.  He told her to go ahead.

They began eating the cookies, which were surprisingly fresh, and drinking tea.  After awhile, Mr. Benjamin began his story:

"I am ninety-eight years old, Terry.  I was born in 1896 in the segregated South, in Wilmington, North Carolina.  Unlike many blacks' parents who had experienced so much pain during the post-slavery years, my parents made sure that I knew our family story.  I was the only child of Martha and Thomas Benjamin.  My parents were both born just after slavery had ended, and they had gone to the school in Wilmington that had been established for blacks.  People back then had so much to contend with, but still they thrived, prospered.  Anyway, my parents worked hard at day labor, domestic work, anything they could find.  My mother even tutored, and she taught music on a beautiful piano that she had inherited.  She used to talk about that piano a lot.  I could see that of all the things she had to leave behind, it was having to leave the piano that made her most sad."

He stopped to eat a cookie before continuing.  His hand trembled slightly as he raised it to his lips and took a bite.  He looked down as he chewed.  His mouth was the only thing that was moving now, the rest of his body still, as if it had been transported, along with his mind, to the past.

"I'm getting ahead of myself," he continued after a few minutes had passed. "Anyway, my parents saved and saved. You see, they had a plan. Many people today don't think far enough ahead, Terry. You should always have a plan, a goal, and be working toward fulfilling it." When he said this, he looked straight into her eyes. Terry sensed that she was getting a lesson.

"In a short time, my parents had enough money to open a carpentry shop. Woodworking was big business back then. Even today, if you go to some of the old black churches in the South, you can find the original, meticulously detailed doors, pews, and what have you, that were done by some of the craftsmen from back then. So my parents had plenty of customers, and they made good money. And so did a lot of other blacks in the town during those days. There were also plenty of black lawyers and doctors, and a black newspaper owner. You didn't know that, did you? It's easy to verify, if you do a little digging. Travel south. Find some old, black people and talk to them." He paused.

"Anyway, the whites in town started to look around and see that the blacks were doing better than many of them, and they got jealous. They decided that they were just going to take for themselves what the black folks owned, and then run them out of town. And they would kill those that didn't leave, if the notion hit them. And that's exactly what they did. It happened in 1898. I was two years old. Many blacks were killed, hunted down in their homes, their churches, and just gunned down in cold blood. The streets and the rivers ran with blood. Blacks hid out wherever they could—in cemeteries, the woods, any hiding place they could find. You can find numerous accounts of this if you do a little research. There is a harrowing, first-hand account of it from the perspective of a black woman, on file at *The National Archives*. Her letter was a plea to President William McKinley to help the black citizens who were under siege. My parents and I were some of the lucky ones—we got to leave town on a train, minus our possessions of course."

Mr. Benjamin paused again. "Are there any cookies left? I don't have an appetite for anything these days except something sweet."

Terry took the tray into the kitchen and refilled the teacups, then added several more cookies. She took the tray back in to Mr. Benjamin and he resumed his story.

"My parents were split about what to do. My father wanted to stay close. He thought the families could move just outside of the city limits, lay low for a while, then regroup and go back in and claim their land and property. My mother said it was no use, that it would take another war to get back what was ours. But Dad didn't want to keep running. He was ready to take a stand. According to my mother, she was not advocating surrender, just a retreat to gather strength and resources so that we would be formidable. She said we had not prepared ourselves this time, because we had been lulled into a false sense of security. Next time, she said, we would be ready. She believed that when you are ready for your enemies, they will think twice about attacking, and more often decide that you are too strong and go on to weaker prey."

Another pause—this time, a very long one. Terry thought that Mr. Benjamin had fallen asleep, and she would have to hear the rest of the story at a later time. Before she could say anything, however, he started talking again.

"My father agreed to go along with my mother's plan. So we rode that train all the way to Annapolis, Maryland. We had some cash because Dad had gone to the bank and cleared out our account when he got wind of what was up. With that money, we were able to rent a row house on Market Street, which was a pretty decent place to live. My parents knew that the money they had would run out in about four months, so again they came up with a plan. Mom said they couldn't get far doing what they had done back in North Carolina, that there was a different energy here, and the people were more progressive. She felt that if we used the same approach, we would just end up near the bottom of the heap. She said she would be damned if she would be on the bottom, fighting other people for crumbs. If she had to fight, she was going to make sure it was something worth fighting for, so she convinced my father to enroll in school at nearby Howard University where he earned his law degree.

"My mother was gifted musically. In addition to playing the piano, she had a great voice. And she missed the piano that she'd had to leave behind. One night, on one of the rare occasions that my parents went out to have fun, they stopped at this classy-looking club called *The Duke*. A jazz band had been playing. During intermission, Mom just got up, went up to the bandleader, and asked if she could sing one set with them. The bandleader thought she was either crazy or drunk, but when she did a mini audition for them right there, they were impressed enough to tell her to come to rehearsal the next day. Now, I've seen my mother perform many times, and I can tell you that she had great stage presence. She could scat and she could sing the blues. Lord could she sing the blues! And rightly so, considering what she'd been through. Anyway, she came back home regaling us with the story of how she had wowed the band. She became a regular singer with them, but she did something beyond that. She signed up gigs on her own, when she did the show solo. And she always had a full house. Martha B. was her stage name, and she became a local celebrity. She cut two albums, which sold decently around the region. That's how my mother was able to support our family while my father got his law degree.

"Anyway, by the time I started school, our family was doing okay, and over the next several years, we started to prosper. That's when we started to travel overseas—when I was about ten years old. And those experiences that I had while traveling helped me to throw off the cloak of oppression. Without them, I doubt that I, a little boy who had had to flee his hometown with his parents, would have had the chutzpah to become an international trader."

Again, there was another long pause, during which Mr. Benjamin closed his eyes. Terry waited patiently for him to resume, but after about fifteen minutes, she thought he really was asleep this time. She got up and carried the tray back into the kitchen. When she looked under the sink for dishwashing supplies, she found that area empty. As a matter of fact, she found that all of the bottom cabinets were empty, so she started looking in drawers and cabinets at waist level and eye level. *Voila!* There was a cupboard on the counter next to the sink that contained all manner of cleaning supplies. Being a nurse, it was easy for Terry to figure that this arrangement kept him from having to constantly bend down to reach or peer into low cabinets, tasks for which the elderly are not well suited. She washed and dried the tray, then went back into the sitting room where she found Mr. Benjamin still sleeping.

Terry started walking around in the room, seeing some things that she had not noticed before. In a corner near the desk that she had marveled at earlier, she saw a guitar case. She wondered if it contained a guitar, but as she walked toward it, she saw something that intrigued her even more. On the desk lay a thick photo album. The condition of the paper and the faded colors beckoned Terry to enter a world gone by. She pulled out the heavy chair that was in front of the desk, sat down, and began flipping the pages. It turned out to be a combination photo album/scrapbook. Each picture had a caption beneath it, with the names of the subjects and a date. There was a picture of a handsome, well-dressed man and woman, with a small boy in between them. The caption read *Martha, Thomas, and Thomas, Jr. – 1902.* There was a picture of Martha standing with a band,

and several of Martha alone at a piano. There were pictures of Mr. Benjamin as an adolescent and as a teenager. There were newspaper clippings with accolades for Martha, Thomas, or both. The photos and clippings had yellowed, but were still in good condition. Terry was flipping quickly through the album, when, on the very last page, a photo caught her eye. The caption read simply *Thomas, Jr. & Eleanor – m. June 16, 1924.* Mr. Benjamin was standing with a woman who looked Caucasian. They were both dressed in evening attire, but to Terry, their smiles looked sad. "What happened to Eleanor?" she wondered. "Did they have any children together?"

Terry looked over at Mr. Benjamin. He had been asleep for more than forty minutes. She went over and moved his feet up onto the sofa, and moved his head down onto a cushion so that now he was lying down. She walked into the nearest bedroom and found a throw, which she placed over him. She would come back to hear the rest of his story another day.

On her way out, Terry took one last look around, and then checked to make sure that the door locked behind her. She walked back out into the cold, started her Mustang, which had decided to be reliable that day, and drove off.

The next week was a busy one for Terry, so she did not get back over to Mr. Benjamin's house, as she had planned. In fact, it wasn't until the following Sunday that she was able to visit. She had worked another night shift, and did not have to work again for a couple of days. After showering and freshening up using her emergency pack, she went out and got into the Mustang. The first time she turned the key in the ignition, the engine made a sluggish sound, but did not fire up.

"This is just what I don't need," Terry mumbled to herself. "Well, at least if I have to get a tow, it's Sunday, so I shouldn't have to wait half a day for someone to come."

The second time she turned the key, the engine started right away.

"Maybe I'll just head home," she thought. "If my car's going to quit on me, I'd at least like to be at home." With that thought, she headed out of the garage and started toward home. Within a minute or so, however, she had changed her mind, and mapped out the route to Mr. Benjamin's house in her head.

When Terry arrived on Mr. Benjamin's block, she found more cars parked on the street than the last time, so she had to park several houses down. As she turned to walk up the path to Mr. Benjamin's steps, she was aware, in a way that was not quite conscious, that things were not the same as before. The house seemed very quiet and closed up. She rang the doorbell and waited to hear that slow, shuffling sound inside, and when it did not come, a feeling of dread came over her. A young boy came out of the house next door, bouncing a basketball.

"If you're looking for the man who lived there, he's dead," the boy said. Terry felt herself enraged by the nonchalant way in which those words came out of his mouth. That man, she wanted to tell him, was a human being. Then she remembered that the person speaking was only a kid—eleven, twelve at the most. He had not as yet comprehended the meaning of death, the finality of it. Terry barely did herself, but still she felt tears forming.

"When did he die?" she asked the boy.

"Sometime in the middle of the week. Wednesday or Thursday, I think."

"Oh. Was there a funeral? Did people come by?"

"I just saw one man there. I don't know about any funeral. You can ask my mom, 'cept she's sleeping now. She worked late."

Terry reached into her purse and pulled out some paper and a pen. She wrote down her name and phone number, and a note asking the woman to call her about the gentleman who lived next door.

"Please give this to your mom when she wakes up," she said to the boy. He stuffed the note in his pocket and walked away, bouncing the basketball. Terry walked back down the street, got into her car, and drove off, feeling that she had unfinished business that may never get done.

Three months went by. Terry never received a call from Mr. Benjamin's neighbor, and she did not make the time to go and try to talk to her. The woman probably didn't know anything about him anyway, she rationalized, and what did it matter now? She had searched all of the obituaries from the week of Mr. Benjamin's death, and even a few days into the following week, but had found nothing. She had almost put Mr. Benjamin out of her mind when she got a phone call early one Friday morning. Terry had been sitting up in bed, reading an article in *Vanity Fair*.

"Maybe it's Cornell!" Terry thought, remembering the date she'd had the previous night. Cornell had taken her to a blues club in Cambridge that Terry didn't even know existed. The crowd was young and old, black and white, enjoying the common bond of excellent music. She and

Cornell had danced and danced. Terry wondered if Cornell would call her again, since that had been their first date.

She picked up the phone. "Hello."

"Hello," said the unfamiliar voice at the other end. "I'm calling for Miss Terry Weeks."

"Yes, speaking."

"Miss Weeks, my name is Nance Taylor. I'm the attorney for the estate of Thomas Benjamin. I'm calling to inform you that Mr. Benjamin amended his will three weeks before he died, and in his new will, he left some significant property to you. I'm wondering if you can come by my office next week so that I can go over the terms that apply to you and arrange for transfers."

Terry was stunned. "Are you sure? I mean, I saw him just a week before he died. I didn't know him that well. Oh, I think I understand. It's probably a piece of furniture or something I admired when I visited him. Or maybe the tea service, the clock, or something like that?"

"Then you can come by my office next week?" Mr. Nance Taylor asked. Terry thought she heard a chuckle in his voice and wondered what it was for.

"Yes, I can, but are you open on Saturdays? Because if you are, I can come tomorrow morning."

"The office is not usually open on Saturdays, but I do want to finalize everything with Mr. Benjamin's estate. Let's make it tomorrow, then. How about ten o'clock?"

"Fine," Terry answered.

"Okay. Ten o'clock it is." He gave Terry directions to his office and his phone number. Before she could ask any further questions, however, Mr. Nance Taylor had hung up.

Since she did not have to work that day, Terry spent a great deal of time wondering about what was in the will. That evening, she called her best friend, Sanaya, and told her about the strange call. Sanaya got very excited. "Oh my God, Terry! What if he's very wealthy and has left you a fortune? You have to call me the minute you find out."

Terry laughed. "Of course, Sanaya, but I don't think I've been left a fortune. The man must have some relatives that he is leaving his money to."

"Terry, that's not your worry. You said yourself that the man was sharp, witty, and alert. So whatever he left for you, he meant for you to have, girlfriend."

Terry thought about what Sanaya had said all night, and did agree that it made sense. She found herself more and more in anticipation of what was in the will. Finally, she was able to fall asleep.

Mr. Nance Taylor's office was on Tremont Street, not far from where Mr. Benjamin had lived. Terry's one-bedroom apartment in Jamaica Plain was less than fifteen minutes away, but in her determination to arrive on time, not to mention her curiosity, she had arrived a full twenty-five minutes early. The Mustang had been running smoothly ever since she'd shelled out $157 the week before to have some work done on it, and she hoped she wouldn't have to put more money into it anytime soon. Maybe Mr. Benjamin had left her a car. Terry kind of doubted it, though. After all, the man was ninety-eight years old. He must have given up his driving license at least fifteen years earlier. However, he could have continued to buy cars and hire a driver. That was definitely within the realm of possibility. The only thing was, he did not mention a driver to Terry, and one certainly did not come to pick him up from the hospital. Anyway, she would soon find out what was left to her in the will, so she might as well stop guessing.

Terry found a parking spot right in front of the red brick building. She decided to go inside rather than wait in her car until the appointment.

She walked up to the building, admiring the mahogany doors with brass plates at the bottom. Terry stepped into a wide corridor with marble floors and walls. A look at the building's occupants showed that Nance Taylor could be found in suite 200. She took the elevator to the second floor. Suite 200 was directly in front of the elevator, and the sign beside the door read:

*Jones, Wooten, Taylor & Hall, P.C.*

*Attorneys at law*

Terry still had twenty minutes to spare, and since Mr. Taylor usually did not come to the office on Saturdays, she thought he might not be in yet. When she tried the door, however, it opened and she walked into a spacious suite, with two sitting areas and a reception area that was unoccupied. One of the chairs near the windows and away from the entrance appeared to offer a good vantage point, Terry decided, so she sat in it. She looked at the magazine rack, but decided she was feeling too much anticipation about her meeting to concentrate, so she turned her attention to the window. There was a good view of the Saturday morning activities on Tremont Street. She was watching two thirty-something guys standing very close and talking, when she heard a door open. She looked toward the sound, and saw that it was an inner door beyond the reception area. An elderly man stood there.

"Miss Weeks, I presume?" and when Terry answered in the affirmative, he motioned for her to come on in.

"Hi. I'm Nance Taylor, attorney for the estate of Thomas Benjamin." He extended his hand, and Terry shook it. "Thank you for coming in today."

Terry stared at him as she shook his hand, as if by so doing she would get some clue as to what was in the will. He looked to be in his late sixties. He was about five feet eleven inches, with a balding head and a slight stoop. He was dressed in dark pants with a white shirt and navy blue, v-necked sweater. Terry wondered if he had been personally acquainted with Mr. Benjamin. He did not appear to view this occasion with any sadness, however. As a matter of fact, he had such a pleasant demeanor that Terry remembered the chuckle she thought she heard in his voice last night. And looking at him now, she saw what she would describe as a chuckle in his eyes.

"So, how long have you known Thomas Benjamin?" Nance asked.

"Not long," she said. "I was one of the nurses assigned to him when he was in the hospital. Did you know him personally?" Nance had turned toward his office and Terry followed him into a smallish room with a desk and two overstuffed chairs. The walls were covered with books and file cabinets. All manner of certificates covered the wall above the file cabinets. There were a few tidy piles of boxes on the floor. Overall, the room had an organized feel to it.

"Not really. He has been one of our clients for many years, but he mostly did business with one of the founders, who recently passed away. That's when I took over his account. You obviously made quite an impression on him. Let's see here," Nance said as he shuffled some papers, peering through glasses that were perched on the tip of his nose. Terry kept her eyes glued to the papers, but there was no way she could read what was written on them from her position. Finally, Nance started reading.

"Mr. Thomas Benjamin leaves to Terry Weeks of 22A South Street in Jamaica Plain, Massachusetts, a three-story, 2,100-square-foot brownstone at 783 Leon Street in Boston, Massachusetts. Said property is free and clear of all mortgages, liens, current-year taxes, and any other encumbrances. Mr. Thomas Benjamin leaves to Terry Weeks all personal property in the house, exceptions noted below." Nance looked up at Terry and handed her a sheet of paper.

"Miss Weeks, here are the exceptions to the personal property that is left to you. They include a rare book collection that go to a local bookstore, and the other items listed there that go to the African American Museum of History."

Terry was beside herself, speechless. Mr. Taylor continued. "He also left a letter for you, which I will give to you as soon as I've finished with the other disbursements."

"Other disbursements? Twenty-three years old. Own a nice house. There's more?" Terry let these thoughts settle.

"In addition to the aforementioned items, Mr. Benjamin has left you a cash amount of twenty-five thousand dollars. I have the check here made out to you, so you will leave this office with substantially more wealth than you came in with."

Terry almost fainted. She took a few deep breaths to regain her equilibrium. She only had about twelve hundred dollars in savings, and maybe another four hundred dollars in her checking account. Her rent was going up, and she needed a new car. She had also been thinking about using a third of her savings to go on a trip next summer with Sanaya. In one morning, all of that had been changed. Someone else would have to pay the higher rent, because now, not only did she not have to worry about it, she didn't even have to worry about a mortgage. And with twenty-five thousand dollars in hand, she could get a new car as soon as she found what she wanted. She knew that her newly found prosperity didn't move her to the ranks of the wealthy, but that didn't stop her from feeling that way.

". . . . .just sign on this line. . . ." Nance Taylor's words were fading in and out. . . . "one more here. . ." "....and here you are, Miss Weeks. The check is in this envelope. The letter that I told you about is in here as well, along with the deed to the house, and a set of keys. I have also enclosed several of my business cards. Feel free to call me if you have any questions."

Terry drove home in a stupor. She could not even remember if she had thanked Mr. Taylor for bringing the good tidings. And now that she was home, she could not bear to open the letter. After all, it was a letter from a dead man—a dead man who had given her a new lease on life. And what had she done to deserve it all? She called Sanaya to come over and help her read it.

Sanaya lived only a few blocks away, so she said she would walk over. Terry kept watch out of her window for her and when she saw her walking up the street, she ran downstairs to meet her.

Terry did not know how Sanaya's mother came to name her daughter, but she did not look like a Sanaya to Terry. She was skinny, but with a to-die-for figure. The two of them had been friends since high school and had seen each other naked in locker rooms and showers. Terry thought Sanaya had the prettiest breasts she had ever seen. But what men chased her for was her ample, firm and shapely butt. Her dark skin was capped by very short, curly (some would say nappy) hair. Terry hugged her and the two of them bounded back up the stairs into Terry's apartment. Terry poured them each a glass of wine, and then Sanaya volunteered to read the letter:

*3 Feb. 1994*

*Dear Miss Weeks,*

*I know you saw the picture of me on my wedding day. Both my wife and son were light enough to "pass," so that's what they did. My wife kept in touch for a few years, then I heard nothing from her. Through some research that I did, I found out that she died some twenty years ago. She had remarried (a white man). I also found out that I have a grandson. He probably knows nothing of his history.*

*This will is air tight, so enjoy your gifts. Remember the lessons I gave you and use your gifts wisely. They represent a lifetime of work.*

*Thomas Benjamin*

# *Two*

---

$\mathcal{T}$erry looked at her phone as she walked in and saw that she had a message from Sanaya. She decided she would return the call the next day. She had too many things to think about. She still was not hungry, but now her lack of hunger seemed to be more from excitement than from anxiety. She walked into her kitchen and made a small salad. The tea service she had used on her first visit to Mr. Benjamin's house was still sitting on the counter, and Terry decided to make some tea. She put a cup on the tray along with her salad. She walked over to the kitchen table and chairs that had also been willed to her with the house, and sat down with her tea and salad.

Terry had been conservative with the money Mr. Benjamin left her. When she spoke to her father about it, he told her not to spend it right away, to sit on it for a while. So she had taken her time shopping around for a car before settling on a brand new Mitsubishi *Galant*. She sold the Mustang for $1,000, and used that money, plus her pre-inheritance savings, for the down payment.

Next on her list was giving her landlord notice, and Terry did that right away. She wanted to be in the house before the first of November to avoid another month's rent. During this time, Cornell called her, not even apologizing for his long silence. When Terry told him where she was moving, he thought she had just found another rental unit. When she told him that no, she was moving into a house that she owned, he was suddenly very interested. He wanted to know how much she had paid for the house, or if she had gotten it at a distress sale. He became very solicitous, even offering to help her move. Terry decided to give him little information. She remembered hearing Oprah say on a show one day, *"When someone tells you who they are, believe them—the first time."* She decided that Cornell was telling her that he was an opportunistic sugar daddy.

Next, Terry had taken out a $30,000 home-equity loan to do a mini renovation on the brownstone. The house had been in excellent shape, but Terry wanted to modernize it—open it up. She accomplished this by knocking down the wall separating the kitchen from the dining area. The foyer was also gone, so when you walked into the house, you could look to your left and see inside the kitchen. There were two columns where a wall used to be. When you looked straight ahead, you saw a combined great room and dining area. Gone were the dark wooden blinds and all of the dark woodwork. The floors had been in such perfect condition that Terry could not bring herself to change them, but she lightened everything else up to compensate. The kitchen appliances, too, had been upgraded. And since real estate prices had been going through the roof in the area, Terry's investment had paid off handsomely.

Having finished her salad and tea, Terry walked up the stairs to her office, which combined with her bedroom and bathroom to form a suite. She had made this area into her private paradise, with expansive views of the courtyard below. She walked past the office to the bathroom, which had an old-fashioned claw-foot tub. Terry had surrounded it with all pampering items imaginable, including the largest, fluffiest towels found anywhere. She liked to take long, relaxing baths, but not that night. She had too many things to accomplish by morning, so she stepped into the shower stall and took a short, hot shower. Then she brushed her teeth, put on her terry robe, and went into her office. Terry was wired, so the steps she had to take the next day came quickly to mind, and she jotted them all down.

Before going to bed, Terry checked her voice mail. Her manager had left a message saying he would meet her in the lobby of Suffolk County Medical Center at seven thirty. When she was typically scheduled to do a *work with*, she would get two, maybe three hours of sleep. That night, however, she set her alarm for five thirty and slept soundly until it went off the next morning.

She got up and dressed quickly. Her bags were packed and at the door; her list on the dining table. She gave Sanaya a call, since she knew that Sanaya was an early riser. She chatted with her for a few minutes, but she didn't give a hint of the day ahead. She did not have time for Sanaya's questions. They would have to be saved for another time.

Then, she called Tyrone.

"Tyrone Brown wishes you a pleasant morning."

"Tyrone, are you all set?"

"Got you covered, my sister."

"Now, play it back to me once more."

Tyrone did as requested. Terry was pleased.

"Sounds great, Tyrone. Your check is in the mail."

"Listen, I've told you that you don't owe me a thing. You're just giving me a chance to practice my drama skills."

"Okay, then. Consider the money a donation to the Tyrone Brown Educational Fund."

Terry hung up and checked her watch. It was 6:15—time to go. She grabbed the bags by the back door and took them out to her car. It had started to rain, but once out of heavy traffic, the rain would not bother her much. When she went back inside, she turned off the heat, made sure all windows were locked and all shades closed, and that most of the electrical appliances were unplugged. She did not know how long she would be gone. She took one last look around, then took the list, along with her purse and the cooler, and locked up. She climbed into her red Mitsubishi *Galant*. It still looked new, since she drove the company-leased car most of the time and kept the *Galant* covered. She put the car in gear, backed up, and drove out onto the street. For the first time in several years, Terry felt free, and that felt marvelous.

# *Three*

---

$T$yrone got up at 5:45 Tuesday morning and turned on the TV to the Weather Channel. He kept the volume low so it wouldn't disturb Robert, another freshman who shared the dormitory suite with him. Robert's bedroom and bathroom were on the other side of the kitchen, but Tyrone knew that Robert had stayed up late the night before studying for his math exam, and he didn't want to take a chance on waking him.

"Today is going to be a wet one in Boston," he heard Natalie Ross say, as the cloud with the dotted lines coming out of it appeared on the screen. A glance outside showed that the rain had already started. "Good," Tyrone thought. "My story will sound that much more credible."

He felt good. He would have done the job for Terry for nothing—he was her fan—but he had to admit the money she insisted on paying would come in handy, giving him spending money for three, maybe even four, weeks. His regular part-time job barely paid for room and board. He was resourceful enough to get spending money when he needed it, usually two to three months worth at a time. He could probably have a little more money by living at home, but he decided that to really excel in college, he needed his own place away from his mom and brother.

The other reason why Tyrone felt good was because he had a chance to do something nice for Terry. He still remembered with such clarity the events of the day they met. He was in ninth grade. Tyrone, his mother Cece, and his younger brother Reginald had moved into the rental unit next door to Terry. It was the best neighborhood Tyrone could ever remembered living in. The triple-decker brownstones were nearly soundproof, and even though three families lived in his building, most of the other houses were single family. His mother had scrimped and saved to get them there, but Tyrone had guessed that the price was going to mean hunger, and he turned out to be right. One particular day, a wintry Saturday, there was no food in the house. Not a bag of rice or grits, not a single egg. Nothing. A peanut butter and jelly sandwich would have been a delicacy. No roaches even dared show up. Tyrone had lived in the city all of his life, but he was leaning toward asking his mother if they could move to the country. At least then, he could learn to hunt and fish. But at that moment, they lived in the city, and they were broke.

When he had gone to bed the night before, Tyrone had been very worried about how Reginald would cope long term. And he was worried about himself and his mother. He saw his studies, particularly drama, as his ticket out. But it was hard to concentrate on an empty stomach. He had lain awake thinking for a long time before finally drifting off to sleep.

Sometime during the night, Tyrone had woken up with the dream he'd just had fresh in his mind. Dollars were falling softly, silently, from the sky. All he had to do was gather them up. He saw himself and Reginald walking around all day gathering up the dollars and putting them in plastic bags that they carried over their shoulders like Santa Claus with all his toys. They took some of the dollars out and went grocery shopping. They came home with enough food to last for a month. They even had enough left to replenish the emergency cash box before dividing up the remainder for pocket change. The dream had been so vivid that Tyrone was tempted to get up right then and look out the window, but he realized this was foolish so he turned over and went back to sleep.

The next morning when Tyrone woke up, his stomach was growling. The beast was contained for the moment, so he pushed it out of his mind. Instead, he thought about the play that his group was producing for his drama class. It was going to be good, and as the group's unofficial leader, Tyrone was very proud of it.

Tyrone and Reginald shared a bedroom, but it was fairly large, with twin beds. Their mother had decorated it nicely. They even had their own bathroom. Tyrone had to give his mother credit. In spite of their poverty, she tried to maintain a sense of style. Tyrone suspected that was her way of keeping her hope alive, and his and Reginald's too.

Reginald was still sleeping. He was two years younger, but he was almost as big as Tyrone, and very muscular. Even so, Tyrone felt a sense of responsibility for him. What were they going to do for the next week with no money for food? Well, at least the house was warm. He was thankful for that, and it wasn't such a small favor.

Tyrone went into the bathroom. The bathroom that his mother used was part of her bedroom *suite*, even though Tyrone thought *suite* was a pretentious word in this instance.

He would just say *bed and bath combination*. But language was something that marketers used very well. And many of them just flat-out lied, if you asked Tyrone.

He brushed his teeth, washed his face, and combed his hair. When he went back into the bedroom to get dressed, he looked around to see if there was something he could sell. His possessions consisted of a CD player and a small collection of CDs, some books, and a few costumes and theatre props that the family sometimes used to put on amateur plays. The CD player and the CDs would bring some money, but his mother would never let him sell them. Also, a part of him knew it was important to hang on to things that brought the family some pleasure.

Tyrone walked out to the family room and stood staring at a picture of the family that had been taken when his father was still alive. Things had been a lot better then. Staring at the picture, Tyrone felt his father speaking to him, telling him that he was old enough now to step up to the plate and do something to improve the family's circumstances. In the background, he could hear Reginald stirring around in the bedroom. Their mother seemed to be asleep still.

Reginald walked into the family room, still in his pajamas.

"Tyrone, let's get the sled out and go to the hill around Jamaica Pond later when there's more snow."

Snow? Tyrone opened the blinds. Sure enough, snow was falling—silently, heavily. And it was sticking. The ground was already covered with about three inches. He felt a sense of déjà vu. That Reginald could think about going out to have fun instead of focusing on his empty stomach almost brought tears to Tyrone's eyes.

"Okay, Reg. Why don't you use the bathroom now and I'll make the beds."

Tyrone made Reginald's bed first. The boys had learned early on that by cooperating fully on their household chores, they could wrap things up quickly and have more free time. When he went to do his bed, Tyrone again had that sense of déjà vu. He was just finishing up when he remembered his dream. Instantly, he became filled with so much excitement that he was giddy.

"Reggie! Reggie!"

He could hear Reginald walking from the bathroom to the bedroom. His face was still wet and he was wearing a scowl.

"Reggie, I know how we can make some money! Come on. Let's get the snow shovels ready."

Tyrone knew he needed the snow to abate before starting the job, and this snowfall did not look as if it would let up soon, hallelujah! He turned on the TV to the weather channel. The snow was supposed to slow up by early afternoon. He sat down to make a list of potential customers. There were several old people nearby who lived alone or as a couple. They would need to have their walks shoveled. The problem with old people, however, was that they were stingy. They would only want to pay a dollar or two for shoveling. Tyrone thought their brains had gotten stuck in the past, because when you talked to them, they only wanted to talk about things that had happened way before he was born.

Reginald finished dressing, and together, they came up with a nice list, with estimated times for each job. He and Reggie could work into the night, if need be, provided they took the time off to buy some food. Otherwise, he doubted they would have the energy necessary to do the work.

Tyrone decided to walk outside to check the snow consistency. He found, to his dismay, that it was the heavy stuff, but the upside was that more people would be willing to pay to have it shoveled.

He was about to go back inside when he heard a car door open. He looked next door and saw the woman who lived there taking something out of her car. She was pretty, and looked affluent. Tyrone even knew her name because the mailman left some of her mail at their apartment one day. He had taken it over and left it at her door. Without giving the idea a second thought, he walked over to where she was standing.

"Hi!" he said. "I'm Tyrone, and I live next door. My brother Reggie and I are going to be shoveling snow as soon as it lets up some. What would you want us to do here, that is if you decide to hire us?"

Tyrone looked at her directly as he waited for an answer. She was fully dressed in her snow gear, but she still managed to look stylish. Now that he had a chance to see her up close, he realized that she was beautiful—kind of exotic looking with her dark skin, sparkling eyes, and perfect teeth. He couldn't see her hair under the hood she had on, but when he'd seen it before, he had liked the funky style that she wore. Tyrone had also sensed that she was kind, and that it was an unusual kindness, at least for this area. He would be willing to bet that she was from a friendlier place—down south maybe, or the West Coast.

Terry looked at him for what seemed like minutes, and it was as if she was trying to look into his soul.

"Oh, wonderful," she said. "I'm Terry Weeks. I'm sorry we haven't formally met before. I have tons of work to do, so if you guys will shovel for me, it would free me up. How much would you charge to do the sidewalk in front of my house, my front steps, and the walkway to them, as well as the driveway back here, and around these two cars?"

"Twenty-five dollars," said Tyrone, figuring he and Reggie could finish the job in about forty-five minutes.

"Deal," she said. Then she said something that made Tyrone think she was telepathic, maybe even an angel.

"I was supposed to have some people over this morning for brunch, but most of them cancelled because of the storm. Only my friend Sanaya will be coming, and that's because she lives close enough to walk. Anyway, I have a lot of perishable foods here that I was planning to cook, so would you guys like a home-cooked breakfast before you start working, or have you eaten already?"

Tyrone was speechless for a minute, but he recovered.

"No, we haven't eaten, and yes, ma'am, we'd love a home-cooked breakfast. I'll go get Reggie. Should we come back right away?"

"Sure, come on back. I don't know if you two know how to cook, but I'm sure there's something you can help me with. And Sanaya will be here shortly. Are your parents home?"

"My mom's at home, but she's asleep. She worked late last night." Tyrone still did not like to say that his daddy was dead. He just hated the sounds of the words. He was glad Terry did not ask any other questions about his parents.

"Well, okay. You can just take something to her for later, if you'd like."

And that was how Tyrone met Terry. He and Reggie filled their stomachs and listened to Terry's friend Sanaya, who kept them in stitches with her jokes and colorful stories. And Terry had given them bacon, bread, pastries, and milk to take home. She had even given them a five-dollar tip for the shoveling. Tyrone had taken it, even though it made him feel guilty. But from that day on, he had decided he would do whatever he could to take care of Terry.

Tyrone decided to make his call from Dudley Square, not only because it would make the story seem more real to him, and thereby improve his performance, but also because he was wary of tracking sophistication. He had even dressed the part, with baggy sweatpants on, and a thick sweatshirt with the hood pulled over his head. He wasn't that tall, about five-ten. He felt that his moderate height made his size thirteen feet more prominent, so he had done his best to make them look as if they belonged in the hood. He didn't wear the expensive brands, but his knock-offs would do fine on just a cursory inspection.

He arrived there at 6:45. Because of the early hour , he did not have to search for a parking place for his *Civic*. As soon as he saw the clerk open the door to *Brothers & Sisters Variety Store*, he got out of his car and walked in. "7 A.M. Good," he said to himself.

He walked to the phone booth over against the far wall. Without hesitation, he picked up the phone, dialed the access code from the phone card he was holding, and then dialed the number Terry had given him.


*Hello. This is John Dunn. I'm out of the office right now. Please leave a detailed message and I'll get back to you as soon as possible.*


Tyrone snickered. Detailed message? Just what details did he want? Tyrone began his message in a voice that was strong and deep, yet disguised. He was deliberately vague:

"Uh, hello. Dis a message from Terry Weeks. She said to call ya. She havin' some trouble, some kinda accident, I think. She say she not hurt, jus shaken up. Says she cain't meet wid ya today." He paused for five seconds. "Bye."

Tyrone had paused after each sentence. He had also taped his message with the credit card-sized tape recorder he had in his shirt pocket. When he returned to his car, he took the recorder out and played the message back.

"Perfect," he said. For him, where Terry was concerned, nothing short of perfection was good enough.

# *Four*

---

*Wilmington, North Carolina*

Jessie got up when the alarm went off and sat on the edge of the bed. These night shifts were turning him into an old man—he felt that literally.

He had gotten home around eight o'clock that morning and made breakfast. When he had finished eating, he showered and then read the paper until he could no longer hold his eyes open. He lay down with an almost audible *aah*. Then two hours into his sleep, a ringing bell brought him up from somewhere down deep. Finally, he recognized the sound as the telephone and groped for it.

"Hello."

"Jessie," he heard his mom say. "Did I wake you?"

"Y e e s s. What's up?"

"I was just talking to Mrs. Anon. You know it's been right hard on her since her husband died."

Jessie thought, yes it has, but five years should give one a chance to adjust.

"Anyway, she said she had to attend a kick-off tonight for a low-income scholarship program. You know, she's the chairwoman for minority recruiting over at the university, and doing a good job, too. Anyway, this is gonna be a dinner function and she needs someone to escort her. I told her I didn't think you had to go to work tonight and I'd ask you 'bout driving her there. She said the whole thing should last only 'bout three hours. It's gonna be held at that new hotel downtown on the waterfront, and you know they serve some good food there. They have that black chef, you know. And there's probably gonna be some good-looking, smart girls there, too."

"Okay, okay. I'm sold. Anything for Mrs. Anon. Is she at the office now? I could give her a call."

"No, honey. She's home right now. I just hung up from talking to her. I know she's gonna appreciate you."

"Okay. I'll call her right now. Bye, Mom."

Jessie didn't mind escorting Mrs. Anon. She was a good woman—an old friend of the family who was always there in a crisis.  He just wished his mother had let him sleep a few more hours.

He called Mrs. Anon, made arrangements to pick her up that evening, and then tried to get more sleep.

Jessie spotted her immediately upon entering the room.  She seemed to be holding court at a table of people who, from the looks of them, made up the diversity panel. She was physically attractive, but it was her aura of self-assurance that made her sexually appealing.  The seating arrangements were such that throughout the dinner, Jessie could gaze at her directly without appearing to be blatantly flirtatious.  He studied the way she appeared to be entirely engrossed in the proceedings, but at strategic moments would whisper something to the person on her right or left, or pass a note to someone seated across the table.

The more Jessie looked at her, the more he appreciated the way she had put herself together.  She had a style all her own.  He could see other people noticing her, as well.

A band took over during a break in the proceedings, and dinner was served. Jessie was barely aware of Mrs. Anon, as she marveled over the various courses. He tried to maintain some semblance of conversation with her, but when he saw the woman he had spent the entire time studying get up and head for the exit, he dropped all pretenses. There were plenty of people at the table that Mrs. Anon could talk to. Without hesitation, he got up and followed the woman.

When he reached the doorway, he paused and looked down the corridor in both directions. The men's room was to his left, the ladies' to the right. If he hurried, he thought, he would run into her on his way back to the main ballroom.

He turned left, and as he walked, he wondered how he could initiate a conversation. Would she be one of those professional women who looked down her nose at the blue collars of the world? True, she wouldn't know right away. He had dressed well. His suit was a few years old, but it was a classic style, expensive, and it fit him well. His shirt was tailor-made, and he was wearing good-quality Italian leather shoes. And he wasn't bad to look at. He worked out regularly, and didn't eat a lot of junk. But unless he planned on lying, sooner or later she would want to know what he did for a living. Lies were okay if you were only looking to have a one-night stand, but for a long-term relationship, those initial lies could spell doom.

"Hello. Jessie Campbell, isn't it?" he heard someone directly behind him say.

Jessie turned. She stood there, his prey, or so he thought until this moment. She was even more stunning up close. And he understood why his eyes had been riveted toward her for the entire evening. She exuded an aura of raw sexuality. The clothes she was wearing, her hair style, the intoxicating fragrance that was so light as to almost be not there, yet you knew that it was—all of these things that when combined, were more than the sum of the parts.

Jessie stood there, enveloped in her fragrance, which was enhanced by his keen sense of smell. He felt himself become aroused.

"Your name is Jessie, isn't it?" she said again.

"Yes it is. How did you know?"

"I read your place card as I passed your table on the way out."

"I find that quite impressive. And you are?"

"Bebe. Bebe Smith."

"Very nice to meet you, Bebe. I must be honest and say that I'd noticed you in there. Actually, I'd done more than notice." He could not believe what had just come out of his dumb mouth. He was sure a warning was going off in her head—*blue collar, blue collar.* Her next words, however, put him at ease.

"Oh, I'd noticed you noticing. That's when I decided to meet you out here."

*Whoa! Talk about the hunter being captured by the game.* He smiled and felt even more at ease.

"So, Jessie, are you anxious to get back to your tenderloin, or can I talk you into going out to the garden for some fresh air?"

"Please, lead me to the garden."

He followed her around the corner, down a long, plush corridor, and out of a door marked with the red *EXIT* sign. As she walked, he watched the way her body moved. He noticed her poise. That lovely butt moved just the right amount. Jessie had the feeling of falling uncontrollably into something mysterious and exciting.

They exited to a garden path and walked for about two minutes to a somewhat private spot that had a bench and a waterfall. They sat on the bench, which was surrounded by flowers that put off a gentle fragrance. The combination of the flowers and Bebe's soft, sensuous smell made Jessie feel as if he had been sipping a very smooth liqueur.

Jessie was now closer to Bebe than he had been all night. He felt as if he were being sucked into a vortex. When he looked down, he could see the clear outline of her breasts in the dress she was wearing.

"So, what brings you to this event? Are you involved in the scholarship program?" Jessie asked.

"Yes, you could say that I'm involved. I'm putting up the seed money to get the program started."

"What?" She had said that without a hint of braggadocio, but her response still left Jessie discombobulated.

"I'm sorry?" she asked.

Her question gave Jessie just enough time to recover. "Oh, I was just hoping to learn more about how you became interested in getting a minority scholarship program going here."

There was a slight, almost imperceptible pause before she answered.

"And so you may. Now, what brings you to the affair tonight?"

"A family friend, Mrs. Anon, needed an escort, since she rarely drives, and never at night."

"Mrs. Anon. That name sounds familiar. Anon, Anon," she whispered softly. "Oh, of course. She works in minority recruiting at the university."

"Yes, she's the one."

"Well, Jessie, I wish I could stay and chat with you longer, but I have to get back inside. Perhaps we can get together later tonight and talk some more. I'm staying here tonight. I had the hardwood floors at my home refinished, and the fumes are too powerful for me. We could meet at the bar, or find a private spot in the lobby."

"Now, that is a superb idea."

She leaned in and kissed him on the cheek. "Okay, then. Come back and ring me after you've taken Mrs. Anon home. Bebe Smith, in case you had forgotten the name."

Bebe got up abruptly and started walking back the way they'd come, hurriedly this time. Jessie was in a fog as he followed her. He was having trouble believing his luck.

They re-entered the conference room, where the servers were removing the plates from the tables, and the officials were getting the stage ready for a continuation of the program. The master of ceremonies walked up to the mike and began to introduce the keynote speaker.

"Ladies and gentlemen, the woman that you are about to hear may be new to the area, but she has taken

Wilmington, North Carolina, by storm. We don't know how long she's going to remain, but I can tell you that if her brief period here so far is any indication, before she's through, the Port City will have one of the most educated minority populations in the Southeast. She comes to us with impeccable credentials, having earned her bachelor's degree in secondary education at Atlanta University. She went on to get two master's degrees, one in educational administration from the University of North Carolina at Chapel Hill, and the other in public policy from Duke University. She worked on the Governor's Commission on Equity in Education during the Hunt administration, where she studied the problems with minority education in North Carolina. It was during her work on the commission that she got a vision of how she could increase the number of minorities who went on to receive post-secondary degrees. Ladies and gentlemen, here she is to share that vision with you, give it up for Miss Bebe Smith!"

Jessie was shocked. While Bebe made her way to the podium, he opened his program booklet for the first time that night. Sure enough, there was Bebe's name listed as the keynote speaker. He felt stupid for the second time that evening.

Bebe took the microphone, and before she relinquished it, she had everyone in the room pulling out their checkbooks and placing contributions for the scholarship program in the envelopes that had been left on each seat. Jessie made a small contribution himself. He had an idea, though, that his one-hundred-dollar donation would be dwarfed by the donations of those around him. But one hundred dollars was all he could afford, if he were to stay within this month's budget.

At the end of the program, Jessie wanted to say goodbye to Bebe and to say that he would see her later, but there were so many people around her, trying to get a piece of her it seemed. He decided that the sooner he could get Mrs. Anon home, the sooner he could get back and spend time alone with Bebe.

Jessie ushered Mrs. Anon out so quickly that she seemed concerned, and asked him if he'd had a good time.

"Oh, it was lovely. I'm glad that you invited me." He opened the passenger door of his Honda *Accord* for her, then went around and got into the driver's seat. Once they were on the road, he decided to question Mrs. Anon about Bebe.

"By the way, I had a chance to meet the guest speaker, Bebe Smith, tonight. Did you know her before tonight?"

"I'd heard of her, but had not personally met her. I don't think she's been here that long. But she does seem to command a lot of attention in administrative quarters."

"Oh? How so?"

"It just seems that her name comes up a lot. And people seem to try to please her, or impress her. How did she strike you?"

"I must say I'm impressed with her, and intrigued. I mean, where did she make her money? How is she able to provide seed money for a project of this magnitude?"

"Is that what she told you, that she is providing the seed money? I suspect . . ."

Jessie hit his brakes hard, cutting Mrs. Anon off in mid-sentence. His only thought as the car slammed into his left rear was that if he'd speeded up instead of hitting his brakes, he would have avoided being hit. "Third strike," Jessie, he thought. "And guess what? This time you're out."

# *Five*

---

*Charlotte, North Carolina*

Sylvia buzzed and Eric picked up the phone.

"Yes, Sylvia."

"You have a call on line one from Bebe Smith. Will you take the call?"

"Yes. Thanks Sylvia." Then, "Hello, Bebe. How're things going?"

"Good, Eric. You sound fine, like things are going your way."

"I can't complain. And if I could, I wouldn't bore you with it. I'm guessing you didn't call just to chat."

"Hey, you know me too well. Listen, Eric. I know you're a tax attorney, but I figure you must have some contacts with plaintiff's attorneys, enough that you can recommend a good one in the Wilmington vicinity?" She made the sentence a question through inflection.

"Why Bebe, are you planning to sue someone? That doesn't seem to be your style."

"First of all, what do you know about my style, Eric? And secondly, no I am not planning to sue. I just have a friend who was in an automobile accident. Not his fault, of course. He was hit pretty hard, and there was enough physical damage that he could use some legal counsel."

"Well, give me time to check with a few of my contacts. Would you like to have your friend call me back, or do you want to give me his name and number so that I can contact him directly?"

"Why don't I call you back, Eric? I'm trying to help my friend as much as possible with the legwork. Would tomorrow be too soon?"

"Let's make it Monday. With the weekend here, I may not be able to get a response back on such short notice. I'll tell you what, I will put in a couple of calls as soon as I hang up with you. Then I'll call you as soon as I get a response. Do call me on Monday if you haven't heard back from me by then. Is it best to reach you on your cell phone?"

"Yes, at 910-799-6243. Thanks much, Eric. Bye."

Eric wondered just what Bebe was up to. She was right, though. He really did not know her style, and she made him more than a little uneasy.

He picked up the phone and called a plaintiff's attorney that he knew. Marcus was not in, so Eric left a message. Ditto for John. He would leave it at that. Even if they were on vacation, or away on business, they would likely get back to him before Monday.

Eric stood up, stretched, and paced the floor a few times, thinking about the trust that he was setting up for a client. Jonas, the client, had an estate worth about six-hundred thousand dollars. He said that although his son, Christopher, was a good kid, he and his wife, Chauntel, did not make a lot of money, nor were they skillful managers of what they did make. He wanted to leave some money to assure his granddaughter a shot at a college education, with a little money left over to give her a start in a small business. Thirty years in a corporate environment, he said, had taught him that that was not the place for most blacks to spend their entire careers, at least not in a mostly white corporation. So he wanted to set up this trust. But he also wanted to spend time with his granddaughter, to teach her some money management skills that he obviously had not passed on to his son. "Must have been too busy working," Jonas had sighed with not a little regret.

Eric started thinking about his own life and work, and about the adrenaline rush he got from building his own business. He was the first family member to own a business of any significance. His gross receipts last year totaled $475,000. He was blessed with low overhead, mainly because he'd had the foresight, many years earlier, before the downtown revitalization project had begun in earnest, to buy the building where he worked. He'd had it renovated, had brought in tenants, and now his mortgage would soon be paid off. He was even thinking about bringing in a partner or two.

How did he come to have the business acumen that he possessed? His mother had had a business of sorts—a beauty shop in a room of their house when he was growing up. But she had never expanded beyond their small community, and eventually gave it up when too many people could not or would not pay for the services.

*Then where?* Eric wondered. He could not put his finger on the answer at the moment. What he did remember was his two-year stint with AtlantiCore Electronics. Eric had gone to graduate school on the West Coast and so had done his internships there. When he graduated, he landed a job with a small, black-owned law firm. Even though he was putting in long hours, he was enjoying his work and learning a lot. Then he'd gotten the call that his father had prostate cancer. The doctors had caught it early, and the prognosis was good, but still Eric wanted to be there to help his mother. He was an only child, and his parents had been very good to him. They had doted on him as a kid, always taking him places, and pulling all kinds of strings to make sure he got the best education possible.

Eric had spoken with Gerald, one of the few white classmates with whom he'd had a genuinely close relationship. Gerald, who had also grown up in the Southeast and relocated to the Los Angeles area, was a sincere, giving person, so when he learned that Eric was looking to move back to the Charlotte area, he put out some feelers. AtlantiCore, he told Eric, was looking to expand. He would get Eric the contact information he needed, but he passed on the warning that the place had a cutthroat reputation.

Almost from day one, Eric knew that he'd made a mistake. He'd gone from working in a supportive, intellectual environment, to one where people would cut you for no other reason than to see you bleed. At least on the surface that's what it looked like. Soon enough, however,

Eric figured out the method to the madness. That was the way people climbed the ladder—by stepping over maimed bodies. Eric looked around and saw how few African Americans there were in the company, and knew that it would only be a matter of time before he became a target. He did not see any sense in spending a significant amount of his time in a war zone and going home shell-shocked each evening. So he scaled back on his workload, and spent the extra time on his exit strategy. He would always remember the satisfaction he felt on the day he handed in his resignation. His property had been fully renovated and was ready for him to move in. His dad had since recovered from his illness, and was able to help Eric supervise the project. Eric had four clients lined up, and he would be interviewing for an assistant the next day.

Eric never looked back. Maybe it was a matter of necessity being the mother of invention. Whatever it was, he was on his way. But he was far from satisfied. Notwithstanding his plans to expand, he wanted to do much more than he was doing to help other young people create more satisfying lives. He believed there were just too many things that kids miss out on if they don't have the proper role models. All they are told is get an education, so you can get a good job—not get an education so you can create a good life for yourself and others. Since his office was located downtown, he was in an area that was fast becoming yuppified. But the underprivileged population had not been completely erased from the landscape, and he knew he had to reach out to them.

Also, Eric wanted the companionship and stability that marriage would offer, but he had no prospects at that time. He had dated Bebe a couple of times, through her initiation. He remembered being manipulated into taking her to a Nancy Wilson concert, with dinner beforehand, and, on another date, to a movie. That last time, she offered to cook omelets at her house, but Eric, for reasons he could not explain, begged off. He told Bebe he had to finish work for a client by nine o'clock the next morning, a statement that was not quite true.

When Bebe got the opportunity to spearhead a scholarship program for low-income minority students, she took it. The position required her to relocate to Wilmington. From what Eric could see, she was performing quite well. She had even talked him into donating twenty-five hundred dollars without his usual due diligence.

Eric thought about the women he'd dated over the past couple of years. He found all of them unsuitable. With Bebe, he was not quite sure why. Maybe it was that she put so much energy into getting him to date her, only to appear disinterested.

When he sat back down, Eric found it difficult to return to work mode. He did what he could until noon, and then decided to take his lunch with him and go for a walk. Sylvia was already on her lunch break, so his other assistant, Ron, was seated at the front desk.

"I'll be back in about an hour," Eric said to Ron, and then walked out of the building onto Tryon Street. He walked four blocks, marveling at the rebuilding that was going on all around him. He wondered how the people who were being displaced felt—having to move and not having a choice about it because they lacked money and clout.

He sat at a bench in the Spirit Square Park. A lot of business people congregated there every weekday to eat, smoke, or just shoot the breeze. He wished he'd brought his newspaper, since he didn't feel much like people-watching. After he finished his sandwich, chips, and water, he decided to walk some more, so he headed to the bakery about a block and a half away. The lunch crowd had started to thin, so when Eric walked into *The Daily Bread,* the normally packed space had a few empty tables. He paid for a cookie and iced tea, and moved to a seat at the window, all the time thinking about the weekend ahead. Maybe he should just go back to the office and pack up his things. His parents were coming the next day, and he wanted to make sure the house was clean, and that there was plenty of food on hand.

He finished the tea and cookie and started to walk back toward his office. About half a block away from the entrance to his building, he noticed a young woman leaving. Something about her made him pay closer attention than he otherwise would have. She was attractive, with an air of self-assurance, but at the same time, she had an unassuming way about her—for instance, in the way she held the door for one of his upstairs tenants. She crossed the street and got into an older model Mitsubishi *Galant*. When she drove off, Eric went into the building and to his office.

Sylvia was back at her desk, and she looked up as he walked in the door.

"Hi," she said. "You just missed a young lady who was here seeking counsel. Maybe you ran into her. She was medium height, slender, wearing a blue dress, and her hair was in twists."

"Oh, yeah. I did notice her outside, but she was getting into her car as I walked up. What type of counsel was she looking for?"

"She said she needed someone to represent her on some employment issues. She said she has been living in the neighborhood for the past two and a half months, and she'd noticed the sign outside. She decided to stop in and see what our specialty is."

"What a coincidence! Maybe I'll have two clients for Marcus or John, or one for each of them. Did you get her name and number?"

"I did," Sylvia said with a slight smile. Amazing how secretaries could read between the lines. "It's Terry Weeks. Her phone number is 704 . . . ."

Eric grabbed the note from Sylvia and looked at the number.

"Thanks, Sylvia. Thanks a lot." It felt a little surreal that he had the name *and* phone number of the woman he had just been admiring.

# *Six*

---

$T$erry got into her car and drove to the cinema she'd spotted a few miles away. She had taken her time making her way from Boston to Charlotte, stopping in Silver Spring, Maryland to spend the two-month holiday season with her family.

Her parents had been so cool, telling her they didn't understand why she had stayed in that job in the first place. They thought she was going to do it for a year or so, just to get some sales training for future endeavors. They knew she was too creative to be boxed in the way she was. What alarmed them, they said, was that every time they called, she was busy writing a report. Besides not being fun, what kind of a job entailed generating so many reports? Unless, of course, you were in a business where the reports themselves generated income. Otherwise, when did you do the actual

75

work that generated income? And how much did they pay her to work so many hours? They contended that a person should add up the hours actually spent doing the job each pay period, then divide the gross wages by *that* number. Then you should go a step further, subtracting necessary out-of-pocket job expenses from that figure, such as the costs of commuting, or the money spent on your wardrobe. Only then, they said, could you get a true measure of how much you are being paid per hour. Once you had that figure, her father said, you could take into consideration what you were learning on the job, and how much value you placed on that knowledge. You should also consider how much pleasure your job is giving you. "As a matter of fact, that should be your first consideration, and part of the due diligence process." her father said. He had spent a number of years specializing in mergers and acquisitions for a brokerage house, and had retained the lingo.

During her visit with her parents, Terry also spent time with her older sister Maya, Maya's husband Brian, and their three-year-old, Monica. She was able to completely relax for the first time in years. Because of her inheritance, and because she had taken her father's money management advice, she did not have the pressure of having to earn money in the immediate future. She could take the time she needed to get into *the natural flow of the universe.* She had picked that phrase up in some yoga classes she'd taken while in Silver Spring.

Once in Charlotte, Terry rented a furnished apartment on a three-month lease. She decided that Charlotte was as far south as she was going, and if she didn't like it, she would trek back north, stopping off first in Virginia. When she had arrived in late January, the weather was still cold, but by late March the spring thaw was well under way. She had one more month on her lease, so she was ready to tie up loose ends before deciding on a permanent move.

Terry had mailed the money to Tyrone before she drove out of town. He would take care of matters—she knew that, so she didn't call him for three weeks. She just wanted to enjoy her freedom. She thought about how Tyrone was always ready and willing to help her with anything. She recalled how he once told her that he thought she was an angel.

"You think I'm an angel? Why?" she'd asked.

"How else could you have known? You know, that day you invited me and Reginald to your house for brunch. You seemed to know we needed that food. It gave us the energy we needed to work. We were going to do one house and then go to the store."

Terry had smiled, grateful for his openness. She explained that when you lend a hand, you don't know how much it means to the other person. You could go through your entire life not knowing. She thanked him for giving her that gift of knowledge.

Tyrone was smart, and a very gifted actor. Terry had helped him get scholarships for college, and he beamed when he opened his high school graduation card from her and found $300 inside. So far, he had done well in school, but Terry told him he needed to take charge of his college experience and create opportunities for himself. That way, he would be farther ahead than most when he graduated.

Terry forced her mind to stop wandering and concentrate on the movie, but she was glad when it was over. Looking at her watch, she saw it was only four thirty. She stopped at *The Green Bar* for dinner, ahead of the Friday night crowd. When she finished eating, it was still only six o'clock. She returned to her apartment and dialed Sanaya's number.

"Hi, girlfriend," Sanaya said in her breezy way. "I just came back from checking on your place. Tell me you're going to rent it out, so I can move in there, with the girlfriend discounts, of course. But I'll tell you, if you sell now you'll make a mint. Real estate prices here are going through the roof."

"Yeah, I know. I'm trying to make some decisions now about my next move. Right now, all options are open. So anyway, how are you doing?"

"I'm okay. I've just been a little tired lately. Maybe I've been working too hard."

"When's the last time you had a checkup?"

"It's been at least a couple of years."

"Then get your butt to the phone first thing Monday and make an appointment. Get a complete physical. And don't go checking on my house if you don't have the energy to do it. I can get Tyrone or Reginald to do that for me."

"Oh, please, Terry. I just said I was a little tired. I'll get some rest this weekend and I'm sure I'll be fine. But I am going to take your advice and get a physical."

"Good. And call and let me know how things turn out. Love you. Bye."

As soon as Terry hung up, there was another call.

"Hello. This is Eric Johnson calling for Ms. Terry Weeks."

"This is Terry."

"Terry, you stopped by my office today. I just missed you. Anyway, Sylvia, my assistant, told me you needed an attorney specializing in workplace issues. As it happens, I'd already had a call out for someone else, so I was able to get the information for you at the same time."

"Well, thank you. You have no idea what a big help this is. Now I can move forward on some things."

"I'm glad I could help. Listen, Sylvia told me that you've only been here for two months. I don't know if you have family or friends here, but if you have no plans for tomorrow, I'm having a cookout in the afternoon. My parents will be in town for the weekend, so I thought I'd put together a coming-of-spring celebration. I've invited John—he's the attorney I called for you, so if you drop by, you can get business taken care of, and enjoy good food and good company. Will you come?"

Terry was taken aback by this invitation out of the blue from someone she had not even met. In the end, she attributed it to being in the South. People here were just friendly and hospitable.

"Yes, I will. Thank you for the invitation." She wrote down directions and hung up. Then she thought about the conversation that had just taken place. Weird, she thought, southern hospitality aside, but she would keep an open mind.

# *Seven*

---

Jessie had just hung up the phone. Mrs. Anon said she was doing okay if you didn't count being emotionally shook up. He had apologized for what seemed like the hundredth time for not getting her home safely. Still, he had a feeling he would not be her escort anymore unless they took a cab or limousine.

Bebe was being so kind. When he called her on the night of the accident, she had rushed right over, helping him with the accident report, and insisting he go to the hospital for x-rays. She was even going to get an attorney for him. She had so many connections. He really felt okay, and thought he didn't need an attorney, but Bebe said that in auto accidents, you never knew when a symptom would show up. She asked him about pain in his back and neck, and when he said he didn't have any, she seemed skeptical. She said she would be surprised if he didn't experience back and neck pain and stiffness. When Jessie thought about it, and began to focus on his back and neck, he realized that indeed they were stiff. Bebe told him he should talk to a lawyer before going back to work, and that she would try to make an appointment for him by Monday.

How capable she was, this Bebe, he thought. Jessie was sitting on his living room sofa, and he leaned back, arms raised and hands folded at the back of his head, legs stretched out in front of him. He thought about the night he met Bebe. He would not have believed it possible that she would have the slightest interest in him, so he was grateful to the point of reverence. After all, the charm he'd possessed when he was in his early twenties was gone. Since he'd been doing shift work, he didn't have the time to get in his regular workouts. Well, on second thought, he did have the time, but shift work did something horrible to his body. He sometimes felt numb after working all night.

But Bebe still liked him. Maybe she could even find a new job for him, he mused. Maybe she had something in her own company that he could do. He would ask her once he got to know her better.

The phone rang and pulled Jessie out of his reverie.

"Hi. It's Bebe. I've got some good news for you."

"Spill."

"I have an attorney who will file a claim for you. He says it's an open and shut case, and if you give him a call on Monday morning, he can get you signed up as a client and tell you everything you'll need."

"That's great, Bebe. You sure know how to handle your business. How much is this attorney going to cost me?"

"Nothing at the moment. I got him to take you on a contingency basis of thirty percent, plus expenses. Don't forget to call him Monday morning."

Jessie wrote down the name and number and they hung up. He was disappointed. He thought he would get to spend time with Bebe, but she had proposals to prepare for Monday. He was guessing he would be away from work for at least another week. Maybe he'd get to spend time with her during that time. After all, she did like him.

Jessie walked to his bedroom. Tucked in a corner, in a hideaway cabinet, was his computer. He turned it on and opened up his personal finance spreadsheet. At that point, his income and expenses were about equal. He seemed to be doing most things right—trying to save and make extra money whenever he could—but lately the income category was barely keeping up. By his calculations, he had enough money to pay all of his living expenses for a little more than a year if need be. But where was the money going to come from to open his gym? His 401(k) money? The IRA's he'd socked away?

He thought of Bebe again. If she couldn't use him in her company, maybe she could help him plan to get what he wanted out of life.

The bandages around his torso had started to itch, but the ten days the doctor said he needed to wear them weren't up. He only needed to wear the collar when he felt stiffness or pain in his neck.

"Wonder how they're gonna react to this?" he heard Ed say. "You can bet they won't be happy." Ed seemed genuinely concerned about Jessie's job security.

"Well, I'm not happy either, so if I can spread my unhappiness to them, all the better," Jessie replied. All of a sudden he was tired of the fear. Ed was a good-hearted man, and if you asked a favor of him, he would deliver over and above your request. But he was trapped in fear like so many of the others at the plant. In that moment, Jessie realized he was free. The others were mentally stuck, but because of his plan, and because of Bebe, he could see a way out.

"Yeah, man, but just be cool 'til you're ready to make your move. You don't want these white folks getting wind of what you're doing, 'cause they will try to cut you off at the knees, man. And that goes for some of the black ones, too."

Ed turned his old Volvo station wagon into the long driveway that led to the offices of *Cape Fear Industrial Works*, or *CFIW* as it was known locally. Jessie could have driven himself, but he thought his injuries would look more authentic if he had someone else drive. He was not looking forward to this, but he could bear it if he just kept his eyes on the prize.

"Do you want me to come in with you?" Ed asked.

"No, man. I can walk okay. It's just that driving requires too much turning of the head and twisting of the body. Just wait for me here. This shouldn't take a long time." Jessie knew his real reason was that he didn't want Ed to suffer any negative fallout from association.

As soon as Jessie walked in, the security guard and the nursing assistant greeted him. They looked very serious and businesslike as they told him that the doctor and nurse were waiting for him. Betty, the assistant, walked him down the hall and around a corner, following the sign that said *Medical*. She ushered him into an exam room where she told him to remove his clothes from the waist up. As soon as he was done, Jane showed up. Since the doctor was off site most of the time, Jane, who possessed an uncanny sense of all things political, had elevated her position from a mere nurse to a powerbroker. She could hand out favors or punishments with equal aplomb. Normally, she wore a cheerful expression, albeit the workers took it for what it was worth. But that day, she didn't even bother with the surface cheerfulness.

"You in any pain, Jessie?" she asked, as she looked him over.

"There's some pain, but a lot of stiffness."

"How did the accident happen?"

Jessie repeated the story exactly as he had told her over the phone. As he finished, Dr. Faustin walked into the room, holding a clipboard.

"So, what's this about your being in an accident? Out racing, huh?"

"No, Dr. Faustin, I was not. I was leaving a fund-raising dinner on Friday night when someone ran a red light and hit me broadside."

"Fund-raising dinner, huh? What type of fund-raising?"

"For scholarships for young people in the area."

86

"Oh, that sounds nice. Have you filled out an accident report?"

"Yes, I have."

"Do you happen to have a copy with you?"

"No, I don't. I can send you a copy, though."

Dr. Faustin started to poke and prod, while Nurse Jane looked on.

"When did you get the bandages and collar?" Dr. Faustin asked.

"That was done on Saturday, after the stiffness and pain had set in," Jessie replied.

"Where did you go? The ER?"

"No, I thought it would be faster to go to a walk-in clinic, so I went to the one on Independence Boulevard. Dr. Perry was the one who saw me."

Dr. Faustin made some notes, and then turned to Jessie. He got up close and stared directly into Jessie's eyes.

"How long did Dr. Perry say you would be out of work?"

"He expects me to be out for ten days."

"Okay. I'm going to approve your pay for the ten days, but before you return to work, I have to examine you again. You'll need to see me one or two days before your expected return date. You can make an appointment on your way out, or call for one later. Keep in mind the physical nature of your job. If you can no longer perform your regular job duties, you may have to be terminated."

While he was speaking, Dr. Faustin kept a steady, penetrating gaze on Jessie. When he made that last statement, Jessie was stunned. He was able to hold on, however, and not let Dr. Faustin see the panic and anger.

"Okay," Jessie said as dispassionately as he could. "I will call back for my appointment. Thank you." *Never let them see you sweat.* As the doctor and Nurse Jane left, Jessie quickly got dressed. When he walked out, Betty and the security guard were huddled together, whispering.

"They give you any flak?" Ed asked as he climbed into the Volvo.

"Shit, yeah. I could feel the ice as I walked in there. Old Faust even threatened my job, and not in a subtle way, either. What they don't know is that I no longer care about that job."

"You don't? Man, what will you do? It's gonna take some time before you get that gym up and running. What you gonna do in the meantime?"

Those questions were exactly why Jessie was in a hurry to get away from there. The average worker was afraid

to make any kind of move unless it was a sure thing, so they just kept living lives of quiet desperation.

"Ed, let me put it to you this way. We live in Wilmington, North Carolina. Let's say that last year you vacationed in Paradise Island, and while you were there, you saw that the people liked drakes. Now, you know how to make drakes, and you know that you can sell drakes to the people there at a profit. On top of that, you were very happy in Paradise Island. So you decide you want to live there. Simply put, you can't live in Paradise Island and sell drakes there until you leave Wilmington."

Ed was silent. After a few minutes he said, "Hey, man, that's deep. That's real deep." He drove on in silence until Jessie asked him if he would be okay eating at a café inside the Cotton Exchange, since Jessie's next appointment was at an architectural firm nearby.

"I'm not paying thirteen dollars for a sandwich and a drink, which is what it'll come to after the tip," Ed replied. "We can just go down to *Amie's* down Barclay Hills Drive and get a full home-cooked meal for half that."

*Jeez,* Jessie thought. "Sure, Ed, you're driving. But I'm paying for your lunch."

"No, man, you are not. I don't take money for doing favors."

Jessie felt ashamed of himself. He had gotten high and mighty over the past couple of days, looking down his nose at Ed and the other workers at the plant. A number of them were just like Ed—generous and humble.

Ed pulled into the parking lot of the diner and he and Jessie went inside. There was a small line in front, and the tables were full. Jessie looked around at the lunchtime crowd. They had streamed in from the surrounding industries, and were a mixture of engineers, line supervisors, and office staff.

The waitress seated them at a window booth, where they could look out at the parking lot. They gave their orders and settled in for a nice meal.

"So when you going back to work?" Ed asked.

"You mean if they let me back? Let's see. My doctor gave me a ten-day leave. I have to go back so ol' Faust can check me out a day or two before returning, but if he approves my return, I will be back on the job a week from Friday."

"So how soon you think you'll have your gym up and running?"

"I'm going to do something in less than a year's time. If I keep saving at this slow pace, I won't have enough money to make the place nice like I want it. So unless I find some outside funding, I'm going to just start small, you know, but try to break even within a few months, and be making a profit within a year. If I can do that, my business will survive."

"Well, if there's anything I can do. . . Holy shit! Speak of the devil. There's ol' Faust in the flesh, with his nurse."

Jessie turned his head to look in the direction Ed was looking. Sure enough, there was Dr. Faustin walking away from a late-model SUV. Right beside him, in what seemed to be earnest conversation, was Nurse Jane.

"Say, if we're lucky, we'll get to hear what they're in such deep conversation about," Ed said. The look on his face, however, suggested that whatever they were talking about, he didn't want to hear, and didn't want Jessie to hear.

The booth was pretty tall, so Jessie didn't think he and Ed would be spotted unless someone was looking for them. As luck would have it, the waitress seated Faustin and Jane in the booth directly in front of them. They took their seats, both checking their watches, and neither bothering to look to see who occupied the booth behind them.

"We'll stay here until they leave," Jessie whispered to Ed. "They seem pressed for time, so I don't think they'll be here that long. We have time to make my appointment."

In front of them, Jessie heard Faustin and Jane give their orders. When the waitress walked away, they started to talk again. They spoke in low tones, but it had to be way above a whisper so they could hear each other over the noise in the diner. This was to Jessie's advantage.

"One thing we can do is pay him with his own vacation time," he heard Jane say. That's well within company policy. I've already checked, and he has three weeks of vacation left, more than enough for his ten-day leave."

"Then that's what we'll do. We'll spare him his job this time, since he's been a decent employee, and Rob said we needed to keep a few of 'em on board, just to keep things looking on the up-and-up. Oh, damn! I told him I'd approve his pay for the ten days he's out."

"Not a problem. He is getting paid, only out of his vacation time. If there are any issues, we can just call Spence in HR, and have it come from their office. Or we could both deny that you ever made that promise. Either way, it's covered."

"Damn, woman. It's good to see you haven't lost your touch."

Jessie and Ed's eyes locked as the two in front of them moved on to more mundane topics. They had both lost their appetites, and sat piddling with their food until Faustin and Jane left. Once they saw the SUV pull out of the parking lot, they paid for their meals, and headed back to Ed's Volvo. Neither of them spoke until they had traveled a few miles.

"Man, those're some lowdown, dirty dogs," Ed finally said. "Can you believe how they just sat in there and plotted against you like that? And they're all in it together, from HR on down, so there's no one you can go to."

"Hey, they can probably smell my ambition. That's why they want to cut me off before I can make it. I don't know why white people are like that, but that's the mentality we have to deal with. And you know what? It's sad to say, but it's not just white folks. Some of us are just like that, maybe not quite as devious. But that's okay. I'm going to make it anyway. White folks have been doing this to us for a long time, and they're not going to change. But we can't let that stop us. We have to do something anyway."

"And did you hear what that scumbag said that Rob said, about keeping some of us on board to keep things looking on the up-and-up? Those low life motherfuckers. I swear to God, Jessie, we can't let this slide. We need to at least pull some of the guys together for a meeting."

Jessie looked over at Ed as he pulled into a parking space in front of the building that housed *G & R Commercial*

*Architecture*. Ed was shaken. Jessie had never heard him swear like that.

"Hey, calm down Ed. This ain't nothing new, bro'. And if I were you, I wouldn't pull anyone together for any meeting. Next thing you know, you'll be left hanging by your damn self."

With that, Jessie grabbed his notebook where he'd written his questions, and got out of the car.

The building was a rather large four-story, red brick that housed a number of businesses, including a beauty parlor on the ground floor. Jessie opened the heavy, mahogany door and stepped inside. The floors were a gleaming, wide-planked hardwood. An affluent-looking blonde was going into the beauty parlor. Everyone in there seemed to look out at Jessie as he walked by.

Jessie spotted the elevators a little ahead to his right. A man and woman in business clothes were standing in front of it. Jessie saw that the *up* arrow was lit, so he stood aside and waited for the elevator to come down. When the doors opened, the well-dressed man and woman got on first and pressed the button for floor three. Jessie stepped on and pressed the button for the fourth floor. The elevator was slow, so there was an awkward silence for a minute or two, then Handsome Couple engaged in some light banter before the elevator stopped on floor three and they got off.

On the fourth floor, Jessie stepped off the elevator into a suite with drafting tables scattered throughout. He stopped to look at pictures of a start-to-finish renovation of a warehouse complex into a shopping center that contained a health club as an anchor. The pictures were impressive.

"You must be Mr. Campbell?"

"Yes. Jessie Campbell." Jessie stuck out his hand and the casually dressed white man gave him a firm handshake.

"I'm Bob Gandolfo. We don't have offices or cubicles here. We just claim a space. Here sit down. Can I get you something to drink?"

"No, thank you. I appreciate your seeing me on such short notice."

"No, problem. Now since you said on the phone that you were interested in opening a gym, and you weren't sure if your space would be a renovation or completely new structure, I put together a packet that will show you samples of our work from both types of projects. I'll give you some time to look through these, and I'll be back in a few minutes."

Jessie felt good about the way Mr. Gandolfo had presented himself so far. He didn't seem to be making assumptions about Jessie's finances or experience. *I'm on my way*, Jessie thought as he began to look through the books. There was one renovation of an old building that took his breath away.

After about fifteen minutes, Bob returned.

"Did you see anything in particular that you wanted to focus on?"

"Yes, very much so," Jessie answered as he turned to the renovation.

"Oh, yeah. This property is in Southport, in a beautiful location right on the waterfront. Naturally, we had to take advantage of the special location in our design, and you can see the result. Look at these before pictures. Unbelievable, isn't it? I will give you the address, in case you want to drive down to take a look."

"Please. I'd like that."

They spent another twenty-five minutes or so discussing the firm's experience, services, and price structures. Jessie left with a folder of information, feeling he had actually begun his project, and that he would figure out a way to move from CFIW, and toward his own passion.

# *Eight*

---

Eric spent the remainder of Friday evening calling to get people to show up at his cookout so Terry wouldn't know he made the whole thing up on the spur of the moment.

First was Guy Pelham. Eric invited him, and then asked if he and Neena were still dating.

"Yeah, man. I'm still hanging in there."

"Good. Then you can bring her with you." Eric was glad Guy was with Neena. This way, he wouldn't have to worry about the unpredictable women Guy could come up with. He remembered the time Guy was dating this woman who was drop-dead gorgeous. She collected souvenirs. The problem was, she neither asked for, nor did she pay for them.

Next, Eric called Pam and Tremain. There was no answer, so he left a message inviting them. He made a mental note to buy enough food for the non-responders, just in case they showed up.

While dialing John DuBois, Eric was thinking John would consider it odd he did not mention this party when they had spoken earlier. But if he was in the least bit curious, he didn't let on. He said he and Deidre had nothing on tap for the next day, but did Eric mind if they brought their five-year-old twins if they could not find a sitter.

"By all means, bring them," Eric answered. Privately he hoped a sitter would be found. It had been a year since he'd last seen the twins, but he vividly remembered the day John had brought them by the house. They were active, to say the least, requiring constant monitoring. And his house was not childproof. Well, he'd have to find a way to deal with it, if it came to that.

His last call was to Andrew Wallace and his wife Vivian. The Wallaces lived next door. They were nice enough, but Eric found them mildly irritating. They were the local braggadocios, but from their tax returns, which Eric prepared each year, they were just blowing hot air.

Vivian picked up on the first ring.

"Hi, Vivian. This is Eric from next door. How have you been? I haven't spoken to you in some time."

Oh, hi Eric. Andy and I are both fine. Always a pleasure to hear from you. How's business?" She didn't wait for an answer. "We've been extremely busy with our real estate. We got listings for two downtown townhouses this week. One belongs to Dr. Marks. You know him, don't you? John Marks, the gastroenterologist? He and his wife are building a huge house out in South Park. They have a three-year-old and another on the way, so they need more room. But that townhouse is immaculate . . ."

"I was calling to see if you and Andrew can come over tomorrow around three o'clock for a cookout." Eric had to interrupt Vivian so as not to be on the phone with her for another hour. "My parents are going to be here, and I've invited a few more couples."

"That sounds lovely, Eric. Maybe some of your young, professional friends are in the market for a house. Yes, that sounds like a great opportunity. I think we can make it, but I better check with Andy before giving you a definite yes. He's always adding to our social calendar at the last minute."

*Social calendar? Give it a rest, Vivian.* Aloud he said, "Oh, fine. Just call me when you've talked to your husband. Even if you forget to call, you can just walk on over. There will be plenty of food."

*Whew!* Eric almost wished they did have other engagements.

Eric had a contemporary house, decorated in a minimalist style. As he walked from his office to the kitchen, he scanned the area. It was two-story, open-spaced, and bathed in light. The maid had been in that day, so everything looked clean and orderly. His concern was not for his parents or the other guests, but only for Terry.

Eric's kitchen was large. In it were two teardrop-shaped, permanent benches that sat behind Plexiglas tables that could be folded away. He sat at one of the benches and made his list of food and supplies. Then he walked back out of the kitchen to the doorway that led to his garage. His SUV was parked in the two-car space. Eric had thought about trading it in for a sports car. Maybe he would keep the SUV, and buy a sports car for Terry.

"Whoa! Get a grip! I hardly know her, yet I'm jumping ahead this way. Why am I so smitten? Maybe she's my soul mate. Hell, I don't know. I just feel something strong." Eric continued with these kinds of thoughts as he backed out and headed for the grocery store.

The *Food World* where Eric liked to shop was six miles away. The parking lot was full. There were a few other stores in the complex, including a video rental shop. When he walked into the grocery store, however, he saw more people than he expected. Many of them looked to be twenty-something. "Why aren't they out on dates?" Eric wondered. "Well, what do I know? Maybe the grocery store is the place to hang out these days, in hopes of meeting someone. At least the lines aren't long yet. I'll try to hurry."

He was reaching for paper plates when he heard a throaty voice behind him say, "Eric? How are you?"

Eric turned, and to his surprise saw that it was Neena.

"Neena, hi. Have you talked to Guy? About tomorrow's cookout?" Eric caught a look of disappointment before she had a chance to make her face into a mask.

"Yes. Yes, I did. Thank you for inviting me, Eric. What's the occasion?"

"It's not really an occasion. My parents are going to be in town, and I just thought it would be a fun way to kick off spring."

"Then you probably need some help. And since I wasn't planning to do anything but go home and watch television, I'm offering you my services."

Her face had suddenly brightened. She was spiffily dressed and groomed. She had shoulder-length hair that was dyed that next-to-blonde color that was so popular with black women these days, and it had a bouncy, just-washed look. Most people would call her pretty, and Eric thought she was attractive. It's just that he preferred a different look and personality. She was wearing a strong perfume, and Eric felt a headache coming on.

"Thanks, Neena. That's so sweet of you to offer, but my mother will be here early tomorrow, and if I know her, she is going to get busy right away."

Neena moved a couple of steps closer to him.

"I'll tell you a secret about mothers, Eric. They go all out for their sons, but secretly, they'd prefer some R&R. So I could just follow you home, and we'll take care of business."

Eric pretended he didn't pick up on the sexual overtones.

"Sorry, Neena. I'm going to spend the rest of the night catching up on the work I left when I ducked out early today. So I'll see you and Guy tomorrow?"

She looked as if she wanted to make one more try, but decided against it.

"Well, okay. But if you change your mind, give me a call. You still have my phone number, don't you? Here, I'll make it easy for you." With that, she reached into her purse for a pen and paper, wrote down her name and phone number, and pressed it into Eric's hand.

"Bye, Eric," she said. She looked him directly in the eyes before turning to walk away.

Eric went about the remainder of his shopping. What was up with Neena, he wondered, throwing herself at him like that? They had never dated. The only thing that had come close was the time he had gone by her office to drop off some papers. He was on his way to lunch, and Neena was getting ready to take her lunch break as well. He invited her to go to lunch with him, since he usually talked to her when he called the office, and frequently had to request her to do this or that for him. The only other times he'd been in her presence was when she was with Guy. As a matter of fact, it was Neena who had introduced him to Guy.

He decided to give her the benefit of the doubt. Maybe she just seemed to be offering herself up for sex. At any rate, Eric didn't play that dangerous game. Besides, he was not interested in Neena.

Eric paid for his purchases, went home and put everything away, and then did some work in his office.

When he finally went to bed, he found himself wondering how he would feel about Terry by that time the next day.

By the time Eric's parents arrived the next morning, he was showered and well under way with preparations.

Eric always felt a pang when he had not seen his parents for some time. It seemed that when he wasn't looking, they just aged. He wondered why grown children weren't warned about the mental shift they have to make from having parents who are powerful and wise to ones they have to look after.

His mom was still spunky, though. She charged into the house after giving him a hug and asked where she could put her things so she could get started. His dad grabbed a cranberry juice from the refrigerator and went out back to set up the grill.

By noon, everything was ready to go. Eric took his parents to the guest bedroom so they could rest for a couple of hours before people started arriving. On his way back to the kitchen, he heard the doorbell ring.

"Surely none of the guests are here this early," he thought. "I hope not, unless it's Terry or John."

He looked at the monitor, and to his horror, he saw that it was not Terry, John, or even a UPS package. Neena was standing there, and Guy was nowhere to be seen.

Eric opened the door. Before he could say anything, Neena offered an explanation. She spoke very quickly.

"Hi, Eric. I had to drive my nephew to his karate class this morning. His mother had to go into the office, and his father is out of town. Anyway, when his class was over, I dropped him off at his mother's office. It's just a few blocks from here. I thought since I was already in the area, I'd come early and help you get things ready. I'll just call Guy and tell him to meet me here."

While Eric was standing there in disbelief, Neena just walked past him. He felt that his brain was on hiatus, and the only thing he could do was watch events unfold. The weather was unseasonably warm for late March, and Neena certainly used that to her advantage. She was wearing sandals—ones with heels, of course—and her toenails and fingernails were shaped and painted. Her hair was fragrant and flowing, again looking just washed. Damn! He didn't know black women washed their hair that often. She had on shorts and a top that, though not so revealing as to look trashy, were revealing enough, just the same.

Finally he felt some brain cell activity. "Sure, Neena. My parents are resting right now, so why don't you start arranging things outside—you know, take out the sodas from the refrigerator and put them in the cooler that is already out there. You'll also have to add ice—you should have enough in the freezer. Cups, napkins, and snack bowls are already outside, but you can start filling the bowls with chips. Let's wait until more guests arrive before setting out the dips. Everything is laid out on the table and counters in the kitchen. In the meantime, I have about twenty minutes of work to take care of."

Eric raced to his office once Neena had gone outside. He found Guy's number and dialed, praying that Guy would pick up.

"Hello," Eric heard Guy say after the third ring.

"Guy, this is Eric. Listen, I was thinking this cookout would be a perfect time to do some networking. There're going to be some attorneys here, some realtors, other small business owners, and just people from many walks of life. Why don't you bring over some samples of your energy bars and drinks, some business cards, and a few of your videos? Also, you could bring promotional literature for your gym or for your personalized fitness programs."

"Fantastic idea, Eric! You know that any chance I get to educate people on how to get fit and stay fit, I'm going to go for it. I happen to have a bunch of stuff here at the house, otherwise I would have to make a special trip to the gym."

"That's great, Guy. Now people have already started to arrive, and I did want to have everything set up, but folks decided to come early. Oh, by the way, Neena is already here. She said something about having to drop her nephew off in the neighborhood. Has she called you yet? She said she was going to. Anyway, can you come right away so we can get this set up before too many more people show up?"

"No problem. I'll be there in about twenty minutes. Tell Neena I'm on my way."

"Okay, brother. Hopefully I can hook you up with a few customers before the day is over."

The two men hung up. Eric went to his office and closed the door. He decided he would wait about fifteen minutes, and then go find Neena. He sat at his desk and started planning his interactions with Terry. God, she looked so delicious to him! He had had crushes before, but this was different. He would let her know he thought she was special, but he would not be overbearing. A little patience might be called for.

# Nine

---

*Tyrone was calling for help. His legs were pumping, but there was nothing underneath. He was falling. All of a sudden, he realized he had a parachute. He opened it, wondering why he had forgotten that he had it. Now the bell was ringing. What bell?*

Tyrone came back to the reality of his room and picked up the phone.

"Hello," he said.

"Tyrone, I need to see you right now. Please, can you come? I'm at the student center. How soon can you make it here?"

"Give me twenty minutes, Yolanda. What's wrong?" Tyrone had a sinking feeling in his gut. Yolanda was the love of his life. What could she be so upset about?

"I'll tell you when I see you." There was a short pause. "I didn't mean to alarm you."

*Didn't mean to alarm him,* she'd said. Well, he was alarmed. He had class in an hour, so he needed to be on time to meet her. He was ready in twelve minutes. He grabbed his books and a jacket and as he was heading out the door, his roommate Robert came in.

"Hi. I'm running," Tyrone said as he brushed past Robert.

"Whoa! Wait up! I saw an ad on the bulletin board that I'm sure you want to know about," Robert yelled after him.

"Sorry. I've got to go. Tell me about it later, or leave me a note," Tyrone yelled as he opened the door that led to the stairwell and bounded down the steps.

When he walked into the student center, he saw her right away. He smiled in spite of himself. Yolanda was one of those women who seemed totally oblivious to her beauty. She was very focused on her studies and all matters social and political. When he walked up to her, she fixed those almond-shaped eyes on him with such a sad, penetrating gaze that he literally felt his chest pressing inward.

They hugged each other, and then Tyrone took her arm and guided her to one of the small conference rooms that were spread along two sides of the floor. He pulled out a chair for her and when she sat down, he sat facing her. Her eyes, usually milky white, were red, with puffy eyelids surrounding them. His heart sank. He took her hands in his and caressed them for a full minute. He had always admired her hands. They were soft and smooth. She never wore the long, manicured nails like many of the other female students. Her nails had a natural beauty, with wide, pink nail beds that were always clipped short.

When he looked up at her, he found her staring with a faraway look in her eyes. After a moment, her face crumpled. She pulled her hands away from him, put them over her face, and started sobbing.

Tyrone moved his chair so that it was side-by-side with hers, and pulled her into his arms. He felt her yield as she put her head on his shoulder. He sat there for several minutes holding her. Finally, she raised her head, rummaged in her purse for some tissue, and blew her nose.

"Wait here. I'll be right back," Tyrone said. He left the small conference room and walked down the hallway to the men's room. He grabbed a handful of paper towels, moistened some of them, and walked back to the conference room.

Yolanda looked relieved when she saw him re-enter the room. Tyrone went over to her and gave her some of the towels. He used a moistened one to clean her face.

"Okay, Yolanda. Whatever it is, you know I'm going to help you deal with it. You know you're not alone. Now, what has you so upset?"

"Tyrone, I'm pregnant."

He sat in stunned silence for a few moments. Yolanda was on the pill, so he thought there would not be a problem.

"Have you had this confirmed?"

"Yes, it's confirmed!" Her answer was sharp. "I went to the clinic this morning. The doctor said I am about six weeks along. I need to make a decision about what to do."

"Hmm. This is shocking."

"Shocking? Is that all you can come up with?"

"Hey, hey, baby. Just hold on. I'm just saying that we've been careful. What happened? Did you miss some pills?"

"No. Well, not technically. But I do remember being several hours late a couple of times. I knew I was supposed to take them at the same time every day. I guess that's what happened. How could I have been so stupid, so careless?"

Tyrone pulled her closer to him and held her tight.

"Look, Yolanda. Let's talk this through. I'm not going to ask you what you want to do right now. I want you to think about that.  Right now, I think you need to rest.  You don't have a class today for three more hours, so go relax as much as possible until then.  My last class is over at five o'clock.  I will pick you up from your dormitory at five-fifteen.  We'll go get a bite to eat and talk.  And remember, we're in this together."  He looked her directly in the eyes when he said this.  "Yolanda, you are not alone."

She smiled for the first time that day.  She felt so unprepared for what she had to deal with, but she was grateful that at least she had Tyrone to help her through it.

Tyrone left Yolanda and headed for his drama class.  He wanted to be on the big screen someday.  He would even go for a television series.  But he also enjoyed being on a live stage and having direct interaction with the audience.  He felt that by learning to write, direct, and produce plays, he would always be able to work in his chosen field, even if he didn't make huge sums of money.

"I have a pressing problem," Tyrone thought, "and I need to find some solutions.  What I'm going to do now is focus entirely on my class—get so involved in it that this thing is pushed out of my mind."  Tyrone knew that by doing this, when he refocused on his problem, a perfect solution that had earlier evaded him, would surface.

Ten minutes into the class, Tyrone was totally focused on what was happening on the stage. The class was Advanced Drama and there were nine students. Each student had to write and direct a small play. Obviously, the play had to be limited in the number of characters and scope, but Tyrone was excited about it just the same. He was trying to learn as much as possible before he got too far into his writing.

The professor was Ary Williams, a fifty-ish woman who had coached some well-known actors and actresses from Hollywood and Broadway. That day, they were talking about the set, and how to use it to create the mood you were looking for. Tyrone was more than prepared for the class. He was fascinated by all the ways a director could set up a scene, and so he had studied well into many a night. He watched teaching videos. He went to amateur plays. He saw every Hitchcock movie. He became so excited about all the creative choices he could make: *Should he use a flat here? A baby spot would work best there. Let's try an apple box in the opening scene.* He had not only mastered the tools of the trade, but he had learned to use them in ways that had not been used before.

When Mrs. Williams asked someone to come up and set the stage for the skit she'd just presented, Tyrone raised his hand. He went backstage and to the room where the props were kept. It took him only a few minutes to find what he needed, and he went to work. When he was satisfied, he motioned for Mrs. Williams to start. Tyrone worked the lights while she did the skit again. This time, when it was over, everyone started clapping. "Very good, Tyrone," Mrs. Williams said once he'd finished his explanation to the class.

"Tyrone, do you have a few minutes. I'd like to talk to you," Mrs. Williams said to him when class was over.

"Only a few, Mrs. Williams. I have a five-fifteen appointment, with only about a five minute grace period."

"This should only take a few moments. Please close the door and have a seat."

"Why does she want me to have a seat if this is only going to take a few moments?" Tyrone thought. Nevertheless, he did as she asked.

"Tyrone, every time this class meets, I become more impressed with your talent and your knowledge and willingness to work. All of my students are good, but you have some special qualities that can take you farther than the other students. Because in addition to all those other qualities, you have charisma, and that is something even the most talented people sometimes lack."

"Thank you, Mrs. Williams. Drama is a very important part of my life, and I guess it shows."

Now Ary Williams lowered her voice. "I'm part of a nationwide initiative to identify gifted African-American performing artists and mentor them. I'm offering to do that for you. I want to work closely with you to help you develop your talents and introduce you to some key people in the industry. Talent will only take you so far, Tyrone, and sometimes not that far at all. You need someone to show you the ropes, someone to tell you how to keep from being bitten by the snakes, because this industry is writhing with them. Sometimes, even the most savvy get bitten, so it's essential to have someone cultivated that you can go to in a crisis. I suspect you know some of what I'm telling you, but you're much too young to know the extent."

Tyrone thought back to the time he had helped Terry by making the phone call. He knew she must have been in a lot of pain. Yes, he thought he knew a little of what Mrs. Williams was saying.

"When I come across a student like you, I try to do everything in my power to help. Also, I get as much out of it as the students do, so it's not all altruism. Now, I have someone with whom I can line up a summer internship for you. I have an application here in my briefcase. I want you

115

to get started on it, and bring it with you to the next class. After class, I'll go over it with you. I will write a letter of recommendation to put with it. And by the way, this internship pays handsomely."

She handed Tyrone the application. Tyrone glanced at it, and then stuck it in his notebook.

"Thank you very much, Mrs. Williams. I can't tell you how much I need that internship. This is the second time in my life that someone has thrown me a lifeline at exactly the moment I needed it."

Tyrone looked at his watch and was dismayed to see that it was five-twenty.

"I'll fill this out and bring it to class next week. Thanks, again. I do have to run now."

When Tyrone arrived at Yolanda's dormitory around five thirty-five, he found her sitting in the lobby looking frantic.

"Baby, I'm so sorry. Mrs. Williams, my drama professor, needed to talk to me after class. She said it would only take a few moments, but it ended up taking twenty. How are you feeling?"

"About the same way I felt when we talked earlier. Come on. Let's go."

They walked the few blocks to a small deli in the symphony area. They each got a salad, some juice, and a cookie, and found a table. Yolanda wasted no time.

"Tyrone, I've thought about this. I love you and I'm sure I'll want to be with you forever. Who knows what this baby will be for us? She could be a perfect baby that grows up to be an amazing adult with many outstanding accomplishments. On the other hand, she could have special needs that we are not equipped to handle. In addition, we want to finish college, and that's expensive. As it is now, you have to work to pay expenses that your scholarships don't cover. My parents are paying all of my expenses, but I don't know if I can count on any help from them once they know that I'm going to have a baby."

Tyrone didn't interrupt the long pause that came next, determined to let her have her say. But he already knew what he was going to propose.

"Tyrone, in spite of all the negatives, we owe it to ourselves to at least think about possible ways of getting by if we married and I have this baby. I mean, there are many…"

"Yolanda, whatever we decide as far as the baby is concerned, there is one thing I'd like to do as soon as possible." Tyrone had jumped in because he had done some thinking as well. "I want to marry you. We want to be together whether we have a baby or not, right? Well, if we do it now, there is no way you'll feel like you're in this alone. Whatever happens with the baby, we'll have each other."

In spite of all the stress she was feeling, a huge grin spread across Yolanda's face and she got up and hugged Tyrone tightly.

"Tyrone, that is so like you. You're a wonderful, wonderful man, and I agree totally with you. I already knew that I wanted to marry you someday. We will just do it sooner rather than later. We can plan for a small ceremony to take place in a few weeks."

"Um, Yolanda. I think the maximum time we should wait is one week. We can get together later tonight to plan."

With that, Tyrone walked Yolanda back to her dormitory. He could see that she felt better. They both knew they would have a tough road ahead. They agreed, however, that with planning and discipline, they could make it work.

When he walked into his dorm suite, Tyrone found Robert sitting in the common area watching television.

"Hey, what's up with you, man? You never let up on the books. What's going on?"

Robert was in pre-med, and the way he studied even then, Tyrone shuddered to think of what it would be like once he got into medical school, and then went on to do his residency. Even though he had not gotten to know Robert very well, Tyrone could see that he was a good brother. What Robert said next confirmed this.

"Oh, I wanted to make sure I caught you when you came in. You were in such a hurry this morning, and I wanted you to know about the ad I saw on the student center bulletin board. It was cut from *Campus Times*. Here. I picked up a copy for you."

Robert handed him a copy of the student newspaper, folded to the ad section. A company called *Pros* was looking for real students to do nationwide college recruitment commercials. Tryouts would be in a month. The ad gave a number to call to get an application. It also gave a post office box address to write for further inquiries. Tyrone's mind kicked into high gear. He shook Robert's hand.

"Thanks, man. That was thoughtful of you, looking out for me like that. I'm sorry I couldn't stop earlier today, but I had a crisis I had to deal with."

"Oh. Sorry. Anything I can help you with?"

"No, no, I don't think so. Not with this. I wish you could." Tyrone went to his bedroom and got paper and a pen. He wrote down his income and expenses. His main scholarship covered tuition, books, and room and board. Two smaller scholarships provided a thousand dollars a year. He used those for emergencies.

Terry had once told him that with his flair for the dramatic, and his charismatic personality, he could sell anybody anything. Tyrone remembered one of his lucrative moneymaking ventures. It was selling knockoff perfumes. He started his junior year of high school and had continued until after the Christmas/New Year's holidays of his senior year. He would work Friday evenings, all day on Saturdays, and most of the day on Sundays. Each hour would bring sales of three to four bottles, for a weekend take of four hundred and eighty to seven hundred dollars. Two holiday weekends of his senior year had brought him fourteen hundred dollars each. One was Valentine's Day, and the other was the weekend after Thanksgiving. At first, he would bring Reginald along to carry packages or scout for customers, and give him ten percent for the effort. Reginald learned quickly, however, and soon staked out his own territory. He and Tyrone opened savings accounts and stashed away money, but they always made sure the cabinets and refrigerator were amply stocked.

The business with the knockoff perfumes was brisk until public tastes changed, seemingly overnight. All of a sudden, people were saying the perfumes were too heavy. They wanted light and natural, and fresh smelling, with names like *Ocean Breezes*, *Spring Rains*, and *Tranquility*. They also began to balk at the prices, even though Tyrone pointed out that generics sold for thirty to forty percent less than the comparable designer labels. Their reply was they never bought the designer labels anyway, but used the store brands of companies like *Bath Expressions* or *Just Fresh*.

Tyrone decided to do some marketing research. He scouted the stores his customers had mentioned. The *Ocean Breezes* and *Tranquility* were selling for ten dollars a bottle in one store. He found *Spring Rains* in another store for eight dollars. Shoppers were walking around with little baskets containing two bottles of fragrant water and often some matching lotion or bath gel. Meantime, in the department stores, fragrance models were handing out samples and begging shoppers to stop at the designer booths. Typical prices here ranged from forty-five to ninety-five dollars and up. This did not look good for his business. He'd noticed that many of his younger customers did not even know what brand name his generic was copying.

Tyrone thought first about starting his own fragrance line, but the more he looked into it, the more he realized he had no passion for giving the world more of what there was already too much. Instead, he contacted *G&L Fragrances* headquarters, explaining what was happening in the market. He received a letter back from the vice president of sales, barely acknowledging his issue. Instead, the letter focused on the sales pitch he should give. He should stress the popularity of the brand, and then focus on the quality of the copycat. He should always demonstrate, the letter said. Let the customer smell. And in a masked acknowledgement of his issue, the VP told him to look for older customers who were familiar with classic scents.

"Great. I should look for little old ladies as customers, never mind that they're still spraying from twenty-year-old bottles sitting on doilies on their dressers?" Tyrone thought when he read this.

Tyrone decided to get out of the fragrance business. Reginald kept at it a little longer before he, too, gave up. But along the way, they had made some money and learned valuable lessons, one of which was to stay abreast of trends. Not that you should be a slave to trends, because there is such a thing as niche marketing. But for fragrance, clothing and such, you needed to be able to adapt quickly.

# *Ten*

---

$T$erry drove up to the house at 398 Robins Way. "Yes, this must be the house. Nice," she thought.

The house was a contemporary that, from the outside, looked very sleek, with a good mix of bright and subdued coloring. There was also the asymmetry associated with contemporaries. Terry saw neither a doorbell nor a knocker. What she did see was a series of colorful shapes. On a hunch, she pressed one and immediately heard the chime of a musical note. She touched a different one and heard a different note. Fascinated, she was about to press yet another of the glass shapes when the door opened. A tall, handsome brother was standing there. He had the kind of looks and carriage that made Terry stammer and forget her name.

"Hello, Terry. I'm Eric Johnson. I know who you are because I saw you as you were leaving my office yesterday. Come on in. My parents are visiting this weekend so you can meet them. I can introduce you to the other guests as well. I take it you don't know many people in town yet?"

"You are so right. Thank you for inviting me. I haven't socialized since I've been here."

Eric ushered her in. Terry looked around as they made their way to the back. She marveled at the home's architecture. There were tall ceilings and enough windows of varying sizes and shapes to play wonderful tricks with the lights. Late March was still usually bleak in Boston, so the brightness made Terry feel giddy.

"I love your house, Eric. How long have you had it?"

"Thanks. I'm glad you like it. I've been here for little more than two years now. Once the party winds down, I can show you around."

There were already numerous people outside milling when Terry and Eric moved to the backyard. They walked up to an elderly couple, and Terry could see some of Eric in both of them.

"Terry, please meet my parents—Louise and Philip Johnson. Mom, Dad, this is Terry Weeks. She's new to the area."

"Hi, Mrs. Johnson. Hello, Mr. Johnson." She shook hands with both as she said this. They gave her warm handshakes, but it was Louise Johnson who seemed to be the more interested in her.

"Oh, you're so cute. And you're not married, I see. Good. We want Eric to settle down with a good woman. And you're not all made up like so many young women today, like they've got something to hide. Honey, you get my vote. Where were you living before moving here?"

"Mom, I'm sure you're embarrassing her, since we just met a few minutes ago."

"Oh, no, Eric. It's okay. I was living in Boston. I'm from Maryland, originally. My parents live in Silver Spring. My best friend and I went to Boston to go to school, and we stayed on after graduation."

"Well, that's very interesting, because we lived in Boston for a short time. I taught in the Boston public schools about twenty-five years ago. I was appalled at how bad the schools were, and at the inability of anyone who gave a damn to do anything to fix things. It was such a shame. I left after two years. We moved back home, and have been here ever since."

Then it was Philip Johnson's turn.

"Yeah, the schools were bad, but there were some clubs around where you could hear some good blues and jazz. *Wally's* in the South End used to hop. I don't think anything like that goes on anymore."

"Oh, I've heard of it, and I've gone by on Saturday nights and it's been packed. But I don't hear of any good entertainment being there now."

Eric stepped in then.

"I'm going to have to deprive you of Terry's company now so I can introduce her to the other guests." He took her arm and steered her away as she said to his parents that she enjoyed talking to them, and would see them later. She liked them and really was looking forward to talking to them some more.

As Eric steered her toward another couple, he bent over and whispered to her.

"These are my next-door neighbors. Whatever you do, do not allow yourself to be cornered by these two. They will hold you hostage in a one-way conversation."

Terry soon found out what he meant.

"What do you do?" both Vivian and Andrew asked in sync as soon as the introductions were made. Terry guessed they were asking how she made her living. She decided she might as well have fun with this.

"Actually, I've been traveling the country trying to decide where to settle."

"Oh." They looked at her with renewed interest. *How does she get to do that? Is she wealthy?* Terry imagined these thoughts were going through their minds. They quickly got back to their favorite topic of discussion, however—themselves.

"Both Andrew and I are in real estate," Vivian Wallace said. "Three years ago, we formed our own company and never looked back. We recently ventured into downtown and currently have two listings for townhouses there. One belongs to a doctor and his wife. They're building a huge house in South Park. They have a three-year-old and one on the way, so I imagine they need more space. Anyway, their townhouse is immaculate and very well designed. And if you're planning to stay in the area, you couldn't go wrong by looking at it. We could set up a showing for you right now."

"I haven't decided just yet, Vivian, if I'm going to make my stay here permanent, but please give me one of your business cards. I'll call you when I'm in the market for a house." If there was one thing Terry hated, it was a pushy salesperson. After all, she had seen enough of them in her former line of work. As soon as she took the card, Eric steered her away.

"See what I meant?" he asked.

"I do, but I don't think your warning was strong enough. It's good you have a garage, Eric, so you can at least get in and out without being fair game."

Eric laughed at this. Did he laugh that easily, Terry wondered, or did she have something to do with it? They seemed to have developed an easy rapport. She took a long look at him. He was really cute, but didn't seem at all stuck on himself. He must not be dating anyone, or she would be here, wouldn't she? Besides, his parents had said as much. And he did seem to be paying a lot of attention to her. She realized she was at a disadvantage, though, being in a new town and not knowing anyone she could call up and ask, *"Hey, do you know Eric Johnson? Yeah? What's the scoop?"*

Terry heard one of the musical notes from Eric's doorbell.

"I hope that's John DuBois. He's the attorney I called for you. Why don't you come with me, Terry, and we'll see?"

Terry followed him back inside and to the front door.

"John," Eric said, as he shook the man's hand and gave him a hug. "And the lovely Deidre. How are you both? And where are those precious twins?" Deidre was indeed lovely, and to Terry, she looked half John's age.

"We're both doing fine, Eric. We were ready to pack the twins up and bring them when Deidre's sister called and volunteered to baby sit. Just out of the blue, she did this."

"Yeah," Deidre said. "We were shocked, because Francois has said on more than one occasion that the twins are too much for her. Well it turns out she's on this mission to find one person each day she can do a good deed for. Today was our day. God bless her."

Terry thought the look on Eric's face was of sheer relief. She made a mental note to ask him later.

"John, Deidre, this is Terry Weeks. Terry, John and Deidre DuBois. John, Terry, I'm going to leave you two alone for a few to discuss business. Deidre, come on out and let me introduce you to the other guests."

This time it was Deidre who followed Eric out to the back. Terry and John sat in the living room, and John pulled out a legal pad.

"So, Terry, I hear your doctor gave you a prescription for sunshine."

"Yeah, that's right. And I may have found the perfect weather mix right here. No more long, bleak winters, but I'm hoping the summers are bearable."

"They are. And the reason they are is that you cannot buy a house or a car here that is not air-conditioned. It's a local ordinance. Now, why don't you tell me the basics, and how you need my services?"

John looked to be around fifty. He seemed self-assured—capable, and Terry felt he was a good fit. She told him how she had left her job one day, that she had sent a letter requesting a six-month personal leave of absence the day after she'd driven off, and that her leave had been granted. She said that now she just wanted to tie up loose ends, return all of her former employer's equipment, have him look over her benefits, and make sure she received any money or other benefits due her.

"This seems fairly simple, Terry. I just need for you to answer a few questions. Are you still covered by the group health insurance?"

"Yes, I am."

"Now, how are your premiums being paid?"

"The cost is being borne by the company now to be deducted from my pay when I return to work."

"Okay, good.  So you can get signed up to continue your health insurance under COBRA.  COBRA stands for the Consolidated Omnibus Budget Reconciliation Act of 1985.  What this act does is guarantee you the right to continue your former employer's health insurance at the level of your participation when you left.  You can get this coverage for up to eighteen months, but you have to pay the premiums, and they are pretty steep.  You can expect to pay a little more than two hundred dollars a month, and more if you include dental.  Now what about life insurance?  Do you have any through your employer?"

"No, I have that on my own.  I was able to get a much better deal that way."

"Wonderful.  I think it's a shame that people tie all their benefits to an employer, as if they're going to be with one company for the rest of their lives.  So you were smart to do that.  And I'll tell you a nasty little secret.  Many of these corporations provide employees with the option of buying life insurance through the corporate group rates.  But what they don't tell you is that the corporation is buying life insurance on you as well.  And guess who the beneficiary is?  Not your spouse, children, mother, father, sister, brother, or even friend, unless of course, it's a family-owned business.  It's called COLI, or corporate-owned life insurance, and the corporation is the beneficiary. The policies for rank and file employees are called janitors' insurance, and it remains in effect even after you leave the company. Picture these guys searching the social security database looking for evidence of your death so they can collect. But anyway, I'm getting off track. When you're on the clock, I don't charge you for my meanderings. Now how long were you with this company?"

"Five years before going on my leave."

"Good. It's likely, then, that you're vested in benefits, such as matching 401(k) contributions, or defined benefit pension plans, if you have one. Those are rare these days. Did you have a pension plan?"

"No. Just the 401(k) plan."

"Hmph. It figures. Okay, why don't you come by my office on Tuesday at ten o'clock? That okay with you?"

"Yes, that's fine. Do you have a business card with you?"

"Sure. Here you are. Now, I'm assuming you have someone back home checking your mail and taking care of things for you."

"Yes, yes, I do. So if there's something that you need, because I brought very little with me, I can have Sanaya or Tyrone send it to me."

"Good, good. Have them send the latest benefit descriptions or handbooks that you have. On second thought, have them send ones from the last three years. Now my fee is usually one hundred and ten dollars an hour, but since you're a friend of Eric's, I'm going to give you a reduced rate of seventy dollars an hour. I don't anticipate this taking more than two, possibly three hours, because everything should be pretty standard and automatic. I'm basically acting as a go-between for you."

"Okay, that's fine. I'll see you Tuesday morning at ten o'clock. Thank you."


Terry needed to find a bathroom. Not knowing the layout of the house, she walked toward the rear, on the lookout for a bathroom as she walked, and hoping she would recognize it as such. She admired the house some more as she passed through.

There was a hallway off to the left, so Terry decided to follow it. The hallway was very wide, and there were original paintings along the wall. Terry didn't recognize the artists, but she loved the art. There were no other decorations or furniture in the hallway——just the gleaming wood floors and the paintings on the walls.

Halfway down the hall, she noticed that a door was ajar. She peered inside. Sure enough, it was a bathroom, beautiful though it was. It was not huge, but with the light colors and almost floor-to-ceiling windows, it maintained the feel of the rest of the house. Terry went in, closed the door, and imagined herself taking a luxurious bath in here. She took a deep breath in and let it out slowly. She felt good.

While she was washing her hands, Terry looked at herself in the mirror. She had lost twelve pounds since the day she'd left Boston. She felt healthier and lighter, not just from the weight loss, but more so from the absence of stress. She liked the way she looked without those extra pounds. Her thick hair was done up in twists, and she wore little makeup. She was surprised that people still commented on how beautiful her skin was. The shorts, T-shirt, and slides that she was wearing were several years old. Terry's new, carefree look liberated her in more ways than one.

When she finished up and opened the door to the bathroom, she was startled. There was a woman standing right outside the door. Terry did remember seeing her outside, but they had not been introduced.

"Hi. I don't think we've met," the woman said. Terry guessed she was late twenties, early thirties. What stood out to Terry was her almost blonde, shoulder-length hair. "I've been so busy trying to keep everything in order that I haven't mingled properly. My name is Neena."

"Hi. I'm Terry." *What did she mean, she's trying to keep everything in order?*

"Are you finding everything enjoyable? I wasn't in the mood to set anything up last night, so I told Eric I would help him this morning. I think things turned out well."

"Oh, it's a great party. And you're the hostess? Eric didn't mention that."

"Oh, no. I wouldn't exactly call myself the hostess. Eric and I are just *very* good friends, and he knows he can call on me to help him whenever or wherever he needs it."

"Hmm. Then he should at least give you more credit. Well, the bathroom's still okay, so you don't have that to worry about. I'm going to rejoin the party. Do you think you'll get back out?" With that, Terry turned and walked away, not waiting for an answer.

"I think Neena's tripping. If she and Eric are an item, why didn't Eric say something, or give some kind of clue? And Eric's mother hinted that he should consider settling down with me. Besides, I haven't seen him say anything to her since I've been here." Terry realized the tacit acknowledgment of these thoughts: She liked Eric a lot.

# Eleven

---

Neena stood and watched Terry walk away. "Uh-uh. This little skinny, northern bitch might think she's going to be some competition. But just wait until she sees what I've got in store for her, and she's not even going to see it coming." It wasn't in Neena's character to consider the appropriateness of such thoughts.

She went into the bathroom and closed the door. Just as Terry had done only minutes earlier, Neena took a deep breath in and let it out. She loved this house, and Eric along with it, of course. He was so good-looking, she thought. She could almost feel her naked body underneath his. He'd been playing hard-to-get, but she was determined to get a grind on with him. And once he had a taste of her, it would be easy to get him to the altar. She wasn't worried about that. That was one advantage to having Guy in constant pursuit of her—free access to a gym. And she made sure she did the pelvic tilts/buttock lifts every time. That was the euphemism for the vagina squeeze, but Neena could understand why that name wasn't used. After all, how awkward would it be in a coed aerobics class for the instructor to say, *"Now, let's do some vagina squeezes."* What would the men think?

Anyway, she had it all together in that department, so Miss Terry need not think she was going to interfere with her plans. She had better just pack up her stuff and get back in her car while it was still winterized and head back north.

Neena splashed water on her face, and then took one of the towels from the open shelf beneath the basin. She looked at herself in the mirror as she dried her face. Her eyes looked a little tired, but her hair was still bouncy. Maybe she should pull it back in a ponytail, she thought. A lot of men found that sexy. She was really glad she had lightened it since it made her skin look lighter.

Next, she looked down at her body and sucked her stomach in. That's one thing she noticed about Terry—that she had a flat, flat stomach. How old was Terry, she wondered?

"I'm not getting any younger here," Neena thought, "so if I want Eric, I need to start playing my best cards now. Like my mom always told me, 'Time and gravity are a woman's worst enemies.' And when they start to do their thing to me, I want to have Eric firmly planted by my side."

Neena decided that she would do the ponytail after all. She pulled out her makeup kit from her purse and found a hair band and a brush. She liked the effect. It made her neck look longer. Looking at it, Eric would probably imagine removing the ponytail band and watching her hair fall loosely around her face. *"How sexy am I?"* was the expression on her face.

When Neena walked out of the bathroom, she was ready to put her plan into action. She was certain, no matter how Terry tried to play it off, that she had planted the seeds of doubt regarding Eric. She needed to get to Terry and plant some more seeds. Then if she could manage one seemingly intimate moment with Eric, in full view of Terry of course, that would cinch it and send Miss T running.

When she emerged from the house, Neena saw that she could not have created a better scenario if she had written it herself. Eric was standing talking with his parents. Terry was a little distance away talking to those hideous neighbors of Eric's, but she was facing them. "Okay, Neena," she said to herself, " you're on."

She walked up to Eric, his mom, and dad.

"Mr. and Mrs. Johnson. Do you mind if I steal Eric away for just one minute? There's just a small matter I need to speak with him about."

Neena could see that once she won Eric over, she would have to put in some work with his parents, too. They didn't seem at all thrilled to be relinquishing their son to her. She steered Eric a short distance away.

"Listen, Eric. Guy would kill me if he knew I was discussing this matter with you, so promise you won't mention it to him." She waited, but Eric didn't say anything.

"Eric, please, you have to promise."

"Okay, Neena. I promise."

"Now I recognize that Guy has a good business, he's dedicated, and he works hard. But he could use some help with taxes and accounting. You know he started this business doing everything himself, but it's grown fourfold over the years, and he hasn't given up control in areas where he should delegate. I mean, he does have someone keeping his books, but to me, that's just what she is—a bookkeeper. He needs someone who is in the advice business. You know, someone with a higher level of sophistication."

"Oh. Is Guy having problems, Neena?"

"I'm not saying he's having problems. What I'm doing is asking you if I could get Guy to agree, would you show him services you could provide that he's not getting right now?" Neena had moved very close to Eric, in the guise of being in a conspiratorial huddle.

"Of course I'm willing to talk with Guy. But it needs to be something he wants to do. I'll tell you what. If Guy calls me, I'll arrange to meet with him. Or even if he indicates to me in conversation that he needs my expertise, I will go forward. How's that?"

"That's good, and that's all I'm asking, Eric."

"Well, then, why don't you go talk to him right now, Neena? That way, he might broach the subject with me before he leaves, and we could get some of the preliminaries over with today."

"Eric, thank you. I know that once Guy starts to work with you, he'll want to kick himself for not doing so earlier. I'm sure you know you have a great reputation."

"Neena, you flatter me too much. But do see if you can talk to Guy before you two leave today." And with that, Eric turned around and walked away. Neena was a little disappointed with his abrupt departure, but she had accomplished her mission.

# *Twelve*

---

Eric wondered if anything had happened. He thought he had connected with Terry, but she seemed chilly all of a sudden. Now that he thought about it, she had not been the same since talking to John DuBois. When she came out of the house, she had walked over to Vivian and Andrew. Eric thought maybe she had not seen him. He went over to rescue her, but she would not allow herself to become disengaged from his neighbors. Finally, he had walked away, thinking he would find John and ask him how their conversation had gone. He found him talking to Pam and Tremain, who had shown up after all.

"John, may I speak to you for a minute." By this time, Eric was so off center that he said nothing to Pam and

Tremain, who were standing there and giving him a quizzical look.

"I hope you guys are having fun," Eric said to them, recovering somewhat. "I'm so happy you could come. Do you mind if I borrow John for a minute or two?"

"Of course not," Tremain answered.

"Eric, you look a little unnerved. Is there something wrong?"

"Oh, I was just wondering about your conversation with Terry. Will you be able to help her?"

"Absolutely. There's really not a lot for me to do. On the surface it looks that way, anyway. Surprises have a way of showing up, however, in seemingly routine matters. Anyway, I hope that's not the case here."

"So everything went well then?"

"Yes, Eric. Everything went well. I'm even giving her a discounted price since the referral came from you. Now what are all these questions about?"

"It's just that Terry's been acting weird since she came out of the house. I don't think it's my imagination."

"I have an idea, Eric!"

"Yeah? What is it?"

"Just ask her. Is there any reason why you can't walk up to her and ask her what the deal is?"

"Hmph! No, I guess not. Okay. I'm going to do that."

"Good luck, man." John turned and walked back over to Pam and Tremain with a broad grin on his face.

Eric looked around for Terry. He saw her standing alone, getting a drink from the cooler. Andrew and Vivian were saying their goodbyes. He would go speak to Terry first, and then go say goodbye to his guests. Besides, if he knew his neighbors as well as he thought, their goodbyes would take another half hour.

As he walked up to her, Terry was turning around, holding a bottle of water. He took her arm and looked her directly in the eye.

"Terry, I'd like to show you around the house once all the guests are gone. Do you mind hanging out here for a little longer? Then afterward, we could catch a movie, or I could show you a little more of the city, whichever you'd prefer."

Eric tried to sound as sincere as possible without pleading. Terry looked at him, stared at him, Eric thought, with wide, questioning eyes. Finally, she answered him.

"I would like to see the rest of your house, Eric. I love what I've seen so far. And a movie sounds good as well." She smiled, and Eric grinned a wide, second chance grin. He felt relief and joy.

"Then that's what we'll do. Please make yourself comfortable either inside or out here. Everyone should be gone shortly." He moved a chair over to where she was standing. "Would you like for me to bring you something to drink?"

Terry just smiled at him and held up the bottle of water she was holding.

"Oh, sorry. Well, can I get anything else for you?"

"No. Please, Eric, go attend to the other guests. I'm going to pitch in and help get things cleaned up. That's okay, isn't it? I mean, I won't be stepping on anyone's toes, will I?"

"No, of course not. Believe me, my mother will be glad for the help."

"Okay, then. I'll just go over and ask your mother what she wants me to do."

Terry walked away. Eric stood and watched as she went up to his parents, and after a brief conversation, they started to gather up the party spoils. He did not see Neena standing back watching in a jealous rage. If he had, he would have known that he needed to take much firmer steps with her than he had earlier in the day.

# Thirteen

---

Jessie had spoken with John DuBois that morning. The conversation had gone well until Mr. DuBois asked Jessie how much he wanted. Jessie was stumped. He hadn't figured that out—he had sort of thought the attorney would give him suggestions.

Finally, he told Mr. DuBois that he would call him back. As soon as he hit the flash button, he dialed Bebe's number, praying she would be in.

"Hello, Jessie," Bebe said.

"Hi, Bebe. I was wondering if you are available for lunch or dinner today?"

"Lunch, no. Dinner, yes. You must be feeling better."

"Yes, I am, thank you. I'm planning on returning to work on Friday. Can I pick you up at six?"

"Six o'clock will be fine. Did you speak with John today?"

"Yes, I did and I'd like to discuss some of the things we talked about with you."

"Great. I'll see you at six, then."

When he hung up the phone, Jessie's mind went into overdrive. First, Bebe could clue him in as to how much he should be compensated by the other driver's insurance company. As for the gym, he could start with a small one. He had already crunched the numbers on how many members he would need, plus the per-month charge. He had analyzed the pros and cons of offering lifetime memberships to get more startup capital. He had surveyed the gyms in the area as to their sign-up fees, monthly dues, specials, facilities, equipment, hours, and staffing. He was still playing with his plan. He had even investigated a franchise, but found that it was too much money for the franchiser and not enough for the franchisee. He thought he could do better by educating himself as much as possible, and using his own network of friends and co-workers to get started.

How much money could he make by working with Bebe, he wondered? In addition to the money, Bebe seemed to have so many valuable contacts. He would ask her about all this. The more time he spent with her, the more dissatisfied he became with his own life. He decided he had to make a change.

Bebe lived in a gated condominium community, one of many that had sprouted up along the highways leading to Wrightsville Beach. What made her community unusual was that it consisted of loft-style units. You could expect to see this downtown, perhaps on the waterfront, but not in the suburbs. Jessie drove up and gave his name to the attendant. Bebe must have just called, because he immediately waved Jessie in, with directions to where she lived.

When she opened the door, Jessie, as always when he saw her, melted. He followed her to the living area just off the foyer.

"I'm impressed with your home," Jessie told her as he looked around. "Did you use an interior designer?"

"Oh, thank you. Actually, I did the design myself. I was lucky in that the furniture I already owned was a good fit. I had some minor renovations done, and worked a lot with colors. I have a friend who specializes in window treatments. He flew in and we discussed what I wanted. He took measurements, went back to his shop and made these, and flew back here to put them up. I can't tell you what a relief that was. And he didn't charge for his labor, so it didn't cost any more than if I had used someone locally."

Jessie walked around. Contemporary was not a big player in Wilmington, especially the severe industrial type of contemporary that Bebe favored. It was a good thing she had the furniture she wanted, because she would not have found these pieces locally; probably not in the entire state or adjacent states. But she had managed a sleek, sophisticated look. The air smelled clean; almost fragrant. He found Bebe's scents intoxicating.

"Just let me grab a jacket, Jessie. I never go to a restaurant in the summer without a sweater or jacket, no matter how hot the temperature outside is."

As he watched her walk to her bedroom, he had the same enchanted feelings as on the night they'd met. On that night, he had anticipated exploring her body. It was so exciting! Since that time, though, she seemed to be cooling towards him. He was glad he was going to talk to her about his plans for the gym. Once she had a glimpse of his ambition, she might show some renewed interest.

"Take your time," Jessie yelled to her. "I'll just look around some more."

In the brief time Jessie had to look around, he noticed an impersonal look apart from the design, which many people would consider cold. There were no family pictures or other personal effects. There was nothing you could look at to give you deeper insight into Bebe Smith and what she stood for. Jessie started to remember something that had nagged him earlier, but just then, Bebe walked out.

"Ready?" she asked.

"Yes, I am. I wanted to try the new steak house that just opened on College Road. The restaurant review said the food is good and the portions huge, and I am a very hungry man. Is that okay with you, or is there someplace else you'd rather go?"

"No, no. That will be fine. No matter where we go tonight anyway, without reservations we can expect a long wait."

"She's right. I should have made reservations," Jessie thought. "I don't even know if this place takes reservations. I should have chosen someplace that does." Jessie was feeling out of his league.

As it turned out, they did not have a wait. Once they were settled and the waitress had taken their orders, Jessie broached the subject of the insurance settlement.

"When I spoke with John DuBois this morning, and he asked me how much to ask for, I had no idea. I mean, how do you figure something like that?"

Bebe looked at Jessie for a few seconds before answering. Sometimes Jessie had the feeling she was sizing him up.

"That's a very good question, Jessie. Let me give John a call and ask for his suggestions."

"Thanks. That's a good idea. I should have done that myself." He said aloud what he knew Bebe was thinking.

"If I can get a decent settlement, I may be able to open my gym sooner than I thought. I've been saving for it for three years now, and I'm still nowhere near having the money I'll need. I don't want to do this shift work for many more years. Actually, I don't want to do it for *any* more years. It's killing me." He paused as the waitress served their salads.

"That's great, Jessie! That you're planning on opening a gym, that is."

"Thank you. Hmmm. This is fresh. High marks so far." Jessie had started to eat. Bebe had barely touched her food.

"Anyway, Bebe, you think you can find anything in your company for me to do, either part time to earn some extra money, or full time?"

Bebe jumped right in, as if she had already given this idea some thought.

"Well, let's just analyze your situation. You've already made a good start, one that many people never make. You know what you want to do and you have a plan to get you there. So maybe it's the execution you need to work on. You've been saving for this for three years, you say? And in those three years, exactly how much have you put aside?"

"A paltry sixty grand," Jessie stated. "I need at least four times that." Jessie actually had only fifty grand, and he'd been saving for four years, not three.

"Maybe not, Jessie. Do you know where you want your gym to be located? And do you plan to rent a space, buy and renovate an existing building, or build from the ground up?"

"I have a location in mind. I've also spoken with an architect, and he told me that it generally costs less to renovate. In addition, with a renovation, I can get my office set up sooner, depending on the condition of the building, of course. Renting would be a last option, since that would put me at the mercy of a landlord. A significant rise in rent at a time when cash flow is low could put me out of business."

"I agree with you one hundred percent. So what we need to do is get you that location for as little money up front as possible. After all, you're going to have to invest heavily in equipment. Now I'm going to throw out some ideas, such as a temporary lease to get your membership built up and to raise capital, so you have more to go to a bank with. Or you could find a distress sale and do a lot of the work yourself, if you're handy that way. Ask friends and family for help. Get some silent partners. The point is, with a little creativity and careful planning, we can get you what you want."

Jessie nodded and gave careful consideration to every idea Bebe threw out.

"And maybe, Jessie, we need to think about how to get more return on your money. How do you currently have it invested?"

"Just in mutual fund money market accounts, and treasury bonds and bills. I didn't want to be in anything risky." Jessie wished he could mention more sophisticated investments, at least a few sexy sounding stocks, but he decided he had done enough stretching of the truth for one evening.

"Well, you've certainly met that objective," Bebe said. "Now, don't get me wrong. There's nothing wrong with your investment choices. It's just that they are more conservative than what you need to be doing right now to get the kinds of returns that are going to help you realize your dreams."

"What are your suggestions? The market has been dismal lately, and since I'm going to need the money soon, I've felt it is too risky a place to put my money. I mean, I don't have a ten-year horizon."

"Jessie, those are very good points, and you're right on target. For someone who is not on the inside, so to speak, and does not have access to the real information about what's happening with a particular company or sector, it is very risky indeed. But there are people, myself included, who are making money during these turbulent times. And since you're a friend of mine, there is absolutely no reason why you can't be one of them. Did you know that I own an investment company?"

"No. I had no idea." Jessie looked at Bebe with even more reverence. "So is that how you've been able to seed the scholarship program? You're a self-made woman? Is that it?"

Bebe laughed. "I can't claim to be self-made. We all get help along the way. But when you know what you want, which you do, Jessie, and are not afraid to act on your plans, you too can be self-made."

She paused to eat a few forkfuls of her spinach salad. Only after she had swallowed the last bit did she resume the conversation.

"I'll tell you what I will do for you, Jessie. Invest your money with me—all of it or any portion of it on which you want to achieve maximum returns. When you get your insurance settlement, you can invest that as well. Now, I cannot guarantee your returns, but what I can tell you is that for the past six months when all of the major indices have been in negative territory, some of it double digit, my investments have had returns of thirty percent or more. Why don't you come by my office this week, and I can show you some of the investments in my portfolio. And although my company is small, I have clients from all over the world."

"Bebe, it looks like you've got it going on, and I would love to check it out. How about tomorrow?"

"Tomorrow will be good for me. If you come at eleven o'clock, we can talk at the office, and then continue over lunch."

"Eleven it is, then."

"Now, you asked me if I had something you could do on a part-time or full-time basis. Well, think about this overnight. My scholarship business is growing, and it's becoming difficult for me to handle all the work. I need someone to go to all the high schools in a four- or five-county area to make sure guidance counselors, principals, teachers, students, and parents know about my general and regional scholarship programs. I need someone to make personal contacts to obtain student data, like names and addresses, parents' names and addresses, grade-point averages, courses of study, and financial information on the family."

Bebe lowered her voice to a whisper.

"In addition, I need someone to solicit donations for the regional scholarship fund. Donations into this fund are pooled according to region, and only students who live in that region can apply. Now, I do solicitations by mail as well, but often, big donations come from the personal contacts. I have lists of people who donate to these types of causes, and believe me, a personal solicitation can work in ways that no letter can. Don't worry. I will give you the proper phraseology, and your looks and personality will take you the rest of the way. Any interest so far?"

"That's an understatement."

"And you haven't heard the best part yet. You could go back to your old job and do this part time. But frankly, I wonder why you would choose that route. You go full time, I will pay you twenty percent above your current salary, plus fifteen percent of the donations you bring in. Then, once you're up and running on your own, which will take about six months, I will increase that to thirty percent above current salary. Take some time and think about my offer. Frankly, I don't see what there is to think about."

Jessie could hardly believe his luck! Not only was Bebe going to get him thirty percent or more on his savings and investments, where he currently was getting three to four percent, but she was also giving him a chance to make at the very least thirty percent more money than he was currently making.

They finished dinner and Jessie drove Bebe home. Emboldened, he asked to come in. Bebe was the sexiest woman he had ever known. But he was not going to get any closer to her that night. She said she was working on a project that had to be completed by eight in the morning. She would only get about three hours of sleep as it was. Jessie would have begged, since his desire had done away with his pride, but he saw it was no use. He would have to content himself with dreaming about how much sooner he would be able to open his gym.

## Fourteen

---

Guy, having just pitched his gym, fitness products, and personal training services to the only person he'd missed that evening, turned to look for Neena. That's when he noticed the way she was looking over at Terry. It was an unguarded moment, and no amount of dressing it up later would convince Guy that it was anything other than what it was—envy almost to the point of hatred.

One reason Guy had achieved success was that he had an uncanny ability to accurately size up people and situations. He was not one to be oblivious to what was going on under his nose. As he watched Neena looking at Terry while in the grips of pure jealousy, he felt sad. He cared about Neena, but she would not or could not reciprocate. And that flimsy excuse she gave for coming over without him, and early, of course, was just embarrassing. He turned and walked over to where Terry was standing.

"Hi. I'm Guy. Eric didn't introduce us, but I understand you're his new lady."

"Oh, God, no! Actually, I just met Eric face-to-face today."

Guy studied her. She was very pretty, but what was most appealing about her was her seeming lack of guile. This sister was *real*.

"Well, Terry, you may have just met Eric face-to-face today, but the brother is tripping over you. Take my word for it, because I know we sometimes have a problem letting a woman know. I'm an observer of people, and I don't think Eric's had his eyes off of you for more than two minutes the whole afternoon. I see why, too. I can tell that your inner beauty matches or even surpasses your outer beauty. That's rare. Eric's special like that, too. The brother is for real. You would do well to remember that."

Guy started walking away, over toward where Neena was standing, and he could feel Terry watching him. When he reached Neena, he put an arm around her, kissed her, and then pulled her along toward where people were saying their goodbyes. Then, just to make sure he had quashed all misunderstandings, he steered Neena over to where Terry was standing.

"Neena, have you met Terry? Terry is Eric's special guest. Terry, this is my date, Neena."

Terry extended a hand, and Neena shook it.

"Oh, we met earlier," Terry said as she shook Neena's hand. "I'm glad you had time to make it back out."

Guy almost said *come again?* but decided he really didn't want to know what that comment was about. All he had to do was look at Terry, who wore a look that suggested, very slightly, that Neena was on the lowest order of the human chain.

"Neena, I was just telling Terry how much I think Eric likes her. I don't think she was aware of it."

"Why wouldn't she be aware of something like that Guy, if it's true?"

"I don't know, sweetheart, but I'm sure she will before the night is over. Let's get out of here. We want to give them more time to clear up misunderstandings." Guy winked at Neena when he said that. "Come on baby. I'll follow you."

Guy followed as Neena walked toward the people saying their goodbyes. He could tell she was pissed, and if not for the fact that he was hurting so much, he would be amused. She was practically running toward her car. He caught up with her, grabbed her, and turned her around.

"Whoa, whoa. Not so fast. Why are you in such a hurry?"

When she looked at him, she was wearing a smile most insincere.

"The night's still so young, Guy. I thought I'd hit a few dance clubs."

"Then let me escort you, my dear," Guy said, and then did a little two-step. "A beautiful woman should not go to these places unescorted. I'll follow you home, then you can join me in the Corvette."

"You mean you don't have to work at one of the gyms tonight? Okay, since you don't, I'll take you up on your offer," Neena said, and then slid into her car—a black Toyota *Solara*. She started the engine and took off before

160

Guy could get in his car, which was parked on the street just behind her.

"I need to find me a real relationship," Guy muttered under his breath as he started the Corvette and quickly caught up with her. He wanted to slow down, but Neena was tearing through the residential streets, doing running stops at all the stop signs.

"I'm going to slow down," Guy thought. "If she decides not to wait for me at her home, then so be it." That decision made, Guy started driving a few miles above speed limit. This gave him some space to think, and he started remembering the time he first met Neena. His infatuation with her began as soon as she walked into his gym about two years earlier. She was a looker, and she made it clear that she was only interested in men of means. Once she found out he owned the gym, and was not simply the manager, she had agreed to go out with him.

Guy was under no illusions that he was handsome, but he worked out religiously, wore tailored clothes, and walked like a man who knew where he was going. Plenty of other women in the gym flirted with him, and most of them he'd managed to resist. He wanted his gyms to maintain a professional reputation, and if word got around that he was up for grabs for the hottest women in town, he would just be working against himself.

But he had fallen under Neena's spell. They started dating, and he even thought he was falling in love with her. It didn't hurt that the sex wasn't bad, either. He had even begun to feel guilty that he was hitting Amber on the side. Then, all of a sudden, Neena was unavailable. At first, she avoided him—not returning his phone calls, and not going to the gym. Finally, she'd called him and asked to meet with him. He had agreed, albeit with a knot in his chest. Sure enough, she lowered the boom. She had met someone else and it was serious. Guy didn't want to know the details.

He rarely saw Neena for the next few months. He would see her in the gym working out every now and then. When they had begun dating, she simply stopped paying her gym dues, and she didn't resume when their relationship ended. He thought about sending her a past due bill, but decided against it. He guessed he was hoping things wouldn't work out with the new guy and she'd come back to him. He would keep the lines open for the time being.

Sure enough, Neena's other relationship ended. The first thing Guy noticed was that she started showing up in the gym more often. And she kept bumping into him. When he finally asked if she'd like to go to dinner with him, she jumped at the chance. Just like that, she was back.

"If I were a crying man, I'd be shedding tears now," Guy muttered under his breath. "I'm industrious, my business is doing well, and I'm not that bad looking, albeit a little on the short side. No matter though. Neena just can't love me. I've wined her and dined her, taken her to Hawaii for a week, and let her work out at my gym for free. In spite of all that, all Eric has to do is say the word, and she would drop me in a nanosecond."

Finally, he reached Neena's apartment building, half expecting her not to be there. When he pulled up in front of her building, however, her *Solara* was parked in her space. He got out of his car, walked the few feet to her door, and rang the doorbell. He stood there for about a minute and was about to ring again when she opened the door.

"Hi," she said. "I was just freshening up. I'll be about twenty more minutes."

She had come to the door wrapped in a towel, having just stepped out of the shower. And she looked good—very, very sexy. Guy thought it should be a crime for a woman to pull a man's strings that way. He sat in her small living room, picked up a magazine, and waited.

After about a half hour, Neena emerged. She had on a very short, very tight red dress, with black stiletto heels and a small black evening purse. Her hair was done in an upsweep, and her lips had been outlined and filled in with a pouty red combination. When Guy walked over to her, he smelled the sensuous body oil she was wearing.

"Wow! I'd be content to stay here and do some dancing in your living room. What do you say?"

"I don't think so, Guy. I want to be out tonight with the other club-goers, you know. I can feel myself now out on the dance floor, moving, showing off my red dress and this figure I've been working out so hard to achieve. Come on now. Don't spoil my mood. Let's go."

"Okay, since you put it that way. I like to dance, too. Just don't use all of your energy on the dance floor. What do you say we spend two hours at the club, then leave and either go to my place or come back here and expend a different kind of energy? By the way, don't you need a light coat or something?"

"You're probably right. Let me get something."

Neena went into her bedroom and came back wearing a very trendy black shiny coat. It was a little longer than her dress, but not much.

"Okay, my dear," Guy said, and he led her out to his Corvette. He was prepared for a long, silent ride. Neena surprised him by starting up a conversation.

"So Guy, do you think you generated any business at the cookout today? You seem to have promoted your services to everyone there."

"We'll see. But five or six people said they were going to try my gym. I offered them a free week. Terry said she was definitely going to come by, since she hasn't worked out regularly since she left Boston."

"That's great. If I run into her there, I'll do my best to get her to join." She stopped talking for a few minutes and seemed to be deep in thought.

"Oh, by the way Guy. I forgot to tell you. Eric told me to tell you to call and make an appointment with him. He said you might be interested in some services he has that would enhance your business earnings."

"He did? I wonder why he didn't tell me himself."

"I don't know. Maybe you were with a potential customer and he didn't want to interrupt you."

"Well, I guess I was pretty busy, even though it didn't seem that way to me. What I do hardly seems like work, so the time just flies. Okay, I'll give him a call. It was nice of him to call me and ask me to bring my stuff over today. He

165

impresses me, so I'm willing to do business with him if he has the right services. Thanks, Neena."

"Oh, he just called you today about that?"

"Yeah, he did. You were there, remember? You were going to call to let me know you had gone over early since you had to drop off your nephew, but since I talked to Eric first, I told him to just tell you I was on my way." Guy looked at Neena out of the corner of his eye when he said this.

"Oh, that's right," was all she said, but she was quiet for the rest of the trip.

# *Fifteen*

---

$\mathcal{T}$erry resumed her self-appointed task. She worked quickly and silently, and was very focused. By the time Eric had finished seeing the other guests off, everything was straightened and back in place. Terry went into the kitchen with Eric's mother and gave the counters a final wipe-down. Louise was still talking and laughing a lot, and telling a lot of things about Eric, some of which Terry was sure he wouldn't want her to know. Eric's father, Philip, was sitting out back on the patio. Terry was feeling natural and comfortable.

When he came in from seeing the guests off, Eric looked surprised, even disappointed, that everything had been finished in his absence.

"I can't believe you guys are finished already!"

"Terry and I were so busy laughing and talking that the time flew and we didn't notice how much we'd done. So now, I'll just go out and join Phil on the patio."

Terry, left alone with Eric, was both nervous and delighted. She was surprised by her feelings. After all, the scene with Neena today had not been pleasant. Guy said that Neena was his woman, but Neena obviously had her sights on Eric. Terry wondered if they had ever been intimate. She decided to bide her time and not ask right away.

"Would you like to look through the house now, Terry, or would you rather chill for a while? Please know that I didn't expect you to clean up. As a matter of fact, I was going to have my housekeeper come in Monday to get the place in order."

"Eric, please, I didn't mind at all. And sure, I would like my tour now."

As they walked through each room, Eric gave Terry his personal history along with the history of his belongings. He told her about why he had moved back to North Carolina from California, and how he had started his practice downtown. Terry filled him in on where she grew up, and how she ended up in Boston living in an inherited house. Eric was fascinated by that story. They talked and talked until finally they were in the master bedroom suite.

"Oh, this is nice," Terry said softly as she looked around. The room was large, yet small enough to maintain some coziness. The bed was the centerpiece, and it was striking in its simplicity. Terry walked over and pulled the shade on one of the windows. The view was of a large, well-maintained park. For some unexplained reason, she sat on the bed.

"Watch this," Eric said. He walked to the wall facing the bed and pressed something, Terry didn't know what, and a panel slid back to reveal a large, flat-panel television screen and a stereo sound system. Eric turned on the stereo.

"Oh, that sounds good! He has the sexiest voice I've ever heard. This is a song to fall in love by." Terry wondered if she should have made the last statement.

Eric stood looking at her for a few seconds too long.

"Terry, have you seen the new movie starring Samuel L. Jackson?"

"No, I haven't, but it does sound interesting. It's received good reviews as well."

"I was thinking we could go catch the show. I can check the times, but there should be one starting around nine thirty. After the movie, we could come back here, talk, and listen to music."

"I'd really like to see the movie, Eric. But I can't hang out afterward because I accepted an invitation to church tomorrow."

"Oh, sure. Some other time, then?"

"Of course."

"Let's go check the movie times. Hopefully, we'll have time to drop your car off so I can take you directly home after the show."

By the time they walked back downstairs, Philip and Louise had retired to the guest suite. Terry and Eric went into his office and checked for movie times.

"The movie starts at nine forty-five at the *Showroom Cinemas*, which are only a few minutes drive from here, so we have plenty of time, even if we drop your car off."

"Eric, I'd like to freshen up. Do you have a spare toothbrush?"

"Sure. You can use the bathroom down the hall here, or go upstairs to the master suite. Just check the closet, and you'll find toothbrushes, toothpaste, soap, and towels. Is there anything else you need?"

"No, thanks. That should do it."

Terry went to the bathroom that she'd been in earlier when Neena had stalked her. She felt excited, but there was still a little apprehension. Eric seemed to like her.

According to Guy, he *really* liked her. And she liked him. He was smart, handsome, accomplished, and she liked his mom. And he seemed so genuine. No wonder Neena was scheming to get him. Terry could not believe herself how quickly and how deeply she was falling for him.

Terry's only apprehension came from not having clear direction about her future. She had given herself this time for reflection. She could not substitute a relationship with Eric for the inner work she needed to do. After all, what if she became involved with Eric, they were a hot item for a few months, and things just fizzled out. Then where would she be? Oh no, no. She was going to tread carefully until she got her bearings. But if Eric turned out to be as genuine, as *real*, as he appeared to be, and as Guy said he was, then she would go for him.

Eric left a note for Louise and Philip, and he and Terry went outside. He watched as Terry got into her car, and then he got into his SUV that was parked in the garage. He followed her the few blocks to her apartment, where she left her car, and then got in with Eric. As they drove off, they got into an easy conversation.

"So, Terry, have you been living here since you moved to Charlotte?"

"No. At first, I was staying at the Queen Suites, which was comfortable, but after a couple of weeks, I moved to this apartment. I wanted to be downtown. My lease is up at the end of April. By then, I will have made a decision on whether to stay here, look for a job, try to start a company, etcetera, etcetera."

"My vote is for you to stay here, if that counts for anything. I'm willing to help you in any way I can. And look at all the people I introduced you to. You can count at least half of them as friends, including my mom and dad. And I'm dead serious about helping you in any way. I have an extra bedroom. As a matter of fact, you could move into my guest suite where you'd have some privacy. Keep that in mind while you're deciding."

It was then that Terry made up her mind. Yes, Eric was very real, and yes, she was going to go for him.

"Eric, that's sweet of you to offer your home to me. And that party today was so warm. I feel at home here, and I'm going to stay. You've got my word on that. But I can't help wondering. Are you dating someone?"

As soon as she said that, they pulled up to a traffic light that was red. Eric and Terry looked in each other's eyes, and he leaned over and kissed her cheek.

"Of course I'm dating someone. How can you ask me that question when you already know the answer?"

Although she was trying not to show her emotions, Terry looked disappointed and confused.

"No, I'm sorry, I didn't know. But it stands to reason."

"Well then, now I need an explanation, because I thought we were dating, Terry." Eric watched the look of relief come over her face. "But maybe I took a little too much for granted. Maybe I should have asked. So I'm asking now. Terry, will you be my steady date? At least until you've given me a chance to let you know who I am?"

"It would be my pleasure," she answered, looking directly into his eyes.

When they looked up again, they both noticed a group of teenage boys a little distance down a side street. One of the boys was being hassled, and at first Terry thought it was just horseplay. Then all of a sudden, Eric turned down the street toward the boys and brought the SUV to a screeching halt. He left the headlights on and jumped out of the car. Three of the boys ran away. Terry watched as Eric walked up to the one left standing there and started talking to him. Then, both of them walked toward the car. When they reached it, they stood outside talking for about fifteen minutes. Terry watched, as Eric seemed to be chastising the boy. The boy appeared to listen respectfully. Finally, Eric opened the rear door and the teenager climbed in. Eric opened the driver's-side door and made introductions before getting in.

"Denzel Mosley, this is my friend, Terry Weeks. Terry recently moved here from Boston, and I'm showing her around this weekend. Terry, this is Denzel, one of my high school summer interns. This year, though, I'm going to try to have him work for the full year."

"Very nice to meet you, Miss Weeks."

"Likewise Denzel."

Eric climbed in and looked at the clock.

"Man! I didn't know so much time had gone by. I'm so sorry, Terry, but we're going to miss the nine forty-five show. Fortunately, the movie's on two screens, so there is another one starting at ten thirty. Would you mind seeing the later show with me?"

"No, of course not."

"I'm sorry I've messed with your date, Miss Weeks. But I'm glad you two happened along. Those guys were trying to hustle me, and it was three against one."

"Some of the known troublemakers from Denzel's neighborhood were trying to take his money. They know he's smart and resourceful, but they don't seem to know that Denzel is working for himself, and not the entire neighborhood." Eric explained all this to Terry before turning back to Denzel.

"Denzel, where were you coming from this time of night?"

"Eric, it's not late. You sound as if it's past midnight. I'd gone to visit my friend Kimba. She lives about seven or eight blocks away. We've been working on this project together for science class, and we worked on that for a couple of hours. Then we watched some TV. Her parents work the midnight shift at Celdon, so they were both sleeping. Otherwise they would have driven me home."

Eric took his cell phone from his pocket. "Here, Denzel. Call you aunt and tell her you'll be with me tonight."

While Denzel was on the phone, Eric spoke to Terry in a low voice. "I'm not sending him back home tonight. Who knows, those guys could be lying in wait for him. I'm going to have him stay with my folks while we see the movie. Are you sure you don't mind seeing a later movie?"

Terry looked at Eric and smiled. If he continued to be so attentive to her needs, he would have her heart before the night was over.

"No, Eric, I don't mind at all." What she was thinking was she didn't want the night to end.

They turned around and headed back to Eric's house. When they walked in, they could hear the TV going. Philip and Louise were watching a movie on *AMC*. They didn't seem to notice the three walking in. Louise looked up first.

"Oh, hi, Denzel. I didn't know you'd be visiting us tonight. By the way, why weren't you at the cookout today?"

"Hi, Mrs. Johnson. Hi, Mr. Johnson. This is sort of an unintentional visit. I'll tell you about it. And I didn't know about any cookout."

"That's because it was an adult party, Mom. Denzel will be spending the night. Can you and Dad get him settled in the other guest room?"

Philip Johnson stood up then, having torn himself away from the movie. "Come on, son," he said, and led Denzel to the guest room.

Eric took Terry into the kitchen and made some snacks for them. He started telling her more about Denzel.

"That boy really pulls on my heartstrings, Terry. His mother, Lonyce, was raising him on her own. She had grown up in the projects and when she was seventeen, found herself pregnant with Denzel. Because she was gifted academically, a teacher convinced her that she could still graduate from high school and go on to college. It was tough, but the teacher helped her find day care and financial aid. Lonyce even went on to get a master's degree, and was working as assistant principal at a middle school. One night, she left a late meeting at the school and never arrived home. Denzel usually waited up for her when she was going to be out later than usual. Two hours past the time he expected her, he tried calling the school, but of course there was no answer. Everyone had gone home—that is, everyone except his mother. Can you imagine how frantic he was? He was only fourteen. To make a long, grisly story short, her body was found about a week later."

Terry gasped when he said that. "Oh, God, how awful!"

"Yes, it is. Denzel's father had not done anything productive with his life, so there was no one to take him in but his mother's sister, Alyce, who still lives in the projects. Denzel's mother left life insurance money in a trust that's to be used for his college education, which was very wise. The other money he had from his mother's estate, plus his social security money, goes somewhere near eighty percent to the support of his aunt and her children."

"Oh, I feel so sorry for him."

"It's a pitiful story, because had I known them at the time of the murder, I could have shown Alyce how to afford the house that Denzel's mother left. They all could be in a better housing situation."

"So how did Denzel come to intern with you?"

"Through a partnership of the public school system, the private business community, and the city government. It's a well thought-out plan that uses government and private enterprise money to pay the interns. Both the employer and intern go through an intensive one-week training seminar before they can participate, and a two-day refresher each subsequent year. Now, Denzel is an ambitious young man, and very talented mathematically, which is why I want to keep him all year instead of just the summer."

Just then, Eric looked up at the clock.

"Oops. It's time for us to get going, or we'll miss this show."

They gathered purse, jackets, and keys, and headed out. Terry was deep in thought when Eric asked her what she was thinking.

"When you were talking about Denzel in there, it made me think about Tyrone, a former neighbor in Boston. He's also a gifted young man who grew up in less-than-ideal circumstances, but of course it doesn't compare with what Denzel has been through."

Eric was curious about everything concerning Terry, so he asked her more.

"Tyrone was also in a single-parent household. His parents were married, though. His father died, I believe when Tyrone was nine years old. His mother was a hard-working woman, but you can imagine times were tough for her living in one of the most expensive cities in the United States, and trying to raise two boys with bottomless stomachs."

"Yep. I think people grow up and forget how much teenagers eat."

"I agree. Anyway, Tyrone and his brother came over after we'd had this unexpected snowstorm, and offered to shovel my snow for a fee. I was more than happy to have them do it. I had been planning to have a brunch that day, but most people called to cancel because of the snowstorm. I had all of this food that was going to be wasted. On a whim, I invited Tyrone and his brother Reginald for brunch. I had no idea until Tyrone told me much later how much his family needed food that day. He said there was no food in their house, and he and Reginald were going to work for a while, get some money, go buy some food, and then finish work after they had eaten. I saved them from having to work for a while on empty stomachs, and I didn't even know what I had done."

"Yeah, I know what you mean. You gave them a gift, but it was as much a blessing for you, even if you didn't know it at the time. If you had never known, you were still given a gift."

Eric stopped talking and drove in silence for a few minutes.

"I have to make some decisions concerning Denzel," he finally said.

"What do you mean? What decisions?"

"Here's the situation with Denzel. Maybe you can help me come up with some ideas. Denzel's aunt has two children of her own to feed. She works and makes almost twice the minimum wage, but do the math and you'll see that even with food stamps and subsidized rent, life is pretty challenging. Then here comes Denzel, and he's got a little nest egg for college, he has his mother's car, and he's getting a social security check. So Denzel is in no way a financial burden to her. The car certainly makes her life easier, and she seems to have first dibs on it. And since Denzel is now working, he takes care of all his expenses. He would even have some money to save, if auntie didn't take a good portion of it. Denzel says that he doesn't mind, that he's glad he can help them. But I'm Denzel's advocate, and I can't help but think he deserves more. What do you think, Terry? Do you think I'm unsympathetic?"

Terry reached over and put her hand on Eric's shoulder. It felt strong and set.

"I understand, Eric. I also understand how Denzel feels. I mean, this is the only family that he has. But I agree with you that the best thing to do is focus on giving Denzel a leg up."

"He inherited his mother's drive and determination. But he needs to be in a nurturing environment. I worry about leaving him in that housing project. I'm afraid for his physical safety. I'm concerned that he doesn't have the space or atmosphere for studying. I also worry that he won't be able to save extra money for college, even though he will be working full time."

"Eric, those are legitimate concerns." She knitted her eyebrows together in deep thought as Eric purchased the tickets. As they walked toward their theater, she turned to him.

"Eric, you say that Denzel is very gifted, especially in mathematics. What if we could find a preparatory boarding school for him that would provide a full scholarship?

Provided that the school is nurturing and inclusive, that could be a solution."

It took Eric about a second to realize the potential of that idea. "Terry, that's brilliant! Let's talk about it more on the ride home."

By this time, they were seated. Eric put his arm around her and kissed her cheek. They settled in to watch the show, and to Terry's pleasure, Eric kept his arm around her during much of it. She felt as if she had known him for years.

On the ride home, the discussion turned to Denzel again.

"The one obstacle to that plan would be selling it to Denzel," Eric said. "He feels obligated to his aunt and cousins. The thing is, if his aunt were not so hostile, I could help her as well."

"I just don't see that Denzel should sacrifice himself," Terry said. "Do you think we could convince him of that?"

"We could if we could make him see that by bettering himself, he would be better able to help them. And we could work on the aunt and try to get her into her own home. There are some good mortgage deals around. People just don't know about them."

"Fabulous idea, Eric. I can start researching the schools tomorrow. Do you want to get together tomorrow evening to see what I came up with?"

"I'd love that. We can do dinner at my house. Why don't you stop over right after church?"

"The problem with that is I will not have finished my search by then."

"Well, come by anyway, and we can do it together."

He had walked her to her door. As Terry stood gazing up into his eyes, Eric bent down and kissed her full on the lips. It was the sweetest kiss Terry had ever, ever known. She wanted to invite him in, to just keep on kissing him, and let events take their own course. Instead, she opened her door, said goodnight, and walked into her cold, empty apartment.

# *Sixteen*

---

There was a new, hip club downtown that Neena wanted to go to. Guy had been there a few times. It was one of the few nightspots in Charlotte where you could go and have more than a fifty percent chance of meeting someone you'd like to date. It was called *The Set* because the dance floor resembled a stage set where you could see yourself on monitors. Also, they sometimes hired local dance groups to perform. Guy had been at one of these shows, and the group performing had brought the house down. They pulled people from the audience, one of whom turned out to be so good people thought he was a professional. He wasn't, but he generated so much buzz that he was featured on a local television news show.

Guy pulled the Corvette up in front of the building. When the valet came over, he handed him a ten-dollar bill and his valet key. Neena jumped out of the car and started walking toward the entrance without waiting for him. Guy felt his frustration growing. He thought it was time to have a heartfelt conversation with her, and he was going to do it soon.

He caught up with her just as the hostess was asking how many there were in her party. They were ushered to one of the larger tables close to the dance floor. As soon as they sat down, Neena started moving in her seat to the beat.

"Come on Guy. Let's dance," she said as she continued her writhing and head bopping.

"Let's just wait a few minutes. I'd like to give the waitress our order first. What would you like, Neena?"

"I'll have a screwdriver."

"What about food? Don't you want something to munch on?"

"Not really. Just order what you want."

"Okay. I'll order some munchies for the table. I don't think it's a good idea to drink and not eat."

"Whatever you say, Guy." A popular dance song was playing, and Neena was throwing her hair all around to the beat. The waitress walked up.

"What can I get for you guys?" she said.

"We'll have two screwdrivers and the hors d'oeuvre tray for starters," Guy answered.

"I'll bring your screwdrivers right away. It'll be about twenty-five minutes for the hors d'oeuvre tray."

"Okay, you've placed the order, so come on out on the dance floor with me." Neena was up and pulling Guy out of his seat.

"Alright, alright," Guy answered, laughing. He followed Neena out among the dancers and she immediately started doing this sexy gyration right up on him. Guy got into the mood and they danced until he saw the waitress bringing their drinks over.

"Come on. Our drinks are here," Guy said, and he led Neena off the dance floor. They sat, sipping and surveying the crowd. It was a racially mixed group, and the ages looked to be from late twenties to mid to late forties. The fashion theme was *too sexy*. For the ladies, it was short and tight, hair and nails. For the guys, it was casual suits with either shirts opened way down, or with tight sweaters. Heads were bald or nearly so, faces clean-shaven or with peach fuzz.

"I'm going to go to the restroom," Guy said to Neena, as he stood up and pulled a fifty-dollar bill from his wallet. "Pay for the drinks and food if our waitress shows up before I get back."

The real reason for Guy's abrupt departure was that he wanted to do some surveillance of the place, which was his practice when visiting crowded, drinking establishments. When places are decorated nicely, cater to more affluent clientele, and have an all-around look of sophistication, people can be lulled into a false sense of security. Guy wanted to check the exits, check out security personnel, and see if a sprinkler system was in place, though he could not go so far as to see if the system worked properly. After making his rounds, he decided that everything looked on the up-and-up.

When he returned to their table, Guy found that Neena was gone. The hors d'oeuvres were there, untouched, and so were new drinks. Guy couldn't believe Neena hadn't stayed for that small amount of time, especially since he'd told her time and again that he did not leave his drinks unattended in public places. He certainly wasn't going to drink it now, so she could have both drinks.

Guy picked up a buffalo wing. The exact moment he held it up to his mouth and took a bite was when his eyes spotted Neena on the dance floor. And she was moving, clearly in the thralls of the music, her body a jumping bean.

Guy watched her and realized that she actually was a good dancer.

Then he noticed the man she was dancing with. He was sexy type number two, with the tight sweater, the head that was nearly bald, and the peach fuzz. Although he, too, was enjoying the dance, he was not swept away in it the way Neena was. He was more into watching Neena. That was to be expected. After all, Neena was a good-looking woman and she was showing her stuff in that outfit. But still, the way the man was sizing Neena up made Guy uneasy. He possessed a smarminess that his stylish looks could not hide.

The deejay decided to slow things down. Couples that moments before were swinging away from each other were now in each other's arms, and that included Neena and her dance partner. They moved as if their bodies were glued together. As he watched them, Guy felt his face getting warmer. Neena was taking things way too far. After all, she had come here with him, and now she was screwing this guy on the dance floor right in front of his face, acting like a slut. He decided he would take her home, and then have no further dealings with her.

Guy was about to get up and go pull her right off the dance floor and out the door. He was stopped by a woman's British accent.

"Excuse me, sir. All of the tables are taken. Do you mind if my friend and I share this table with you?"

The one speaking was a white woman, late twenties, with long red hair, freckles, and blue eyes. Standing with her was a black woman with long store-bought braids.

"No, please. Join me. It seems I've been abandoned, so there's nothing I would like more than to share my table with you lovely ladies. Here, have some hors d'oeuvres. What would you like to drink? It's on me."

"I don't really know. What do you want, Andrea?" the redhead said to the braids.

"I'd like one of those sweet drinks, but without the alcohol——a strawberry daiquiri, virgin. But you don't have to pay for us, you know. After all, we've imposed on you."

Guy looked at her again. He found her exotic—this black woman with the British accent.

"Since you've imposed on me then, why don't you buy me one of those sweet drinks, as well?" Guy said as a mock Briton.

"We'll be happy to," the redhead said. "You Americans like yours extra sweet, don't you, with lots of tropical fruits?"

Guy laughed.

Andrea waved to the waitress. "Is there anything else you'd like?"

"Just some friendly conversation. My name is Guy."

"I'm Andrea, and this is my friend Judy."

"Nice to meet you, Andrea and Judy. Do you two live in the area?"

"Yes. We both just graduated from the International Classics Culinary School. I landed a job as assistant chef at *Chez Louis*, and Judy is working as assistant chef at the Convention Center Hotel. What about you? Do you live in the area?"

"Yes, I do. And if you ever want to work off some of those calories, because I know you have to do a lot of tasting, just sign up for membership at my gym. Here, let me give you my business card."

"I usually ride my bike in the mornings. That's about all I have time for. But I must admit that it's scary sometimes riding on the streets. Drivers don't seem to think I belong out there." Andrea said this with a look of consternation.

"Yeah. Some of the stories she's told me about her rides, you would not believe them," said Judy.

"So, are you two roommates?"

"Yes we are," Judy answered. We live in a small house that we've been renting now for three years. Small by your standards, that is. For us, it is quite comfortable."

"You're right, Andrea, to be concerned about riding your bike on the streets. I wouldn't do it at all. If I had to ride, I would pack my bike up and go to a park where biking is allowed. There are a few around, but you might have to drive some distance to get to them. I'll tell you what. I will give each of you a free month's pass to my gym. Just call me and let me know when you can come in, and I'll show you around. You might be pleasantly surprised at how much you get for your money."

"You're very generous, Guy. We intruded on your table. First you ask to buy us drinks, and now you're letting us work out at your gym for free. So, I'd like to make a proposal. I will take you up on your gym offer. In return, I'd like to extend an offer to you. You can have a lunch and a dinner on *Chez Louis*. Here. I have some complimentary invitations. Just let me sign them." Guy watched as she signed the two cards.

"I don't have the fancy invitations," Judy chimed in. "But if you come by the Convention Center Hotel and ask for me, I will arrange lunch or dinner for you *gratis*. Just call ahead to make sure I'm on. Here, take one of my cards."

Guy took the card from Judy, and then sat smiling. He was suddenly feeling much better, being in the presence of two friendly and generous women. He looked at Judy's pleasant freckled face that was framed by a cascade of red hair. Then he turned to Andrea and he saw something very surprising. Her hair was in locks, and it was her own. He must not have been looking that closely at her. He also noticed how smooth her skin was. And she had a pleasant face, too. He turned back to look at Neena still on the dance floor, still with the same partner.

Andrea and Judy had started to talk quietly to themselves. They were recounting tales from the kitchen. Guy listened as Andrea became pensive.

"I don't know, Judy. I just can't see myself staying there, waiting to be put in charge of the entire kitchen. I envision a less frantic pace for myself. Do you know what I mean?"

"Yeah, I do. The pace is hectic, especially when there is a major convention. Maybe I can get myself hired off to some wealthy person, like Oprah. I should contact her right now, so that when she makes her current chef rich and famous, and he goes off to a life of yachting and golfing, I will have a good chance. But first I need to get more practice on the low-fat stuff."

Guy decided to jump in.

"I hear you ladies are trying to find out what to do with the rest of your lives. And so am I, except for me, it's not in the business arena. For me, it's my personal life. You see that woman straight ahead on the dance floor, the one that's wearing the very short, tight red dress? She has on the black, stiletto heels."

They both nodded.

"Well, that's the woman I came here with. Take a good look. Look at how she's dancing with that guy. They've been dancing like that for some time now."

"Well, looks to me like you two had a bit of a row before you came out."

"No, not really. She just likes coming in and out of my life, which is why I need to make some decisions."

Guy watched Judy and Andrea look at each other. Andrea nodded.

"Why don't you come on the dance floor with Andrea and me?" Judy asked, as both she and Andrea stood up. Guy sat for a moment with a look of *"Why didn't I think of that?"* on his face.

Not for long, though. He stood up, took Judy's hand in his right one, Andrea's in his left, and led them to the dance floor. They weren't dancing the way Neena and her partner were, but they were having fun. They danced for close to an hour. When a slow song came on, the two women laughingly pulled Guy back to the table.

"I'm afraid we have to go," Judy said. "I have to do brunch tomorrow."

"If you must go, then. Andrea, what will you be doing while Judy is at work?"

"I don't have anything planned. I'm thinking about trying to find one of those parks you were talking about, and ride my bike."

"Then let me make a proposal. If you let me take you to Judy's brunch, I'll show you where the bike paths are."

"That's fair enough. I can meet you there if you'd like, say around one o'clock?"

"Well sure, but why take two cars? I can pick you up at your house."

"Okay," Andrea said. "Let me write my home address and phone number down for you." She got a pen from her purse, wrote the information on one of the club napkins, and handed it to him. "Do you need directions?"

"Nope. I know this city as well as any cab driver. Let me walk you to your car."

"There's no need for that. Besides, you'd really better keep an eye on your date. She may not know who she's mixing it up with."

Guy extended a hand to both of them.

"Ladies, it was a pleasure meeting you. I will see you both tomorrow."

"Oh, the pleasure was ours," Judy said, and they both turned to leave. Guy watched until they'd reached the door, then turned his attention back to Neena. He didn't see her, but he spotted the guy that she'd been dancing with. He was sitting alone at one of the tables surrounding the dance stage. Guy had started to study him closely when he saw Neena coming back to the table. Apparently, she had been to the ladies' room.

"What happened to your friends?" Neena asked him as she reached their table.

"You mean the two women who were sitting here with me?"

"Yeah, and dancing with you."

"Humph.  I thought you were too busy to have noticed."

"So, were they friends of yours?"

"I actually just met them tonight.  They asked if they could sit here because all the other tables were taken.  So, what about the guy you were dancing with?  Did you know him before tonight?"

"No.  The guy's a weirdo."

"Neena, you've been dancing intimately with this guy all night.  Now you say he's a weirdo.  What does that make you?"

"There's no need to get nasty, Guy.  Anyway, could we go now?"

"Yes, indeed," Guy said.  He waved their waitress down and paid the bill.  He and Neena started toward the coat check area, and when they reached it, Guy handed the attendant a dollar.  He was about to hold the coat out for Neena, when all of a sudden another hand was grabbing her arm.

"Don't tell me you're leaving without saying goodbye.  That's not nice."

"What are you talking about?  I said goodbye to you fifteen minutes ago."

Guy cleared his throat loudly and looked directly at the man who had been dancing with Neena earlier. He looked into Guy's eyes, and Guy felt a chill go through him.

"I'm Guy, and I see you've become acquainted with my date, Neena. Is there a problem?"

"No. There's no problem. There's no problem at all. I didn't realize you were here with Neena, being that you didn't dance with her, you know."

"Well, now you do realize it, and also, I did dance with her. I didn't catch your name."

"Jerome."

"Good night, Jerome." Guy helped Neena put her coat on, and steered her out the door and to his car. He didn't have to look around to see Jerome staring at him. He felt the burning in his back.

# Seventeen

Jessie leaned forward and turned off his car radio. He was in a euphoric mood, and he wanted to think about the events that were responsible.

He and Bebe had met that morning in her office, which was in the black student union on the university campus. Her office was small, but nicely decorated. It quickly became clear to him that she was running a first-class outfit. He'd had to wait while she helped a parent and student apply for scholarship money, and since she kept the door to the inner office open, he could hear the exchange. Bebe maintained the attitude that she was giving them so much value for their money that they couldn't afford not to use her services.

She finished with the customers in about twenty minutes, and after they had gone, she apologized to him, saying that her customers had been ten minutes late. But she got right down to business, showing him slick brochures for her scholarship program, and explaining how it worked. She spent much more time, however, on her investment services, describing in detail the different investment options that she offered. Even though Jessie was in awe of her level of sophistication in financial matters, after a while his eyes started to glaze over. All of the different options started to sound alike. But the returns were all good. He did remember that. He didn't hear anything lower than twenty percent.

He told Bebe that he would take her up on her offer of employment. His plan was to go back to work for a week, and then give his two-week notice. He had thought about hanging on to his job, and trying Bebe out on a part-time basis, just to see if things would work out. In the end, though, it was *what the hell! Things already were not working out.* And so his decision was made.

The decision to invest his money with Bebe was an easier one to make. It was a no-brainer. Her investments did far better than his current ones, and he needed to maximize his returns if this gym was to become a reality. He would go to the bank the next day to get a check to give to her. He should probably hold back a few thousand for emergencies, though.

Jessie broke out of his reverie as he came upon the driveway to CFIW. He slowed way down before turning in, more from a feeling of dread than from an attempt at safe driving. He hated the thought of being examined by Dr. Faustin again. It was enough to make him want to just leave without giving the two-week notice. But since he had gone that far, he guessed he could manage a little more patience. And, since he wouldn't get his vacation pay, the extra two weeks would come in handy, he reasoned.

He felt the rage rise in him again ; it filled him up as he thought about the conversation between Faustin and Jane that he and Ed had overheard. He was finally getting away from this rat hole. He just had to be cool during this exam, and hold on for another couple of weeks.

There was a small parking area reserved for people going to the clinic, and Jessie found a spot there. He got out and walked toward the building. The day was overcast and on the chilly side, which further dampened Jessie's mood.

"Hi Jessie," he heard someone behind him say. He turned around and saw Maureen, a nice white woman who worked his shift.

"Hi there. What are you doing here? You haven't been sick, have you?"

"Worker's Comp. I cut my hand at work yesterday and had to go to the hospital to get stitches. The nurse told me to come in today for her to look at it, and since we're on the night shift, I had to come in earlier. How're you doing? I heard you were in a car accident."

"I'm doing okay. Dr. Faustin has to examine me before giving me the go ahead to return to work, so that's why I'm here."

They had come to the entrance to the clinic. Jessie opened the door and allowed her to go in first.

"Well, good luck, Jessie," she said as she went to sign in.

"Hey, thanks. Same to you." Jessie signed in and sat in one of the waiting room chairs. He was about to reach for a magazine when he heard his name called.

"Jessie Campbell?"

Jessie stood up.

"Hi. I'm Ellen. Would you follow me, please?"

Ellen was new. She stood out here because she seemed focused on the task at hand, and not on what she could find out to go gossip about. She led him into an exam room and instructed him to take off everything except his socks, and to put on the gown with the opening at the back. Jessie thought that was peculiar, since he didn't have to undress so completely last time.

"Faustin must be getting ready to start some shit," he thought. "Well, let him bring it on. If he tells me I can't come back, then that'll be my opportunity to get some things off my chest."

The assistant left and Jessie started taking off his clothes. No sooner had he removed everything than Faustin showed up, as if he had been standing outside peeking. Jessie hurriedly put on the gown.

"Hello, young man. How are you doing? You ready to get back to work? Probably not, Huh?" He chuckled when he said this. "Well, let's just see what we have here."

He put on his stethoscope first and listened as he instructed Jessie to take in deep breaths and hold. Then he checked Jessie's blood pressure. He took a moment to write the numbers on his clipboard, and then put the clipboard down on the table. He told Jessie to open his mouth wide and stick out his tongue, while he looked inside. When he started to poke and prod where the bandages had been, Jessie had just about had enough.

Dr. Faustin stopped for a moment and looked directly at Jessie. Then he started to poke and prod again, moving his hands down.

"You know, Jessie, I may not be able to approve your return to work. Are you sure you're not in any pain?"

As he was saying this, his hand had moved further down Jessie's back. Then all of a sudden, his hand had moved around and was on Jessie's penis, fondling. Jessie drew in a sharp breath, temporarily stunned. Then he went into action and hit the doctor with an uppercut that sent him sprawling across the room.

"What are you doing, you low-life motherfucker? You pansy-assed bitch! Don't you ever put your hands on me again."

The doctor was cowering, and holding his chin. Jessie jumped up and started grabbing his clothes.

"Get your punk ass out of here so I can get dressed. Now!" Faustin moved skittishly out of the room, a shadow of the power image he had once portrayed.

Jessie got into his clothes faster than he had ever remembered doing. He was trembling as he grabbed his shoes and ran out with his shirt and pants open. He stopped outside the exam room long enough to put on his shoes, zip his pants and button his shirt. Then he walked down the hallway and out the door to the parking lot without encountering a single person.

Jessie was muttering aloud. Anyone seeing him would swear that he was crazy. "Did that asshole have this all set up? Did he plan it all night, or was it a spur of the moment thing? I'm going to kill him. I'm going to hunt him down like the bitch that he is and blow his brains out."

He was driving quite fast, enraged and traumatized at the same time. He was still talking to himself.

"Who would've thought? Faustin's a fairy. And him getting all up in my face like he's threatening me—trying to get his thrill and intimidate me at the same time."

Jessie drove on, but the rage did not subside. He did start to think a little more clearly, though, a little more deviously. He knew he couldn't kill anyone. But he would make Faustin pay. He wanted to talk things over with Bebe, see what she thought was the best way to get him back. But it didn't take him long to realize he couldn't tell Bebe, or any other woman, what had happened.

Jessie made it home, still stunned by the afternoon's events. He sat in the first chair he came to. The scene kept playing over in his mind, like a song that gets stuck in your head. Faustin saying *I may not be able to approve your return to work*, and the next thing Jessie feels is that scumbag's hand on his penis. He had to get revenge, but the kind of revenge where he was not hurt and Faustin was.

Jessie had been sitting for almost an hour when he was startled by the sound of the phone ringing. He checked the caller ID box. *Unknown Name, Unknown Number*, it said. He picked up the receiver and pressed *Talk*.

"Hello."

"Hello. May I speak with Jessie Campbell, please?"

Faustin! Jessie recognized the voice, which had been permanently imprinted in his memory. Play it cool, Jessie. This may be your moment.

"Hello, Dr. Faustin. This is Jessie Campbell speaking." Jessie made his voice unemotional.

"Hello, Jessie. I just called to let you know that I've arranged to reverse the decision on your short-term disability coming out of your vacation time. Plus, I'm giving you permission to take an additional two days off before you have to return to work."

There was a long silence as Faustin's words sank in. By then, Jessie was a quiet, hot furnace, burning away. He felt no need to fill in the silence, not until he was good and ready.

"I'll get this taken care of right now, Jessie. I just wanted to call to let you know."

"Oh, no he doesn't," Jessie thought. "No, uh-uh. He doesn't think he's just going to throw me a few crumbs, hang up, and that'll be the end of it."

"Oh, you did, did you? Well, you've let me know what you're thinking. Now I'm going to let you know what the deal is, and it's a lot more complicated than what you just laid out."

"I beg your pardon?"

"Oh, don't try to go indignant on me. You don't have a leg to stand on. Now, the first thing you're going to do is write some things down, while they're fresh on your mind."

"Listen, you're getting a good deal here . . ."

"No, no, no, no, no. You don't seem to understand that you're no longer in charge here. The reason you're no longer in charge is that you don't want to lose the prestige and money that comes with being Doctor . . .what's your first name?"

"M."

"No. That's just an initial. What is your fucking first name?"

"Myrtle."

Disbelief registered at first, but it didn't take Jessie long to appreciate the humor of the situation, and when he did, he let out a huge belly laugh.

"Myrtle?" and he laughed again, but there was coldness in the laughter, and Dr. Faustin probably noticed.

"Okay, so you don't want to lose the prestige that comes with being . . . . okay, I agree with you. The name should be *M*." Jessie snickered again. "The prestige of being Dr. M. Faustin should be guarded, don't you think?"

"Get to the point, please," M. Faustin said in a quiet voice.

"Okay. Here's the POINT! You are going to get some of your personalized CFIW stationery that I know you have. You are going to write today's date on it, and then you're going to write down the events of my visit to you today. You are going to be brutally honest, Myrtle."

"Now wait a minute . . ."

"Excuse me. EXCUSE ME! You are taking orders now, and this is your prescription. When you write this, don't leave out the part where you planned to have me alone in the exam room with you. It's very important that you don't leave that out. You're going to sign this document. In addition to your hand signature, you're going to stamp it with your signature stamp."

"If you're going to turn me in, then there's no point . . ."

"Who said anything about turning you in? I'm not turning you in. I'm not even going to squeeze you financially. But as for your pitiful little proposal, you're going to take that way further. Of course, the time that I've been out is not going to be taken as vacation time. But in addition to that, you're going to arrange for me to be off from work on short-term disability for an additional three months. And, of course, that is with full pay and benefits. And there's one other thing."

Silence.

"Okay, I'll tell you anyway. Since you're so cozy with Rob in HR, you're going to persuade him to give me a three-month severance package when I turn in my resignation at the end of my three-month leave. That shouldn't be difficult for you to do. Tell him you feel sorry for me, since I've ruined my health and may not get meaningful employment again. Tell him that's the least he could do, considering my long, faithful service to the company. Hell, tell him anything. I don't care. Buy him some drinks after your golf game. What else do you two do together?"

Just then Jessie inhaled sharply, audibly.

208

"Don't tell me Rob's a fairy, too! I'll be damned."

"Now, I didn't say that . . ."

"Save it. Do you think I care? I don't. I just want you to take care of business. Now, we're wasting time here. I'm going to get off the phone so you can write your letter. You're going to put it in an envelope with my name on it. Have it done within an hour and wait for me at the office. And don't think I'm the only one who knows about this. Are we clear?"

"Yes."

"Then hang up the phone and get busy."

Jessie didn't tell the doctor that he had a few phone calls of his own to make.

# Eighteen

---

Neena was in the foulest of moods when she woke up. Eric seemed to have slipped completely away, she had alienated Guy, and she could swear that the man she was dancing with at *The Set* a month or so ago was following her. She needed to clear her head and make some plans. Things were not exactly going her way.

She got out of bed and went to her kitchen to make coffee. Just as she opened the cabinet to get the coffee, she remembered that she didn't have any. She hadn't been grocery shopping in weeks. She opened the door to her refrigerator to see if somehow it had replenished itself. It hadn't.

"I'll grab something on the way," she spoke aloud. "That is, if I have the cash. And there're still four days before I get paid."

Neena went to her bedroom and glanced at the stack of bills on her dresser. On top was the bill from Guy's gym. "If he thinks I'm going to start paying now, he's crazy," she muttered. "He's just upset because I danced so much with Jerome that night at the club. Okay, I don't blame him. I was wrong. But for God's sake, did he have to throw Eric and Terry together the way he did?"

She lay back on her bed for about thirty minutes. A smile slowly spread across her face. She had a plan to get things back on track.

Neena got up and moved to her closet. She wanted to find something to wear that would suit her new and improved mood. She had a lot to choose from, which was the main reason for the stack of bills. The other reasons were the hair, the nails, the diets, and the lack of tax deductions. But, she always figured, why should she buy a house when she was going to marry someone who had one that was nicer than anything she could afford?

She finally decided on a casual suit. She would wear a pair of high-heeled sandals with it. Flats were much more comfortable, but the heels were definitely sexier. She thought it was a good trade-off.

Neena brushed her teeth, showered, and began her long ritual of putting on makeup, getting her hair just so, and putting on various lotions and potions before getting her clothes on and heading out the door.

Even though she'd gotten up early, with all she'd done, she was pressed for time. As she walked up to her car, she clicked the door open. She didn't even notice the man sitting in the car parked next to hers.

"Hi, Neena."

Neena jumped almost a foot into the air as the man appeared from nowhere. She turned around and looked into the smiling face of Jerome Dyson, her dancing partner from that night at *The Set*.

"Jerome! You startled me! What on earth are you doing here?"

"I live here."

"You live here? I thought you told me you live in South Carolina? And the last time I checked, the city of Charlotte had not seceded."

Jerome laughed. Neena noticed that he did not look as nice in the daylight as he did that night in the club. In fact, she did not like his appearance at all.

"I moved here last week, Neena. It's closer to my job."

"Let me get this straight. You move to get closer to your job, and the place you move to just happens to be the apartment complex where I live?"

"Yeah, baby. What's the problem? You certainly aren't acting as friendly as you did at the club. The way you were dancing then, I wouldn't think you'd be so uptight. That guy you were with hasn't been giving you a hard time, has he?"

Neena was nonplussed. She just looked at him for a few moments.

"Well, I have to get to work," she said. "I suppose you do too, unless you're so close to work now that you don't have to leave home."

She had never seen anyone's demeanor become so ugly so quickly, and she hoped never to again.

"What do you mean by that statement?" His lips were curled in a sneer, his eyes a window into hell. "Do you think I don't have a job? Is that what you think?"

Neena couldn't get into her car fast enough. She half-expected him to grab her, but he just stood there looking. She locked her doors and drove off, her heart beating extra fast.

"Whew! What a way to start the day," she said to herself as she pulled up to her parking space. The tenants of the building where she worked all had spaces in this lot. Neena sat in her car and took several deep breaths, watching familiar people walk by. "What is up with Jerome? Is he psycho? Well, whatever he is, I don't have time for his madness. I've got to get my own life on track." And with that, she got out of the car and walked confidently to her office. She never looked around to see if she had been followed.

"Good morning, Irene," Neena said as she walked past the receptionist's desk. Irene was the typical receptionist, who knew all the comings and goings, and the insides and outs of everyone in the operation.

"Good morning, Neena," Irene answered her. To Neena, Irene looked as if she wanted to say something else, something troubling, but she apparently changed her mind. Neena didn't stick around to coax it out of her. Instead, she went down to her cubicle, dropped her purse, grabbed the file she was working on, and walked to the law library. The attorney she usually worked with, Brenda, would not be in that day, so Neena planned to finish with this file, and make some personal calls.

The research took longer than expected, and it was almost noon before she finished. She looked at her watch, and then dialed Eric's number, hoping to catch him before he went out to lunch.

"Hi, Neena," Eric said after Sylvia had connected them.

"Hi, Eric. How are things going?"

"Just fine. Can I help you with something?"

"I was just calling to see if you and Guy had gotten together yet to go over his business matters. I thought about it this morning, and I just wanted to fulfill my part of the mission."

"Well you can rest assured that you have. Guy and I are meeting just after lunch today."

"Oh, great. I wish you luck. By the way, how is that young woman I met at your house a few weeks back? Terry, I think her name is."

"She's just fine, Neena. I'll tell her you asked about her. If there's nothing else, I have some work I need to finish before I meet with Guy."

"Oh, that's it. Goodbye."

Neena wasted no time feeling miffed, but went right to work, dialing Guy's number at his main gym.

"Guy Pelham."

"Guy, this is Neena. I was just thinking about you, so I thought I'd call and see if you could join me for a quick lunch."

"Oh, hi Neena. Sorry. I have a previous engagement. As a matter of fact I'm late, and I'm heading out the door right now. I'll have to talk to you later."

He hung up.

"What a day!" Neena said, after hanging up too. "Should I just go home, go back to bed, and start all over again tomorrow? Naw. Neena Marcelle does not give up that easily."

Neena dialed information.

"Bell Atlantic 411. What city and state?"

"Charlotte, North Carolina."

"What listing?"

"Terry Weeks."

"One moment, please."

Neena wrote down the number the computerized voice read out to her. Then she dialed.

"Hello," she heard Terry's voice say.

"Hi, Terry. My name is Neena Marcelle, and I met you at Eric Johnson's house at a party a few weeks ago. I don't know if you remember me, but I was rude to you, and I've been feeling guilty about it ever since. I wasn't raised to be that way, acting territorial and all. And with your being new in town, I should have been trying to make you feel at home. Anyway, I'd like to make it up to you. Could you have lunch with me today?"

"Neena, yes I do remember you. Of course your apology is accepted. I can't have lunch with you today, though. . . ."

"Don't tell me. You have a prior engagement."

"As a matter of fact, I do."

"Well, what about dinner tonight? My treat."

"Sorry. I can't do dinner tonight either."

"Oh, okay. Well, one day when you're free for lunch or dinner, give me a call. You can call me at home or here at the office." She gave Terry the numbers and hung up.

"What next? What next?" Neena sat for a few minutes and let her mind wander. She thought about the morning's events. She thought about the look on Irene's face when she walked in. "Ah-hah. Why didn't I think of that earlier?"

She picked up the phone and made another call. This time the recipient seemed happy to hear from her.

# Nineteen

---

"There it is. Just up here on the right."

Jessie pulled up to the building and he and Ed got out. It was an old warehouse, but from the outside it looked pretty good. It was red brick, with lots of windows. The windows were high off the ground, so Jessie and Ed could not peer in, but to Jessie, it looked like a loft. He got excited thinking about the possibilities. He could have gleaming hardwood floors in an aerobic room, with free weights and stationary equipment all around it. He envisioned a walking/jogging trail on the second floor that looked down on the first floor. It even looked large enough for a pool, steam room, and sauna. And if he could buy this building, he could do it all in stages. It might take him five years to complete, but at least he would be on his way.

"Are you sure it's for sale? There's no sign."

"Yeah, man. I thought about you soon as I heard about it. And from what I hear, the seller's looking to make a quick sale so he can get back to California and not have to travel back here much."

"Well, I need to talk to either him or his realtor, if he's using one."

"I think he's trying to sell it on his own."

"Well, can you get the number for me? I want to take a look inside."

"That shouldn't be a problem. I'll call you later today with the info."

Ed and Jessie got back into the car, and Jessie dropped Ed off at his home. As soon as he got home himself, Ed called with the number.

Before calling the seller, Jessie took some time to contemplate his next moves. Old Faustin had delivered the letter just as instructed. Jessie was surprised at how easily he had acquiesced. And because the doc had made good on all of his promises, Jessie decided not to give him any further grief. After all, who knew how far you could push the guy? He didn't want to be the one ending up behind bars—for blackmail. But if, down the road, someone else brought a case against Faustin for similar deeds, then Jessie would come forward, letter in hand.

Despite everything, he was in pretty good shape. He had used the time he was on medical leave to bone up on Bebe's operation and to study various investing strategies. A lot of it he didn't understand, but Bebe talked about the various concepts so fluently that there was no questioning her knowledge of them. He had decided to let her invest nearly all of his money, reasoning that since he would be moving to her payroll, he would be making a lot more cash that he could use to shore up his emergency stash.

And boy had he been making a lot more money! He had proved to be an invaluable employee, with bonuses to show for it. He had kept the bonus money, putting it in very low-risk investments, so he had a tidy little sum apart from what Bebe had invested for him.

Jessie thought that he should pinch himself. Only four months earlier, he had been in a dead-end job, living in quiet desperation, and not so quiet at that. He had been making plans, but at the rate he was going, they were going to take many, many years to materialize. Then, because he did Mrs. Anon a favor, he met Bebe and his life seemed to change overnight. He was making a lot more money, he was enjoying the work and the creativity that it involved, and his investments were growing. And to top it all off, he had a chance to get started on his real passion.

All of a sudden, thoughts that had been nagging just below the surface burst through. *How much money had Bebe made for him so far? Suppose his investments had lost money?* Although Bebe had practically guaranteed results, Jessie knew there was always risk. He had not received a statement since the initial one. He wondered how often she sent them.

He called the number Ed had given him. It turned out that the owner of the warehouse—Jules was his name—was selling it himself and said he would be glad to show it that day. Jessie made an appointment to meet him in an hour. He called Ed to see if he could go with him, but Ed's wife said that he was sleeping.

Jessie made it there with about twenty minutes to spare. Jules was an elderly white man, Jessie guessed about sixty-three to sixty-five. He was tall and skinny, with a huge beak nose, and the most extreme comb-over Jessie had ever seen. He was very pleasant, though. He told Jessie that his father had left the property to him. Jules had lived in California most of his adult life, and since he no longer had ties to this community, he wanted to sell and get back home.

When he unlocked the door and they walked in, Jessie couldn't believe his eyes. He was glad he had come while there was plenty of daylight left. This way, he didn't miss the way the place was bathed in light. And it was quite expansive, with two stories that contained more than enough floor space for what he wanted to do. It was in excellent shape. The floors were made of some type of rubberized material. It had exposed brick walls. The more he looked, the more nervous he became about the price. He was determined not to be the first one to bring it up, though.

"What was this building used for?" he asked Jules.

"Storing furniture and appliances. That was the line of work my father was in, and his father before him. At one time, it was a showroom where people could come with their trucks or U-Hauls and make purchases. Later, it became a storage facility for furniture and appliances that Dad didn't have room for in his retail stores. He had a retail store in Wilmington, and one in Whiteville."

"How many bathrooms are there?'

"There are two bathrooms on each floor, but they're not working. You have to understand, this place has been vacant for going on three years. I'm sure it wouldn't take much to get them going. I had the water turned on a few weeks ago. There's also a small kitchen on this floor. Come on, we can walk down to look at it."

They walked all over the place, with Jessie looking for signs of structural damage, water damage, anything that would be expensive to repair. All in all, the building looked good, but of course he would have an inspection prior to closing the deal.

"Do you have a specification sheet?" Jessie asked once he had seen everything.

"Yeah, they're right in my car. I was running late, so when I saw you were already here, I jumped out without picking them up. Come on, I'll get one for you."

They walked to Jules' car—a rented white Cadillac. Jessie looked at the spec sheet that Jules handed him. The warehouse was listed as ten thousand square feet. The price: $450,000.

Jessie was reeling. Sure the place was nice, but he guessed it would take another three-hundred thousand to get it operational as a gym. And he was leaving out many of the things he would put in eventually, such as the pool, steam room, and sauna.

He thanked Jules for his time, got into his car, and drove home. He sat at his computer and went to work. He figured that with the investments he had with Bebe, plus the money he had saved from his bonuses, he had about one-hundred thousand dollars. He could sell his condo to free up another fifty- to sixty grand. He pulled up the numbers on the income he could generate from memberships and monthly dues. And he couldn't forget that he still had his job with Bebe, where he could expect to keep earning good commissions.

He decided he would spend the rest of the day crunching numbers, and playing with different scenarios. Then he would call Bebe in the morning.

# Twenty

---

The day was pleasant for an August day in Charlotte. It was very warm, but Neena and Sylvia managed to find a bench under some trees, and there was a nice breeze. Neena was wearing a sleeveless dress, and after looking at Sylvia's arms in her sleeveless blouse, Neena uttered a silent prayer of thanks that she had kept up her workouts.

Sylvia was talking about the exploits of her two high school children, and Neena wanted her to hurry up so she could get to the real reason for her being there. "At least she hasn't pulled out the pictures," Neena thought. "If she does that, I'll have to waste time looking at them and pretending to be interested."

Finally, Sylvia seemed to have exhausted her supply of tales from the world of adolescence. "Thank God!" Neena thought.

"I understand you've been with Eric from the time he opened. It must be interesting being privy to people's financial information. That's sort of like me, being a paralegal. I get interesting scoops on people's lives based on their legal entanglements."

"Oh, I love working there. You couldn't ask for a kinder employer than Eric. However, I don't see the financial information on his clients. Eric and Ron, his assistant, handle that. Occasionally, I assemble documents and mail them, and I do filing and such, but I only scan as much information as I need for the job."

"Yeah, right. And I'm the Easter bunny," thought Neena.

"Oh, really. I'm sorry. I thought you were Eric's assistant. Well, I'm sure you'll be moving up to that position eventually. I mean, you're intelligent and hardworking. But in addition to that, you have integrity. Eric can't go wrong, and I would vouch for that."

"Thanks, Neena."

"I'm just calling it as I see it. I've known Eric for years, and I know he'll do the right thing by you. If there's anything I can do to help you, just call. Eric owes me a couple of favors. As a matter of fact, I brought him a new customer just recently—Guy Pelham."

"Oh, yes, Guy. He was in just the other week. He's a very nice young man."

"Yeah, he is. I go to his gym, and we go out from time to time. We were talking, and he told me about needing help with financial planning. He sounded like he was having trouble. You know how it is. A person starts a business on a shoestring budget, so they do everything themselves. Then when the business starts growing, they find themselves in over their heads. They can't keep up with the details."

"Well, he might be in over his head with work, and he may need Eric to help him with a few things, but that young man has done well for himself. It's my understanding that he's a millionaire many times over."

Neena was stunned. *Guy, a multi-millionaire? Imagine that!* She was a pro, however, so she recovered before Sylvia could see how surprised she was.

"Yeah, Guy is wealthy, but since he doesn't flaunt it, you know, you kind of forget."

"Oh, then darling, you should remember, because from the way they've been talking in the office, he is a man of considerable means."

Neena began to recalculate. Here she'd been stepping all over Guy to get to Eric and various and sundry other men. She could kick herself for not doing her homework. She knew she was resourceful enough, however, to turn things around. What she wanted to do right now was get rid of Sylvia, so she could give some thought to getting back into Guy's good graces. It would be a little harder this time, considering the way she had carried on at the nightclub. But if he hadn't fallen hard for the Brit, she still had a shot.

Neena looked at her watch and feigned surprise at the time. She grabbed her purse and stood up.

"Sylvia, I need to head back to the office." As soon as the words left her mouth, Neena happened to look at a bench across from, but slightly behind the one where they were sitting. She took in her breath and put her hand to her mouth. Jerome was sitting there, grinning at her.

Sylvia noticed Neena's reaction, just as Neena grabbed her arm and practically pulled her up from her seat.

"Please, Sylvia. Can you walk back to my office with me? See that guy sitting over there? Yes, the one right across from us. I swear it seems that every time I turn around, he's there. I think I'm being stalked."

Sylvia peered over at Jerome.

"Do you know who he is?"

"I just know his name. It's Jerome Dyson. I met him at a nightclub a few months ago. After that, he moved into my apartment complex, and now I see him everywhere. I mean, what's he doing here? I don't think he works down here. I don't know what kind of work he does, or if he even works. Sylvia, I'm afraid."

"I don't blame you. I think you should call the police."

"But what can they do? He hasn't done anything to me."

"True. But just get it on record. Who knows what their initial investigation will turn up? If for no other reason, Neena, say you have to defend yourself against this man, and he ends up being the one hurt. The fact that you have a complaint on record will make things go a lot easier for you."

"I guess you have a point, Sylvia. I will give the police a call once I get back to my office. Can you walk back with me?"

"Sure, I will. But you should call them right now, while he's here and you can point him out to them. You can use my cell phone if you don't have one."

"Thanks, Sylvia. I do have one, but I'd be more comfortable calling from the office."

"Okay, then. It's your call. But just be sure you make that call as soon as you get back."

Sylvia and Neena made their way back, all the time looking around to see if they were being followed. When Neena walked into her office and saw Irene's familiar face, she stopped. She had never really had the time of day for Irene, but that day, she stopped and asked her how was her lunch. Irene looked surprised.

"Oh, it was quite nice. My husband's been out of work for several months, so he's taken up cooking. He enjoys fixing me these exotic sandwiches. I never know what's going to be in my lunch bag. Today, it was falafel and chopped vegetables in a pita pocket. For dinner, he'll probably stick with the Mediterranean theme, but it's still going to be a surprise, and I like that."

Neena guessed that Irene was fifty-two or three, and quite attractive, once she had taken the time to really look at her.

"At least you can still afford to eat what you want, with your husband being out of work and all. I couldn't afford the basics if I were out of work for a week." What Neena left unspoken was that Irene couldn't be making much more than half of what Neena made.

"Oh, fortunately that's not an issue with us. My husband sold a business that he'd started more than thirty years ago, so we're pretty set."

Neena's jaw dropped. "Oh," was all she could manage. She hurried off to her office.

"Imagine that. Millionaires all around me, under my very nose, and I don't know it," she muttered to herself. "Well, there's one I'm going to hook back up with." She dialed Guy's direct number at the main gym. There was no answer. She tried the other gym. Same thing. Ditto for his home number. She decided to leave a message there.

"I hope I haven't let him get away for good," she thought as she got started on the stack of folders on her desk. Then she remembered that she was supposed to call the police, but she couldn't bring herself to do it.

"One more chance, that's what I'm going to give him. If I catch him following me just one more time, I'm going to call the police."

Before she left the office for the day, Neena tried Guy at his main gym once more, but he still didn't answer. She decided to leave another message. It looked like she was going to have to get creative so as not to seem to be chasing him. She'd give that some thought once she got home.

When she walked into the outer office, she found that Irene had gone for the day, as had most of the partners. She felt herself missing Irene's comforting face, and she began to feel uneasy. She decided to use extra precautions going to her car. She would ask the security guard to keep an eye out for her. She would also scan the area round her car, and check inside before getting in. Thoughts of Jerome made her feel really creepy.

"Hey Marcus," Neena said as she walked up to the security guard. "Would you keep an eye on me until I get into my car. There's this guy that appears to be following me."

Neena saw Marcus put his game face on, ready to play the hero and come to the rescue of the damsel in distress.

"Of course, Miss Marcelle. I can walk you to your car if you want me to."

"Oh, Marcus, would you? I was going to call the police to make a report, but I decided to wait to see if he does it one more time. Who knows, maybe he's tired of the whole thing by now."

"Well, you can't be too careful these days, you know. And when you come in tomorrow, if you want me to call the precinct for you, just let me know. Come on, let's get you to your car."

Marcus wasn't carrying a gun, but he was strong-looking, though not that big. He escorted Neena to her car and wished her a safe night.

"Thanks, Marcus. I'll see you tomorrow," Neena said, and she drove off.

The evening traffic was worse than usual, so the commute took an extra twenty minutes. Neena used the time to hatch a plan to get Guy to date her again. She had pushed thoughts of Jerome Dyson out of her mind, but as she pulled into her parking space, she went into high alert, looking behind and to the sides of her. She tried to remember what kind of car he was driving that day he was parked next to her. She did remember that it was white, but otherwise nondescript. She didn't know that she would recognize it if she saw it again.

Having assured herself no one was waiting to pounce on her, Neena got out of her car and walked to her apartment. She hurriedly opened her door and went inside, taking off her shoes the moment she stepped in. She went into the kitchen. It had been a stressful day. She wanted to get a glass of wine, put on some smooth jazz, and lie on her sofa.

After she'd poured her wine, Neena thought she could relax more if she took a hot bath.

"I'll put on some music and drink the wine while I'm pouring my bath," she said aloud. She drank half the glass, and then refilled it. She already felt better.

She moved to the living room to put on the music, but before she could reach the stereo system, she saw something that made her stop dead in her tracks.

Sitting in the middle of her coffee table was a vase of white roses. There was a ribbon tied around the vase, with a note card attached. Next to the coffee table, on the sofa, some white, skimpy, lacy underwear was laid out. Neena walked toward the coffee table. She felt like she was moving in very slow motion—that it would take her minutes to reach her destination.

She put down her glass of wine and took the card from the vase of flowers, still in slow motion. She opened it to reveal the note:

*What man without a job could afford this?*

Neena's eyes grew very wide. She was more frightened than she had ever been in her life. She suddenly felt hot and lightheaded. "I shouldn't have had the wine," she thought, and then fainted.

# Twenty-one

Eric was packing his things, getting ready to leave for the day, when Sylvia buzzed him.

"Call on line one from Bebe Smith," she said.

"Thanks Sylvia. Hi Bebe."

"Hi, Eric. Just wanted to let you know I'm in town. I'll be doing seminars here—for a few months at least. During that time, I'll be operating from two bases—Charlotte and Wilmington, with the goal of making Charlotte a permanent part of my operation."

"That's great, Bebe. It sounds like things have taken off for you. Your Wilmington office must be coasting, or do you have someone who can handle things there while you're gone?"

"Actually, I have hired an assistant, and he's working out quite well. He's a quick study, and he's hungry—a powerful combination. And how is your business, Eric?"

"It's doing very well. I'm busier than ever, and signing up new clients all the time. I may have to take on a partner."

"Then you must be making lots of money. If you're wondering where to put it, I've got some great investments I can show you. Not everybody is losing money in the market these days."

"Of course not everybody is losing," Eric thought, "because when one person loses, someone else gains. And I bet you'll be on the gaining end."

Aloud he said to her, "I appreciate that you want to make me as rich as you are, Bebe. But I prefer to stick with my slow, steady approach. Besides, I'm trying to build cash reserves to finance some long-term projects."

"Fine. Just thought I'd ask. When you decide you want stellar returns, give me a call. So, Eric, who are you dating? Or rather, are you dating anyone exclusively?"

"Yes, as a matter of fact, I am. Her name is Terry, and we're very serious about each other. Things clicked with us as soon as we met. What about you Bebe? Do you have a love interest?"

"Yes, it's money, honey."

"Oh, I'd forgotten. Well thanks for letting me know you're in town. Where are you staying?"

"I'm buying a loft out near UNC-Charlotte. Since I'm going to be here so much, I might as well be comfortable. If I decide to move on, I can sell. Which brings me to the other reason for my call. I'd like to make an appointment with you to lay out a tax strategy."

"Sure. When do you want to meet?"

"Friday afternoon would be good for me."

"Okay. How about Friday at two o'clock? Will that work for you?"

"It's a date. Bye. See you then."

Eric hung up. He was shocked that Bebe was buying a place here, and it didn't sound like a place she could get on the cheap. That was an exclusive area she was talking about. He had been in a couple of the lofts, and they were spectacular. He was happy for her, but he knew one thing for sure: He didn't want Bebe Smith investing any money for him. He had worked too hard to entrust his money to some pseudo-investment specialist. It would be hard for him to watch his nest egg go *poof*, which it had a good chance of doing with Bebe. At least that was his opinion, and where his money was concerned, that was the only opinion that counted.

Eric gathered his remaining things together, placed them on his desk, and walked down the hall to where Denzel was making copies.

"As a going-away present for you, I'm going to let you take off early and pay you for the entire day. That is, if you'll go with me to pick out a ring for Terry."

"How about that? You and Terry, you're getting married. Congratulations, man." Denzel grabbed Eric in a bear hug. "I'm not surprised. You two are so good together. And Terry is good people. They don't come any better."

"Thanks, man. But I'm afraid I can't accept congratulations just yet, because I haven't put the question to Terry. I want to have the ring when I do, though, so she can't turn me down."

"Believe me, Eric. The way she looks at you, she's not about to turn you down."

"Let's hope you're right. Now, are you ready to go?"

"Sure thing. Just let me give these papers to Sylvia for assembly."

Eric walked back to his office for his things. He wanted to surprise Terry with the ring when she got back from Boston. Sanaya was going to be renting her house, and Terry had gone to get her settled. Sanaya, who had been feeling more tired, was hit with the news that her landlord was changing the apartments in her building to condos. She couldn't afford to buy, nor did she have the energy to find another place. Terry did not want to sell her house, since she felt that selling it would go against the spirit of the inheritance. So she agreed to let Sanaya move in for the same amount of rent she had been paying. Terry also went to nudge Sanaya into finding the reason for her tiredness.

Eric and Denzel had driven Terry to Boston in a U-Haul, and stayed with her for three days, helping her pack and load the furniture that she wanted to bring back to Charlotte. Eric kept wondering why Terry wanted to bring back so much, when she would be moving in with him when they got married. Then it dawned on him that they hadn't discussed marriage. So he and Denzel packed her things and drove back to Charlotte, while Terry stayed on with Sanaya. Later, Eric was going to meet Terry at her parents' house in Maryland.

Eric's comment—about getting a ring as insurance against being turned down—was made in jest, but it did reveal his anxiety. He had attempted on one occasion to broach the subject with Terry. Before he could, however, she started talking about her need to discover what she wanted to do with the next few years of her life. She told him not to feel she was turning away if she became very busy or preoccupied. Eric had accepted what she said, but he also knew what he wanted—to marry Terry right away and start a family. He was building a significant business, and he and Terry could have fun nurturing their children to take over.

Denzel came in and interrupted his reverie. "All right. Let's get this done." The two of them headed out.

"We're taking off early today, Sylvia. Call me on my cell if anything comes up that needs my attention."

"Now that your big moment has come, Denzel, how do you feel about it? I mean, a full scholarship to Triangle Academy, that's something else!"

Triangle Academy was in Chapel Hill, and it had a good reputation for preparing students for a rigorous college curriculum. It was also where many of the wealthy black families in the area sent their kids. Denzel would not feel isolated since there would be a good racial mix, and since he had known middle class life before moving in with his aunt, he was less likely to feel economic intimidation. He was to spend his entire junior and senior years there. He could remain during the summers, but that was yet to be determined. He wanted to continue to work with Eric during the summers, and Eric wanted that as well. Eric, however, still had concerns about Denzel staying with his aunt.

"Eric, I've thought long and hard about the chance you and Terry are giving me. Thanks for being there for me."

"You can thank me by doing your best. And if you ever need help with anything—anything at all—call me. There are some pre-paid phone cards in a travel pack that I've made up for you—enough to last you until next summer. Hell, they'll last the entire time you're there since you're going to be too busy studying to be on the phone much."

"Tell me you didn't do that. That was Terry's idea, right?"

"What are you trying to say?"

"Just that that's something a mom would do."

"Let me hear if you still think that once you've seen what's inside."

"Uh-oh."

"That's right. You're going to get that lecture."

Denzel managed a laugh, hoping the lecture could wait.

Eric found a parking spot near *The Diamond Place*, a store that had come highly recommended.  Inside, they were greeted by a very pleasant woman whose name was Peggy.  Eric had done his homework, so Peggy didn't have to educate him on color, clarity, and cut.  She did, however, give him some interesting details on various rings as he and Denzel looked around.  Finally, Eric settled on a one-and-a-half carat classic-styled ring, but as soon as he had, he began to wonder if Terry would want a more contemporary look.  Peggy chimed in right on cue.

"Mr. Johnson, I think you've made a very good choice.  You can't go wrong with a style like this.  It's always in fashion."

"She's right," Eric thought, and he finalized the order.  Then they walked next door to a shop called *Tailor Made*.  The gentleman who greeted them seemed to have known Eric well.

"Oh yes, Mr. Johnson.  We've been waiting for you.  Is this the young man?"

"Yes, this is Denzel Mosley."

Eric saw the confused look on Denzel's face.

"Hi.  I'm William.  Come with me and I'll get your measurements.  You're going to be pleased with the look of these clothes. And since you're tall and slender, they're going to look that much better on you."

Again Denzel looked at Eric, who was smiling.

"The travel pack is ready for you to take with you. These clothes are going to take a little time, so I'll send them as soon as they're ready."

"That will be about three weeks," William chimed in.

Denzel pulled Eric aside.

"Look. This place must be pretty expensive. I don't know if I can afford any of this."

"So who asked you for money? I'm getting you some custom shirts and casual jackets, and one suit. Now, do you have your checking and money market accounts set up the way I told you?"

"I took care of that last week."

"Good. Make sure you leave me some deposit slips so I can deposit this week's pay. And have you arranged to have your social security checks deposited into your checking account?"

"I did, against Aunt Alyce's wishes. I thought at first she wasn't going to agree to it. She said she still had to provide a home for me for holidays and school vacations, so I told her that I would send her some money every month. She let up then."

"That's up to you, sending her money I mean. But you might as well get into the habit right now of taking care of your own money. It's better that you send her what you want her to have, rather than the other way around."

"I guess you're right. Although I feel sorry for Aunt Alyce and my cousins, I'm mostly just glad to be getting out."

"Don't worry about all of that now. You're too young to have so much on your shoulders. Enjoy this time, and do well."

After their shopping binge, Eric dropped Denzel off, saying he would see him in the morning. He was nervous about leaving him. This section of town, and this housing project in particular, was starting to have a murderous reputation. Eric often kept him at his home on weekends. But Denzel said he needed to pack, and that he wanted to spend the night with his aunt and cousins, since he wouldn't be seeing them for a while. Eric understood. For all of Alyce's failings, at least she had taken him in and was probably doing the best she knew how. Sure, she had access to the social security money, and had taken over the car as her own. But until he had walked a mile in her shoes, Eric thought, he should not judge her harshly. He never went up to the apartment, though. The one time he had, Alyce was much too attentive. He left quickly.

By then, the rush hour traffic was full blown. As Eric inched along, he found he was missing Terry. He could hardly wait to talk to her that night and to see her again. He was looking forward to the trip to Maryland to meet her folks. He even thought about asking Terry if they could meet up in Maryland sooner than planned.

The traffic was almost at a standstill. Eric picked up his phone and punched in some numbers.

"Hello."

"Hi. Sanaya, it's Eric. How are you doing?"

"Oh, hi Eric. I'm okay. I'm just waiting to see what the lab results show. But there's a part of me that is hoping for no news, if you know what I mean."

"I understand, but I also know that the sooner you find out what's wrong, the sooner you can work on making it right."

"Very true. Thanks for reminding me to keep a positive attitude."

"You are very welcome. Sanaya, is Terry there?"

"No, Eric, I'm afraid she isn't."

"Oh. Then will you tell her I called? I will call her again when I get home. Do you know when she will be in?"

"No, Eric, I'm sorry I don't."

"Oh, okay. Then just tell her I called."

"Sure. Bye."

"Bye."

"Is it my imagination, or is Sanaya being evasive?" Eric wondered. He decided that it was his imagination. Sanaya had been so tired lately. She could have been sleeping when Terry went out.

All of a sudden, the traffic started moving again, and within five minutes, Eric was turning onto the ramp leading to his street. The remaining drive home was a breeze, so by the time he pulled into his driveway and hit the garage door opener, he was much looser. Then came the surprise: Terry's car was parked there! So that's what Sanaya's evasiveness was about. He wanted to know if she had driven all this way alone. That idea did not make him happy.

He rushed inside, calling her name.

"I'm upstairs," she yelled. Eric bounded up, two steps at a time. He was not prepared for what he saw there.

The door to the bedroom was closed. Without even thinking about it, Eric opened the door, and it was like he had stepped into another world. His windows had shades that shut out the light almost completely, and Terry had lowered them. There were candles and incense burning on a

246

small table that Eric didn't recognize. An animal print throw was covering his bed. But the centerpiece was Terry herself. She was dressed, or rather undressed, in, well, what could he call it? It was a shimmering, clinging fabric that had a lot of spaces in it. It barely covered one thigh, and did not even touch the other, ditto for the shoulders. Both breasts were teasingly covered. She had on much more makeup than she normally wore, and lots of bangles and earrings.

Eric watched as she walked over and turned on the stereo. He didn't recognize the music. Terry started to do a slow, sexy dance. Soon she walked over and took him in her arms, and he started to move with her. This did not go on for very long.

"Hang on for ten minutes while I freshen up," Eric said.

He took off his clothes, brushed his teeth, and showered in record time. When he went back into the bedroom, Terry was lying on her back, the material that had partially covered her on the floor, and her long, dark, shapely legs sprawled across the bed. After a little foreplay, they were both over-excited and practically clawing at each other. Eric managed to get control and slow things down, and Terry followed suit. When he finally came, it was so intense and so satisfying. He held Terry's still trembling body very, very close for a long time.

All of a sudden, Eric remembered the ring he had ordered. Should he ask her now? He thought he would wait just to set the right mood, but he changed his mind. After all, this could be his only chance. He remembered reading somewhere that the present is all we can be sure of.

Eric took a deep breath and began:

"Terry, there's something I want to talk to you about."

# Twenty-two

$\mathcal{N}$eena started to stir, and then she came into full consciousness. At first, she had to look around to see where she was. Then she was confused. What was she doing on the living room floor?

She sat for a few seconds, and then her eyes moved to the coffee table. When she saw the vase of white roses and the lacy underwear nearby on the sofa, the full force of the terror that she had felt just before she passed out came back. She lay back down on the floor and curled herself into a fetal position.

Then came the stream of awful thoughts. "My God! He's been in my house. What am I going to do? I've got to call the police.  Okay, in just a minute.  I can't do it right now.  Not right now."

Neena lay on the floor rocking for about twenty minutes.  Then she dragged herself up, went to the phone, and dialed 911.  As she was waiting for the operator to pick up, she saw the note that had been attached to the flowers on the floor, evidently where she dropped it on her way down.

"911 emergency."

"My name is Neena Marcelle.  I live at 6804 Parkway Drive, Apartment 33.  Someone broke into my apartment earlier today. . ."

"Ma'am, are you okay?"

"Yes, I am."

"Is the perpetrator still in the apartment?"

"No.  But I know who it was.  His name is Jerome Dyson, and he lives in this apartment complex."

"Do you have an address for him?"

"No, I don't, but the apartment manager can tell you."

"Were you in the apartment when he broke in?"

"No.  It happened between the time I left for work this morning at eight thirty and the time I got home at five thirty."

"And how do you know it was Jerome Dyson who broke in?"

"He left a note, and he's been stalking me. He was even following me today at lunchtime."

"I thought you said he broke in between eight thirty and five thirty? Are you saying that there was time during those hours that he could not have been in your apartment?"

"Yes. Yes I am."

"Now ma'am, you say Mr. Dyson has been stalking you. How long has he been stalking you?"

"For several months now."

"And has he done anything to hurt you physically?"

"No, he hasn't."

"And have you made a police report before regarding this stalking?"

"No, I haven't. I was going to today when I saw him following me at lunchtime, but I didn't."

"Okay ma'am. I'm going to send some officers over. Will you be safe there until the officers arrive?"

"I guess so."

"Okay. I have two officers on the way."

"Thank you."

Somehow, Neena didn't feel any better. Then a chilling thought came to her. *What if he is still here?* After all, she hadn't been in her bedroom or bathroom since she'd been home. He could be hiding out in there.

Her heart pounding, Neena got up, grabbed her purse and car keys, and went out the front door. She would wait outside until the police came.

It took the officers about twenty minutes to arrive, and Neena had been standing outside all that time. They got out of the cruiser slowly, and she approached them as they walked up to her door.

"My name is Neena Marcelle, and I'm the one who made the call about the break-in."

The two policemen looked her over. One was black, the other white. The black one spoke first.

"I'm Detective Blakely, and this is Detective Sharpe. How did the suspect get in?"

"I don't know. I didn't notice anything unusual when I unlocked the door and went in."

"Have you checked the entire apartment? Are you sure the suspect is no longer inside?"

"Well, no I haven't. That's why I've been waiting out here. When I saw the things he'd left in my living room, I was so frightened, I passed out. Then, after I'd come to and called 911, I remembered that I hadn't been any farther than my living room. Of course, I didn't hear anything, but it is possible that he's still inside."

"Okay, ma'am. You stay here. We're going to check it out." Detective Blakely had done all of the talking, while Detective Sharpe seemed to be studying her closely and looking around. They both moved toward her door, hands on their guns. When they got to the door, they drew their guns, stopped to listen, and then went inside. Neena stood in the same spot, very tense, expecting to hear gunshots, or see Jerome come running out.

Nothing of the sort happened. After about ten minutes, Detective Sharpe came to the door and told her she could come inside.

"Now, ma'am, you say you know who came into your apartment?"

"Yes. His name is Jerome Dyson."

"Is this Jerome Dyson a friend, an acquaintance? Does he have a key?"

"He's an acquaintance. I met him several months ago at a dance club, and he's been following me around. I did not give him a key to my apartment."

"You said he left a note. Did he leave anything else?"

"Yes. He left these roses and the lingerie."

Detective Sharpe used a gloved hand to pick up the note. He read it, showed it to Blakely, and then put it into a plastic bag.

"This note have any special meaning to you?" Blakely asked.

Neena told the detectives about the time she was getting into her car to go to work and Jerome popped up from nowhere. She told them about the conversation that ensued, and how angry Jerome had gotten when she insinuated that he might not have a job.

The detectives took plenty of notes, bagged up the remaining evidence, and then went about checking all of her windows and checking the door again. They asked her if the apartment manager lived onsite, and if she had a twenty-four-hour number to call in case of emergencies. Neena gave them the emergency number.

"Miss Marcelle, we're going to see if we can find Jerome Dyson, and have a talk with him. We're also going to check out the evidence here, see if we can get some prints. Did you touch anything besides the note?"

"No. No I didn't."

"Good. Now, you should get a locksmith over here to change your locks, and make sure he installs a deadbolt. Also, you should get bars on your windows, but make sure you have the kind that you can remove from inside. You don't want to trap yourself in here. Now, do you have a place where you can stay until all these things have been taken care of?"

"Yes," Neena lied.

"Alright then, we'll just see if we can find Jerome Dyson, and call you with a report as soon as we find out something. What's a number where we can reach you?"

Neena gave the detectives her cell phone number and watched them leave. She felt so alone and frightened. She wished she hadn't alienated Guy. He would have taken care of her. A great weariness settled over her. She had no energy to figure out what to do. Where could she go? She had no place to go. She didn't even know if she could get a locksmith to come tonight.

Neena's head was suddenly filled with memories of her strict upbringing. If she told Mom and Dad she was being stalked, they would swear she had done something to cause it. Had she? After all, would any of this be happening had she stuck with Guy that night at the club? She didn't want to think about it anymore.

Then she remembered the thick, wide board that she had in the hall closet. It might be the right size to fit under her doorknob. She went to the closet and pulled it from behind a lot of other junk. When she tried it, she found it a perfect fit. She then went into the kitchen, took out a sharp carving knife, and went back to the door. She sat in front of it, staring straight ahead, the knife in her hand. She leaned against the wall, and after about thirty minutes, she was asleep.

The sound of a phone ringing woke Neena up. She got up quickly and went to the phone, only to realize there was no ring coming from it. It was the cell phone in her purse. She went to get it.

"Hello," she said, her voice low and cautious.

"Hello, Miss Marcelle, this is Detective Blakely of the Charlotte/Mecklenburg Police Department. Are you okay?"

"Yes, I am. Have you found out anything?"

"Well, ma'am, the only thing we've found is that no one by the name of Jerome Dyson lives at your apartment complex. In fact, we have not been able to find anyone by that name in the state of North Carolina. Are you sure that's the name he gave you?"

"Yes, I'm sure of it," Neena said, her heart sinking even further.

"Okay, ma'am. We're going to keep checking. In the meantime, though, we'd like for you to come down to the precinct to give us a description. Do you know of anyone else who has seen this person?"

"Yes, my friend Sylvia. Sylvia Bonhie."

"Then see if you can get Sylvia Bonhie to come down to the precinct with you, say around eleven o'clock tomorrow morning."

Neena hung up the phone and felt so overburdened. She would call Sylvia in the morning. Sylvia had an active family life, though, as evidenced by her running narrative today. She might be out early tomorrow, driving the kids here and there. The best thing would be to call her now. But Neena couldn't do it. Not now. She would take her chances.

"Maybe I should get a hotel room for a few days," she wondered aloud. "But how am I going to pay for it? My credit cards are maxed out and I have no money."

Neena picked up the knife and her cell phone and settled back in her place in front of the door. At first, she felt more alone than she had ever felt before. Once that feeling was gone, she was left with just numbness.

# Twenty-three

---

$T$erry had been up for about thirty minutes when the alarm went off. Her present experiences were real, she knew, but they felt surreal just the same. In the space of about nine months, she had walked away from a dead-end job and an unfulfilled life, to a city where she had found a wonderful man and a life of much promise. The sparkle was back in her eyes.

On the way back from Boston, she had stopped in Maryland to pick up her sister Maya, and her brother-in-law. They wanted to come with her to see Charlotte, and take a much-needed break from their daughter. They were staying in Terry's apartment, so when Eric went over with her to meet them the night before, he had cleverly suggested that Terry stay with him, and let Maya and Brian have the apartment to themselves. So she had packed some things and moved in with Eric, for a few days anyway.

Maya liked Eric right away, so she was thrilled with the news of the engagement. She wanted to call everyone immediately, but Terry wanted to wait until she had at least set a date. Sanaya would be ecstatic. She would call Sanaya that night, not only to tell her the news, but also to find out if she'd gotten her test results back. At least Terry had been able to help with her living situation.

One thing Terry knew, and that was she would not be having one of those headache weddings. If she had her way, she and Eric would elope. The families might not like it, but she had no intention of spending the next year of her life planning an elaborate party.

She heard Eric getting up, so she moved into fast gear, all the while smiling as she thought about the ways she had surprised him the day before. If only she could have captured his face on film.

"Good morning, sweetheart," Eric greeted her, adding a big hug.

"Good morning. Do you feel like eating? I can go downstairs and get breakfast started while you get dressed."

"Sure. I'm starved, since we didn't take time to eat last night. When we finish, we can pack something for Denzel, in case he doesn't get to eat breakfast this morning."

Terry went downstairs and turned on the television. A local news anchors was giving a rundown on the murders, rapes, and robberies that occurred while the good citizenry of Charlotte were asleep. She turned the television off, opting instead for some music with soothing guitar sounds. "That's a much better way to start the morning," she said to herself as she beat some eggs.

By the time Eric came downstairs, everything was ready. They ate quickly, and then packed a breakfast for Denzel. They were supposed to pick him up at eight thirty, so they needed to get going.

The ride to Denzel's house didn't take long since it was Saturday morning, and people had not yet come out in force. Eric parked as close to Denzel's building as he could. He told Terry to stay in the car while he went to see if Denzel was waiting downstairs. In less than a minute, he was walking back to the car.

"He's not waiting downstairs, so I'm going up to get him."

"I'll come with you," Terry said, and got out of the car.

They walked up one flight and down a narrow, dark hallway until they found *204*. Eric knocked, and Terry noticed the worried look on his face.

After what seemed like at least a minute, Denzel opened the door. His luggage was sitting just inside, and he started putting it in the hallway. Terry looked around as she and Eric helped. The place was small, and by most people's definition, not even modest. The linoleum floor was curling up at the edges, and had long since faded. She saw light coming through the wall straight ahead of her, but she couldn't tell if it was from a room in this apartment or from the adjoining apartment. The place was clean, though, and looked as if the occupants had done their best under the circumstances.

A woman came into view from somewhere in the house and started toward them. Terry assumed that it was Denzel's aunt, so she stepped forward and extended her hand.

"Hi. I'm Terry Weeks, Eric's fiancée. I'm riding with them to the academy."

"I'm Alyce Jackson, Denzel's aunt, and the one who has provided a home for him all these years. I guess you two are the smarties who told him he could have his check mailed to him at school now."

She left Terry's hand hanging, and Terry was shocked. Alyce had dismantled the theory that all southerners were friendly.

She looked like a woman who had once been pretty, but whose face was now showing the wear and tear of a life that had not been kind. She was lean, and her skin looked dry, like it was not accustomed to being pampered. She was wearing Capri pants and a T-shirt. Her hair was in one of those wrapped styles, but it was not colored. Her best feature to Terry was a pair of very full and shapely lips. It seemed incongruous that these ugly words were coming from such a beautiful mouth.

Eric stepped in.

"Mrs. Jackson, in no way did I intend to minimize what you've done for Denzel over the years. But since Denzel will be at school most of the time, he needs his check to pay for incidentals that his scholarship won't cover. That just seems fair. After all, the money does belong to Denzel."

"Fair?" she snapped. "Who will provide a home for him when school is not in session? Isn't it fair that the money help pay for that?"

"But Aunt Alyce, I told you I'd send you part of the money each month," Denzel piped in.

"Miss Jackson, if it's going to put a strain on you, Terry and I will be more than happy to have Denzel stay with us when he's away from school."

"So now that I've raised him, and he's become a smart boy, you want to just snatch him away and take all the credit. Is that it?"

"Aunt Alyce, please . . ." Denzel began.

"Mrs. Jackson, I assure you that is not the case. Denzel loves you, and if we all pull together now and help him, I think you will be better for it in the long run."

Alyce Jackson stood there and glared at them.

"Denzel, have you said your goodbyes to everyone?" Terry asked.

Just then, two adolescent girls walked into view. Terry wondered if they had heard the whole exchange. They looked to be around ten and twelve years old with the aloofness that typically began at those ages and continued through the late teens. They soon made it clear, however, that they were going to miss Denzel. They both hugged him for a long time. When they said goodbye to each other, Denzel had tears in his eyes. He let them go, and then picked up his one remaining bag—a backpack.

"Let's go," he said. The look on his face was so sad that Terry's eyes began to tear.

Maya and her husband had gone back to Maryland, and Terry was back in her apartment. She and Eric spent most evenings, and often the nights, together. That night, they were having dinner at her house, and Terry was in the middle of preparations.

The plan was to discuss their wedding, but the biggest item on Terry's mind was *The Ring*, or rather her lack of one. As a matter of fact, Eric had not even mentioned one. What could he be thinking? He didn't appear to be a tightwad. Terry was about to get upset.

The phone rang and she picked up on the first ring.

"Hello."

"Hi, love. I'm hoping you can have lunch with me tomorrow. I'm meeting an old acquaintance for business, and I'd like for you to meet her."

"Sure. Dinner will be ready in about an hour. What time will you be arriving?"

"I have an errand to run first, so I should get there at seven."

"That's perfect. I'll see you then. Bye."

"Bye. Love you."

Terry hung up and resumed dinner preparations. She was making Shrimp Creole, which would be served over rice. She had already prepared the salad and lemonade. For dessert, she had made a graham cracker-pineapple-banana-almond dish from her *Golden Door* recipe book. There was no point in making herself and Eric fat before their wedding day, she had thought.

She had a lot on her mind. When she had spoken with Sanaya last weekend, Sanaya still had not received her test results, and her symptoms remained. She could barely make it through her workday. Terry was very concerned about her friend.

She also needed to call Tyrone to tell him her good news, and to find out how things were going in school. She had no doubt that he was doing well, since he was smart and ambitious. Still, she wanted to call him within the week.

And last, there was the matter of her career. Not only had she not made any decisions, she also had done nothing to pursue the recommendations of the career counselor based on the results of her Campbell Interest and Skill Survey.

And now she had a wedding to plan. "It's time to get serious," she thought. "I have to make a list and structure my days based on it for the next three weeks. First on the list will be to call Tyrone and Sanaya."

Terry turned the stove to *simmer*. By the time Eric arrived, the shrimp would be ready to serve. She went to set the table, but was interrupted by the phone again. When she picked up, to her surprise and delight, she heard Tyrone's voice.

"Tyrone, how're things? How's school going?"

"My classes are going very well," he began. Terry found herself mentally finishing his sentence with a *but*. Something was wrong.

"One of my drama professors has begun mentoring me. She even helped me get an internship. She believes I'm more talented and ambitious than the average student."

"Tyrone, that's true, and anyone who is around you for very long would recognize it. I'm just glad you've been discovered early in the game. How are your mom and brother?"

"Things are looking up for them, too. My mother is making more money. Reggie's doing well in school and he has a weekend job."

"So, you bring nothing but good news. And last, but not least, how's the girlfriend?"

"Not girlfriend, but wife. Yolanda and I were married almost five months ago."

Terry was speechless for a moment. The doorbell gave her a chance to regain her composure.

"Best wishes, Tyrone! Could you hold for just a minute? I have to answer the door."

She went to let Eric in. He had a key to her apartment, but only used it if she was not at home. When he came in, he stared into her face.

"Is something wrong?"

"I don't know. I was talking to Tyrone, and he told me that he and Yolanda have been married for five months. He's still on the phone. Excuse me."

Eric followed her back to the kitchen, where she resumed her conversation with Tyrone.

"Tyrone, I would have sent you a wedding present had I known. Of course, I'm still going to send a gift. Oh, by the way, I'm engaged. My fiancé is Eric Johnson, and he's smart, and handsome, and kind." She turned toward Eric, a big smile on her face. "We haven't set the date yet. But, Tyrone, are you happy? I know being a full-time student with a wife and a job can't be easy."

Terry was silent as Tyrone talked. Eric was trying to read the expressions on her face as she listened.

"Oh, I see. How is she feeling about this? Uh-huh. . .Uh-huh. . ."

The conversation went on like this for fifteen minutes more. By the time Terry got off the phone, Eric had set the table. Terry went into the dining area and sat down. Eric said a grace, and she filled him in as they started to pass the food.

"Not only have Tyrone and Yolanda married, they are also expecting a baby in two-and-a-half months. Yolanda's parents are disappointed in her, so they haven't been supportive at all. Tyrone says that she has an aunt who has helped them. He also said that his mother has given what little help she can. I have a lot of sympathy for them. I wonder if they have any idea how difficult the next several years are going to be. God, I wish . . ."

Eric reached over and put his hand over hers.

"Sweetheart, don't despair. Look at how things looked for Denzel. But right around the corner, there was a solution waiting. They are both bright, promising young people. I'm sure something positive will turn up. Now let's eat."

With that, they began to eat and discuss their marriage plans.

# Twenty-four

Jessie had just scored another big donation, thanks to a tip from Mrs. Anon. She had learned about a foundation that had moved its headquarters from New York to a suite on Gordon Road. The foundation had been set up by the heir to the estate of one of the wealthiest black businessmen in America in the 1980s. Margaret Baird was the president, and Jessie submitted a proposal to her that he had done himself. Bebe had been in Charlotte, and he was glad because this gave him a chance to try his wings. And, to his delight, he had pulled it off. He was becoming more confident each day. His portfolio had to be looking good.

Then came the nagging feeling he'd been having. He still couldn't determine what was causing it. If he could totally relax, he thought, it would all come to him.

As soon as he got home, he took off his suit, put on some lounging clothes, and called Bebe. He was put through to voice messaging. She was supposed to be back from Charlotte that afternoon, so he decided not to leave a message. He wanted to pass the good news on to her live. He would call later that night. He entertained the idea of taking her out and telling her over dinner. She would be proud of him. He even wished the evening could have a romantic twist, but he harbored no illusions of that anymore.

Jessie thought about the night he met Bebe. Surely it had been no illusion, the way she came after him. Boy did she turn him on. Things would have gotten interesting, too, had it not been for the accident. Since that accident, however, she only seemed interested in helping him professionally and financially. He didn't know what happened. Maybe the accident had given her time to realize that he was just not in her class.

Well, she could just take her classy self on. One of his mother's adages was "love the one who loves you." Like a lot of folk wisdom, it made sense. There was bound to be a woman out there who would love and appreciate him just as he was. But he couldn't help it if Bebe still excited him.

Jessie sat at his computer to complete the documentation for the day, as well as do some planning for follow-up. Before he knew it, three hours had gone by. He sat still and closed his eyes for a minute. *He was driving and he had some passengers in the front and back, except he couldn't tell who they were. He swerved suddenly to avoid a car headed right for them.*

Jessie drifted out of his dream, and the thoughts that had been nagging below the surface were suddenly crystal clear. He remembered his conversation with Mrs. Anon just before they had the accident. They were talking about Bebe. Jessie had asked Mrs. Anon if she'd known Bebe before that night. Mrs. Anon had answered no, but that she had heard of her. She said Bebe commanded a lot of attention, and that people tried to impress her, even please her. Then Mrs. Anon asked Jessie about his impression of Bebe.

*I'm impressed with her, and intrigued. . . Where did she make her money? How is she able to provide the seed money for a project of this magnitude?*

*Is that what she told you, that she is providing the seed money? I suspect . . .*

Then there was the tire screeching. What did Mrs. Anon mean? Did Bebe misrepresent her role?

He dialed Bebe's number again, and again he got her voice mailbox. This time he left a message.

271

Feeling anxious, Jessie went for a walk to clear his head. After about an hour, he returned home. His mother had called, but still no word from Bebe. He decided to drive to her house and take a look around.

After he'd freshened up and changed his clothes, Jessie headed toward Bebe's condo on Eastwood Road. What would he say if he found her at home—*I just couldn't wait to tell you about the huge donation that I got today?* What if she was not alone? He decided not to go there after all. He would just stop somewhere for dinner.

He saw the sign for *Mrs. Jones,* the new southern cooking restaurant that people had been raving about. Jessie loved good home cooking, and this was the next best thing. He pulled into the driveway and got out, not thrilled about going in alone. The alternative was carryout, and he didn't want that either.

There was a waiting line about ten deep. Jessie gave the hostess his name and sat on a bench. When he looked around, he felt even more self-conscious because the dining was communal style at. If you didn't come with a large party, chances are you would end up being seated with total strangers at one of the long tables. That was a very likely scenario for Jessie. Maybe he should have opted for takeout.

Just as he was about to go to the takeout area, however, the hostess called his name and he was instructed to follow her.

Jessie was led to a table in the rear that was populated by a diverse group of people. He sat next to a sister—Colleen Rivers. She looked in her late twenties, or early thirties, and she was friendly in an unobtrusive way. She told Jessie she managed the Millennium Gym on College Road, but when she told him she wanted to open her own gym, one just for women, he really became interested. He opened up to her about his plans, and they began an animated discussion.

The waitresses brought over large bowls of steaming collards, black-eyed peas, rice, candied yams, fried chicken, barbequed chicken, barbequed pork, biscuits, and corn bread. The diners were to pass the bowls around as if they were seated at the family dinner table. Sharing the food that way made the dinner more intimate for Jessie and Colleen, even though they had not come here together. After dinner, they did not want to part.

"Colleen, I've enjoyed your company. May I call you this weekend?"

"I'd like that. Would you like to go to my place for coffee, tea, or a nightcap?"

"Very much so," Jessie said, vowing to himself to drive very carefully this time. He reached for her bill, but she stopped him.

"No, you don't have to do that. I don't expect you to do that."

"I insist, and it's my pleasure." He didn't know how she would take this. Some women might think he was trying to put them under obligation. But he relaxed when Colleen looked into his eyes and smiled. This was turning out to be a pleasant night.

Colleen lived about a half mile from where Jessie lived. He was surprised he had never seen her before. After directing him to a visitor parking space, she headed to her door. Jessie sat in his car for a minute after he turned off the ignition and took a deep breath. He didn't know what he was about to get into, but he was too excited to turn back. He got out of the car and followed Colleen inside. She turned on a few lights and they sat on her sofa.

"There's been a strange, but nice, turn of events tonight," Jessie said to her. "First of all, I decide on a whim to stop at *Mrs. Jones*. Then the hostess seats me next to someone who is also interested in owning a gym. And to top things off, you live only a half mile from me. You weren't adopted, were you? Or maybe I was."

Colleen laughed. Jessie liked her full laugh. He liked her looks, too. She was petite—only about five-four and slightly more than one hundred pounds, with most of that being breasts.

"It's called serendipity."

"That's right. Serendipity. So, Colleen, do you have family in the area?"

"No. Most of my family is in Monroe. That's where I grew up. I came here to go to business college, and stayed on after finishing."

Colleen's apartment was interesting. It was obvious that her furnishings were not expensive, but her personality showed through what she did have. The light, low-slung sofa looked fragile but was comfortable. Each chair at the dining table was different in an artsy-craftsy way. When she opened the refrigerator, Jessie saw that it was very well stocked.

"I'm guessing that either you just went grocery shopping today for a big party this weekend, or you won a grocery sweepstakes."

Colleen laughed again. Jessie had fallen in love with that laugh.

"I guess it's a habit left over from when I grew up," she answered. "I love having a well-stocked refrigerator, extra soap, an excessive number of towels, you know, the essentials for unexpected guests."

"Okay, so she's quirky," Jessie thought. "Quirky's not bad, though. I can deal with that."

Colleen had several trays stacked on a kitchen counter. She took one and placed two glasses, two small plates, and some knives and napkins on it. She opened the refrigerator and took out some type of cheese or dessert ball covered by a crystal dome. Then she opened another cabinet and came back with some brown bread slices that had golden raisins baked in. She added these to the tray. She told Jessie to take the tray over to where they had been sitting.

While Colleen was in the kitchen mixing and pouring, Jessie sampled the bread and spread.

"Mmmm, what is this?" he said to Colleen, who was still in the kitchen. "This is delicious!"

Again, there was that sweet laugh.

"It's from an old family recipe. I made it all this morning, just on a whim."

As she said this, Colleen walked over to Jessie. She was holding a brightly colored pitcher, and she filled the two glasses with a dark-colored, carbonated liquid. Jessie took a drink and had a repeat reaction.

"Let me guess," he said. "Another family recipe."

"Actually, this drink is a tradition in the community where I grew up."

Jessie looked at her and smiled, wondering how many other pleasant surprises he was in for.

Somehow, and Jessie didn't know how it happened, he and Colleen were sitting very close on the couch. He turned to say something to her, and she pulled his face down to hers, her lips finding his. Her lips were plump and soft, and he'd never tasted any as good. Pretty soon they were breathing heavily.

"How far is this going to go?" Jessie wondered. He stopped and looked into Colleen's eyes for an affirmation that he could continue. He got more than that. She unbuttoned her blouse. Jessie looked down to see beautiful breasts with large, erect nipples. By the time he bent his head over and started to taste them, they were both too far along.

Colleen moved away from Jessie and took a deep breath. Then she stood up and beckoned him to follow her to her bedroom. They undressed very quickly. Somehow they found the restraint to prolong their lovemaking, even in all of its intensity. The first time Jessie came, he thought, "No, quirky's not bad, not bad at all." The second time, he was saying to himself, "Damn! Give me quirky all the time."

# Twenty-five

---

$T$erry was the first to arrive. She sat nursing a Pepsi, anxious to meet the intriguing Bebe, and wondering if she would turn out to be another Neena. She knew Eric was considered a good catch. She hadn't done any planning or scheming to get him either. Maybe that was why she ended up with him, and someone like Neena did not.

She looked up and saw Eric coming toward her. He was alone. He smiled at her and she smiled back. She was fiercely in love, but that still didn't stop her from wondering if he was going to get a ring for her. She might just have to break down and ask him, even though that would take away from the romance of it.

She stood up when he got to the table, and he hugged and kissed her.

"Hi. How's it going?" he asked.

"I have good news and bad news. I spoke with Sanaya last night. The good news is that she knows what's wrong with her. The bad news—she has diabetes. It's an insidious disease, and it can wreak havoc. The doctor immediately prescribed medication and a diet and exercise program. He said had she not come in for testing when she did, she would have been gravely ill or worse. She's depressed, but I think once the effects of the medication and her eating and exercise programs kick in, she'll feel better and be in better spirits."

"Oh, I'm sure. I'm sorry. Are you okay?"

"Yeah, I am."

From her peripheral vision, Terry saw someone walking toward them. She turned and saw an attractive, confident woman who smiled as she approached.

"Hello, Eric. So this must be the fiancée, Terry. Hi. I'm Bebe Smith."

"Hi. Yes, I am Terry, the fiancée. It's nice to meet you Bebe."

"Hi, Bebe. Good to see you. Have a seat." Eric pulled out a chair for her.

"So, have you guys set a date, yet?"

"Not exactly. We've narrowed down some dates."

"Bebe, I wanted you and Terry to meet, so I asked her along. Hope you don't mind. A young man that she's mentored is now a college student in Boston, and he needs scholarship money. I told her you'd be the person to talk to."

"Oh? Tell me about him."

"Eric is so special," Terry thought as she looked at him. Last night, when she was worrying about Tyrone, she didn't think he was paying much attention. She looked at Bebe, who was staring straight at her. Bebe was also genuinely interested in what she had to say about Tyrone.

"It's Tyrone's wife, Yolanda, who needs the scholarship. Tyrone has a full scholarship and an internship. He and Yolanda were facing an unexpected pregnancy, so they married. Yolanda's parents were financing her education, but when she got pregnant and married, they were very disappointed. You might think it's harsh that they cut her off. I'm not judging any of them. I'm just trying to help. Their chances are so much better if they finish school. And Tyrone is so talented. The odds of him making it are greatly increased if Yolanda can finish her undergraduate degree as well. Anyway, if you could help, I will do whatever I can to facilitate.

Terry's determination must have been evident, based on what Bebe said next.

"Don't worry, Terry. I don't see this as a problem. As a matter of fact, we've recently had a spike in donations since I hired an assistant in Wilmington. Listen, why don't you and I meet tomorrow. I'm staying nearby, at the Executive Suites Hotel, until the loft that I purchased is ready. If you meet me there, I can plug some information into my computer to get the process started. I'll just need some data from you, such as Yolanda's full name, date of birth, social security number, grade point average, the school name, etcetera. We'll go from there."

Terry was swept away. Bebe had turned out to be a godsend. She was smiling from ear to ear, but when she looked over at Eric, she thought she saw skepticism.

As soon as they finished eating, Eric and Bebe pulled out briefcases and prepared to discuss tax issues.

"Hey, guys. I'm going to walk to the bath shop next door and browse so you two can have some privacy. I'll meet you back here in about twenty minutes." Terry picked up her purse to leave.

"Oh, please don't leave," Bebe protested. "If Eric doesn't mind your hearing this, I don't. Besides, I love bath items, and maybe I can find a gift for my new assistant, Jessie. We can go together when Eric and I have finished here."

"Good. I'd love that," Terry told Bebe. She settled back down and listened to everything she never wanted to know about taxes. She was astonished by the amounts of money they were talking about, and she listened as Eric outlined a tax strategy for Bebe's business ventures. Their meeting went on for about forty-five minutes. Afterward, they all walked to the bath shop where they spent another twenty minutes before saying goodbye.

"I have to get back to the office. Where are you going now?" Eric asked Terry as soon as Bebe had walked away.

"I'm driving to the outlet shops that are about ten miles away. Someone told me they have great wedding dresses at bargain prices. It's really time to start making the big decisions." Terry decided that Eric needed less subtle hints about the ring.

"Can I talk you into spending the evening with me? I can pick you up after work. I'll even make dinner."

"Eric doesn't get it," Terry thought. "Typical man."

"Uhm, Eric, I'm sorry, but . . ." Terry started, but she could not keep up the tease once she saw the pitiful expression on his face. She gave herself away with a laugh. "Of course I'll spend the evening with you. I'll wait for you to pick me up."

Eric left and Terry began the walk to her car that was a few blocks away. She sauntered, stopping to look in some of the store windows. The afternoon was full of sunshine, and she felt good. At the end of the first block, she was standing, waiting for the light to change. Directly across the street from her was a medical office building. It was tall for the area—about ten stories—and had around thirty angled parking spaces out front. What caught Terry's eyes was the late model Ford Taurus that had just pulled into one of those spaces.

Terry knew it had to be a drug rep—she had been part of that world long enough to tell. She watched as the black woman, who looked to be in her late twenties, got out from the driver's side. She was wearing a generic business suit and nondescript pumps. Her color scheme was black. It dawned on Terry that the reason many of the reps wore black was that they were in mourning for their lives.

The light changed and she crossed the street. She was much closer to the woman—close enough to see that familiar anxious look on her face. The reason for the anxiety climbed out of the passenger side of the car—a young white man who might as well be wearing a sign saying *District Manager*. His physical bearing reeked of the newly empowered. He was wearing a dark suit and tie and sunglasses. He walked with a swagger. Terry recognized the situation as she had witnessed it countless times. This woman was on horror duty—otherwise known as a *work with*, when your manager follows you around all day and watches your every move.

As Terry watched, the young man walked around to the trunk of the car where the woman was putting samples into a duffel bag. She stopped in the middle of the sidewalk, riveted to the scene unfolding before her. She felt a rush of strong emotion.

Terry could see the manager's mouth moving and his hands pointing. Then he turned, put his hands in his pockets, and started looking around, checking out *the lay of the land*. A very strong feeling of repulsion swept over Terry, and she felt nauseated.

Terry saw people who were slaves—men, women, and children, working in the cotton fields of southern plantations. It must have been *haaard* work, because the sun was beating down on them, and they were tired, but they were not allowed to take a break. There were whole families there, just working, working for someone else's bank account, someone else's meal table, someone else's school, and never their own. Walking around, checking everything out—checking out *the lay of the land*—was the white overseer. He was holding a whip in his hand, and a gun was in the holster around his waist. He held all the cards.

"The gun and the whip are gone," Terry thought, "but that's just a cosmetic change. Today you can leave, but you still must plan your escape years in advance, or you'll be sucked right back in."

She wondered where the vivid images were coming from? Something she'd heard elderly people in her family talk about? Did they come from something she'd read or seen on television?

The rep had closed her car trunk, and she and the manager had begun walking toward the office building. Still, Terry stood there, another vivid image washing into her mind. This time, she pictured a migrant farm family, the children working the few morning hours before school begins, and again during the daylight hours left after school. The parents have stashed away some money, planning to leave for greener pastures. When they go to settle their last bill, the owner of the farm tells them they are mistaken, that they owe twice what they thought. The father knows this is not true, but he also knows it is futile to dispute. So he has his family wait it out, because he knows the owner's mind will be filled with suspicion. After all, the owner *is* a thief and a liar.

Finally, after four long weeks, the migrant feels that the farm-owner's suspicions have abated. Sunday is the only day they don't have to work in the fields, so the man and his family steal away on Saturday night, figuring they won't be missed until Monday. By that time, he plans to be far away.

The drug rep and her manager were, by then, inside the building. Still the images came. They came from different times and places. The stories, however, were the same: the white foreman in a sweatshop, now standing guard over black prisoners on road detail; the black secretary and her demanding white boss; the black physician who is now an employee of a white-run hospital or HMO. The images kept coming, except the *overseers* appeared in different genders and a variety of colors.

A man touched Terry's arm.

"Are you okay, ma'am? You've been standing here and you look a little faint."

"Oh, I'm fine, thank you very much. I was just deep in thought. I have to get to my car." With that, Terry began to walk much more quickly. She got into her car, but instead of driving to the outlet mall, she drove to her apartment. Once there, she raced inside, grabbed a pen and a thick pad of paper from her desk, and began to write.

# *Twenty-six*

---

Neena was waiting for the locksmith to come. She would have to use her grocery money to pay him. She might as well, since she couldn't go out for groceries anyway. She didn't even go to the precinct so the police could do a sketch of Jerome, or whatever his name was.

How could she go anywhere? She'd have to come back home and face the possibility that Jerome had been in her apartment again. Not only that, he might decide to leave behind more evidence of his filthy mind. Or what if he decided to stay this time? No, there was no way she could go anywhere yet. Maybe after she had a new lock and a deadbolt. She would see how she felt then.

When the doorbell rang, it startled Neena, even though she was expecting the locksmith. She looked out the living room window first, and relaxed somewhat when she saw the truck with the *Open Anytime Locksmith* painted on the side. Still, she looked through her door's peephole, and asked who was there before opening the door.

"It's Jay, from *Open Anytime Locksmith*," the young man replied.

Neena opened the door and introduced herself to Jay. He explained that the type of lock he was installing was one of the best, and he went over the cost with her.

"Unless you have some more questions, I'll get started."

"Oh, go right ahead," Neena answered, but she stayed at the door. Jay went out to his truck and came back with his tools.

"Is the bulk of your business from emergency calls?" she asked.

"No, although we do get a fair amount of emergency business. We do a lot of work for new construction and rehabs." Already Jay seemed to be completely involved in his work.

"Oh, I see." Neena was going to have to work to keep a conversation going. "I'll bet your own home is a fortress."

"No, not really. We just have locks on all the doors, similar to the ones I'm installing here. We also have locks on our windows. That's basically all you need, unless you put in an alarm system. Some people put bars on their bottom floor windows, but we haven't seen the need to do that. We live in a pretty safe neighborhood."

"Well, someone broke into my apartment. I don't know how he got in, because I didn't detect any damage to the doors or windows. Will the locks you're installing prevent that from happening?"

"Ma'am, if someone tries to get in with these locks, they would have to make so much noise, they'd attract the entire neighborhood. The lock that you had on this door was pretty flimsy. The guy probably just used a credit card. I'm surprised they even install locks like this on the doors here."

"Maybe I should have you do a security sweep of my house, you know, check the windows, and tell me what I need."

"Sure, I can do that. We even work with another company that installs alarm systems, so if you're interested, I could set up something with them as well. I can't do that today, though. I only scheduled a half-hour for this job. I'll leave my card with you, though, and you can call the office to schedule another appointment."

"Oh, okay. I'll do that."

Jay was finishing. He asked Neena for a broom to sweep up the dust. She took her time walking to the kitchen to get it, not wanting Jay to leave. His presence was comforting, and once he left, she would be alone again with her fears.

By the time Neena got back to the door, Jay had put away all of his tools. He explained to her how the lock worked, gave her two keys, and watched while she tried them. He swept up the dust and put it in a plastic bag.

"Okay, you're all set. That will be seventy-five dollars."

Neena went inside again to get the money, her steps heavier this time. She paid Jay, he gave her his business card, and just like that he was gone. Neena was alone again.

She stayed inside the rest of the day and all day Sunday. Her mother called her Sunday evening. Neena couldn't get into the conversation about other people and their problems. She had a crisis on her hands here. Finally, Neena's mother asked how her church service had been that morning.

"Oh, Mom, I didn't go to church this morning. I haven't been feeling well for the last few days."

"I thought you sounded a little under the weather. What's wrong?"

"I don't know. Maybe I've just caught a bug of some sort."

"Well, take care of yourself. You haven't been staying out late partying, have you? That kind of life takes its toll, you know."

"No, Mom, I haven't. I'll be okay. I just need to rest, so I'll talk to you later." Neena hung up the phone. "I thought a mom was supposed to make you feel better," she muttered. "How come I feel worse?"

On Monday morning, Neena called into work saying that she was very ill, and that she would be out for a few days. She called very early in the morning so she wouldn't have to talk to Irene, and therefore wouldn't have to lie to her. Eventually, she would talk openly about this situation, but she was too tired at that point.

She did a lot of sleeping that day. The thought of a shower frightened her. Hadn't Norman Bates taught all women the dangers of taking a shower when they were alone? No, a tub bath would be safer. In the end though, she couldn't even do that, so she took a sponge bath, ate canned soup, and drank juice. By Tuesday, she felt better. She had heard no more from Jerome or from the police, and she was thinking of returning to work before the week was out.

By Tuesday night, the fears had dissipated even more. She still couldn't take a shower, but she soaked in the bathtub for a long time, and the water and soap seemed to cleanse her spirit along with her body. She could go into work a couple of hours late the next morning so she would have time to stop by the precinct.

" No, no. It will be better to go in at the regular time. That way, I can get Sylvia to go to the precinct with me after work. Yes, that's what I'll do." These thoughts comforted Neena. She had a plan. She would call Sylvia as soon as she got to the office.

Neena got out of the tub and dried herself. She wanted to wash her hair, but since she usually did that in the shower, she decided to pass. She put on her pajamas, and then checked all the windows and doors, even though she knew they were locked. She still kept the board under the doorknob, even with the dead bolt.

As she was passing through her living room, Neena's eyes happened on the text of *A Course In Miracles*. An old acquaintance from years back had given the book to her. She had always thought him kind of weird. He used to make abstruse statements, and when she asked him to explain, the explanations were more enigmatic than the original statements. He had given her the book as a birthday present, for heaven's sake, so that should tell you something. Neena had never done more than thumb through it. Now, however, she thought she might take solace from the words. The publisher was the *Foundation for Inner Peace*, and if there was anything she needed right now, it was some inner peace.

The book was lying beneath several others on a shelf built into her end table. Neena removed it and took it into her bedroom. She turned on the reading light, climbed into bed, opened the book to the introduction, and began reading. She was confused by what she read. The *"course in miracles . . .is a required course. Only the time you take it is voluntary."[1]*

"What does that mean?" She read on:

*"The opposite of love is fear . . ."[2]*

Neena was intrigued. She thought the opposite of love was hate. But fear?

Neena closed the book and put it on the nightstand. She turned out the light and kept thinking about the passage she'd read. She thought of the things people did when they

---

[1] A Course in Miracles, Foundation for Inner Peace, 1993, Introduction.
[2] Ibid.

were afraid. If you were afraid of an insect, what would you do? Step on it. What about an animal you thought was vicious? Chances are you would try to kill it. Wouldn't she try to kill Jerome if she had the chance? Would she even care if she heard that he had been killed? It all began to make sense to her. She dozed.

Neena was jolted out of her sleep by the phone ringing. Normally, she would have just picked up the phone, but something stopped her this time. She looked at her clock and saw that it was three a.m.

She let the phone keep ringing as she checked the caller ID. *Unknown Name, Unknown Number*, it said. The phone rang again, and she heard her answering machine go through the clicks to indicate her outgoing message was playing. She started to listen intently to see if the unknown name was going to leave a message. She didn't have long to wait.

"Neena," she heard a deep voice say. There was a long pause.

"N-e-e-n-a," the voice said again, this time somewhat playfully.

"That's Jerome's voice! My God, that's his voice!" Neena said in a hoarse whisper. "Oh, my God, make him stop! Make him stop!"

The voice on the phone stopped, the same time that Neena heard a voice in her head say, "Try Me, Neena. You've tried everything else. Your way is not working. Try Me."

Neena got very still. The message was finished, so the machine turned off. She sat on her bed for about ten minutes, very still, her mind silent. Then she got off the bed and got down on her knees beside the bed. She had not prayed in years. She couldn't remember the last time. But the words to *The Lord's Prayer* came effortlessly to her mind, and she said them aloud. She said them with feeling, especially when she said "But deliver us from all evil."

Then Psalm 23 came to her mind, and she repeated that as well. She was tired of this evil and she was tired of being afraid. God was going to deliver her from evil that night.

Neena stayed on her knees in silence for almost an hour. She got up feeling a calmness that she had never known. She even felt joyous. She didn't know exactly what had happened to her, but she knew that her life had changed for good. A weight that she had been carrying was suddenly gone. She knew she wouldn't be hearing from Jerome again.

She got up, turned on the lights, and reached for *A Course in Miracles*. She read from Chapter One:

> *"There is no order of difficulty in miracles. . . . They are all the same."*[3]

Neena moved down the page. The next sentence that she saw was so profound, it made her get absolutely still:

> *"Prayer is the medium of miracles."*[4]

Had she experienced a miracle? Neena knew that she had! She kept turning pages in the book, picking out passages and reading them.

> *"If you knew Who walks beside you on the way that you have chosen, fear would be impossible."*[5]

Neena stayed up for the rest of the night reading similar passages. She took out a highlighter and notepad, and began to study the book. About thirty minutes before

---

[3] A Course in Miracles, Foundation for Inner Peace, 1993, text, p.3.
[4] A Course in Miracles, Foundation for Inner Peace, 1993, text, p. 3.
[5] Ibid, text, p. 378.

she got up to get ready for work, she closed her eyes, and when she opened them, she took the notepad and made a list for herself:

- No more excessive clothes shopping. Shop only for necessities, and be thrifty in your purchases.
- Save the money to pay Guy for the time you used his gym without paying (you may have to work out a payment plan)
- Send Terry and Eric a sincere note congratulating them on their engagement

She could begin with the last item on her list. Before she did, she called the office and told them she was feeling much better, and that she would be in this morning at her regular time. She got out her stationery and went into the kitchen to put on a cup of coffee. Oops. She had forgotten she didn't have any. She had spent her grocery money on the locks, so she would have to eat creatively this week. Neena put the stationery on her dinette table and went to get her address book. She found Eric's address, and addressed the envelope to him and Terry. Then she wrote the congratulatory message, put it inside the envelope, and sealed and stamped it. She would drop it into the mailbox in the apartment complex.

Neena was about to get up when she thought about how she had feigned an interest in Sylvia, when all she wanted was information on Eric and Guy. She resolved now to have a real interest in Sylvia. She took out another sheet of stationery and wrote a note expressing her gratitude for the way Sylvia had shown such concern for her the day they had lunch. She addressed this envelope and sealed the note in it. She put the two letters in an outside pocket of her purse and went to get dressed.

Anyone familiar with Neena who watched her emerge from her apartment that morning might not have recognized her. She smiled and spoke to everyone she saw. She was dressed nicely, but didn't look like she owned stock in *Fashion Fair* or *Dillard.s*. She had on a short skirt—after all, that's what was in her closet, but she had paired it with her only flat shoes. Her feet felt wonderful. Her hair, which had not been washed for days, was pulled back in a large braid and wrapped in a bun. In short, she looked as if her workday would consist of more than trying to catch a man.

Neena dropped the two letters off at the mailbox. When she arrived at work, Irene was already at her desk.

"Neena, we were all very worried about you, since you're never sick and never miss a day. If you hadn't come in, I was going to call to see if I could do anything for you. You do look a little thinner today."

The sincerity in Irene's voice and facial expression touched Neena.

"I guess I am since I've barely eaten since Friday. But I'm well now, Irene. Thank you so much for your concern." She gave Irene a big smile. She even felt like hugging her, but thought that might be a bit much.

The day went on like that. People Neena had barely noticed before, and who she thought barely noticed her, came up to her asking how she was, and saying they missed her quiet efficiency at the office. Was this a new world? She had the presence of mind to know, however, that the world had not changed. She had.

Since she would have no money until she was paid on Friday, Neena decided to work through lunch. She was sorting through some paperwork that had piled up during her two-day absence when Irene entered the small conference room where she was working. Irene was carrying a plastic bag.

"I hope you didn't bring lunch today. Last night was soul food night at our house. My husband said that with soul food, it's impossible to cook just enough for two. It wouldn't taste right. So to keep from eating leftovers for the next three days, I brought some in. I didn't know if you'd be back, but I figured I could get someone to take it, since my husband is such a good cook. You didn't bring lunch today, did you?"

"No, I didn't, so I was going to work through lunch, but I can't resist a sample of your husband's cooking."

"Good. And this is more than a sample. You can take it all. I'm sure it's enough for your dinner tonight, too, even if you have company. Here. You can bring the bowls back to me whenever you're done with them. I'm going to go for a walk to try to get rid of some of the calories I took in last night. See you later. Enjoy."

Just like that, Neena had not only lunch, but dinner as well. And it tasted s-o-o good. She ate what she wanted, and then placed the rest in the refrigerator. She made herself a note so she wouldn't forget to take it home with her.

Before going to her apartment, Neena stopped and picked up her mail. Since there was several days' worth, her box was overflowing. She carried the bundle to her door, unlocked it, and went in without hesitation. After placing the food in the refrigerator, she walked through all the rooms and, seeing nothing amiss, said a prayer of thanks. She got down on her knees and prayed for twenty minutes, asking God for peace, security, and the strength to stick with her new resolve.

Next, she removed the rubber band from the bundle of mail and started flipping through the envelopes.

"Credit card bill, credit card bill, utility bill, phone bill, IRS, char . . .IRS? Hmm. I was expecting a refund. I hope this isn't bad news. Lord, please don't test me now. My finances are in bad enough shape."

Neena tore away the back flap as best she could, removed the letter, and quickly scanned it.

The letter stated that she had some miscalculations on her return, and that the IRS had corrected the mistakes, resulting in a bigger refund for her. She had expected a refund of two hundred and sixty-four dollars. The letter said she would be receiving one thousand four hundred and forty-nine dollars.

Neena closed her eyes. "God is good," she thought. "Are these the kinds of miracles I will see in my life? Yes, they are. I believe, no, I know they are."

She put the letter aside. Further down in the pile, she saw the brown envelope from the United States Treasury. She opened it, hands trembling, and there was her check for $1,449.

Neena started figuring what she would do with the money. True, it wouldn't do much to pay down the eighteen thousand dollars that she owed on credit cards, but at least she could double—no, probably triple—this month's minimum payments. That was something, at least.

Then she remembered. She owed Guy and she had promised to pay him. Membership dues were thirty-nine dollars a month. She estimated she had gone for twenty months without paying. That came to seven hundred and eighty dollars. She used paper and pen to figure that she would have six hundred and sixty-nine dollars left.

With only slight hesitation, Neena pulled her checkbook from her purse. She tore out a deposit slip, filled in the check number and the amount, and entered the amount of the deposit in her register.

Next, Neena opened the nightstand where she kept her bills and found the one Guy had sent for membership dues. She remembered how upset she had been when she opened it. Now she thought of how kind he was to send the bill for only one month's payment, when it was clear she owed much more.

She wrote a check to the gym for seven hundred and eighty dollars, and put it in the envelope he had sent with the bill. She would go out to the bank branch that was open late and deposit the check. Then she would drop the payment in the mailbox.

After brushing her teeth, Neena drank some water, grabbed her purse, and headed out. As she drove down the highway to the bank branch, she thanked God over and over that He had made it possible not only for her to pay her debt to Guy, but also to have hundreds of dollars to spare. The Lord is good indeed!

# Twenty-seven

---

Eric was singing when he rang Terry's doorbell. At first he was going to give her the ring at his house, but he decided he wouldn't wait. He didn't want to push his luck. He had noticed the digs that started out being subtle but had escalated to blunt. He was hardly able to keep a straight face the day she commented that it was time to make big decisions. "Well, let's see how she likes this big decision," he thought.

Terry opened the door, but her eyes didn't light up the way they usually did when she saw Eric. She seemed preoccupied. She kissed Eric, and then asked if he would mind waiting for about fifteen minutes. She dashed off to her bedroom without even waiting for his answer. There was nothing for him to do but make himself comfortable, so he sat down, put the ring on the cocktail table, and turned on the television.

Terry came out about twenty-five minutes later. She had on a jacket, and was carrying her briefcase along with her overnight bag.

"Why are you bringing your briefcase?" Eric asked.

"Eric, I didn't get to the outlet shops today. I was walking, and I had these vivid images, you know, and I had to rush here and get them down on paper before I forgot. I was finishing just as you drove up. I don't know how I'm going to use it all yet, but I had to write it down." She finally stopped talking and looked at Eric, who was smiling.

"God, Terry. Those sparkling eyes may not be for me this time, but I love to see them just the same. Now, take off your jacket and sit down for a few. I want to see the last of this show."

He pulled her down and put an arm around her. Since the ring box was sitting on the table in front of them, Eric wondered when Terry would pick it up. "Apparently never," he thought, after some ten minutes had gone by.

"Eric, what's in the box?"

Finally! Eric turned to her and gave her the most serious look he could muster.

"It came in the mail today. The box was addressed to me, but when I opened it, your name was on the package, so I brought it over."

Terry gave him an *I know you're joking* look. Eric did not give an inch; instead, he kept the same serious expression. Terry picked the box up and opened it. As he watched, she went from curious to ecstatic.

"Oh my God, Eric! It's so beautiful!"

When she slipped the ring onto her finger, Eric could not tell which had more of a shine—the ring or Terry's eyes.

Eric watched as Terry set the dinner table. It had been three weeks since he'd given her the ring, and if he'd known how happy it would make her, he would have given it to her much sooner. In the future, he would shower her with diamonds.

"Dinner's ready," Terry called out to him, and they sat down to a simple meal of roasted chicken with red bliss potatoes, and a mixed green salad.

"Has Bebe called you yet with finalized plans for the scholarship?" Eric asked.

"As a matter of fact, she called me this morning with great news. We can call Yolanda and Tyrone when we've finished dinner, but Bebe said she was going to FedEx a package to them today outlining the details. I can hardly believe she did this so quickly, but she's arranged a full scholarship for Yolanda's remaining two years, plus next semester's tuition and room and board."

"Wow! So Bebe came through in a big way."

"Oh, I forgot. There's more. The package includes a small stipend for miscellaneous living expenses."

"Terry, that's wonderful. I can see how happy that makes you, and I'm happy about it as well. I can't help wondering, though, what does Bebe want in return? Their first born?"

"Eric, that's not fair. She's gone out of her way to make this happen in record time. I don't know what your beef is with her. All you've told me is that you just have a feeling about her."

"Okay, you're right. That was unfair. Now let's finish dinner so we can call the lucky couple and give them the good news."

They ate in silence for a few minutes.

"Guy was in the office today. He brought some papers for me to take a look at. He's doing very well, and he's wondering if he should expand. I told him about the note we received from Neena, how sincere it seemed, and how shocked we were to get it."

"Is he still seeing her?"

"No. According to him, he hasn't talked to her in months. He said she left two messages some time ago, but he was with someone else so he didn't return her call. He felt guilty about it, he said, because she sounded troubled, but she had shown such disrespect for him, he couldn't respond any other way."

"Guy is a good man. I liked him the first day I met him. It's too bad Neena doesn't appreciate him."

"The thing is, when I told Guy about the note we got from Neena, he told me something very interesting. He said that Neena had taken advantage of their relationship, and never paid her gym dues. Now Guy said that when they were seeing each other, he didn't object. But their relationship has been on again, off again, and when it was off, Neena still didn't pay. Well, apparently the same week we got the note, maybe even the same day, Guy received a check from Neena for all of her back dues. He said he was so surprised, knowing Neena's attitude, but also knowing how she lived on the edge financially."

"Interesting. Perhaps the lady has changed."

"Maybe. Why don't we call Tyrone and Yolanda now? I'll clean the kitchen later."

Eric and Terry moved to his office. Terry dialed the number.

"Hello," Terry heard Tyrone's voice say.

"Tyrone, hi. It's Terry. Eric's here with me. I'm going to put him on speakerphone."

"Okay. Hi, Eric. Don't tell me you two have eloped, and cheated us out of a wedding."

"No, not a chance. So how are the newlyweds doing? Where's Yolanda?"

"She's at the library, doing some research. I have to pick her up in about an hour. We're both okay, but things are going to get much more demanding. Yolanda's parents have remained cold and distant, and I know she's heartbroken. The bright spot is her aunt Eloise, her mother's sister. She keeps in close touch with us and says she's looking forward to having a baby in the family again. She even gave us five thousand dollars for a wedding gift."

"I know it's hard now, Tyrone," Terry piped in. She could hardly contain her excitement. "But things do get better, and for you and Yolanda, they already have."

"Already have what?"

"Gotten better. I met someone through Eric who manages an endowment for scholarships, primarily for African Americans. Eric was the one who thought about this, and he introduced us. Her name is Bebe Smith. Anyway, I gave her your story, which is why I asked you all those questions a few weeks ago. By the way, I'm sorry for not telling you the real reason for prying. I just didn't want to build your hopes needlessly.

"And you still haven't told me what would build our hopes needlessly."

"Oh, sorry. Yolanda now has a full scholarship for her remaining two years of college, plus next semester's tuition and room and board. A letter outlining the details was sent out to you today by overnight mail."

No sound came out of Tyrone's mouth; nevertheless, Terry could sense his excitement.

"Oh, Terry forgot to tell you that the package includes a small stipend for living expenses," Eric chimed in.

Finally, Tyrone was able to put voice to his thoughts.

"Terry, Eric, you cannot know what a help this is. Both Yolanda and I were determined she pursue her degree, but frankly, we didn't know how we were going to make it. Thank you. Thank you from the bottom of my heart. I know Yolanda's going to you when I give her the news. And

Terry, this is the second time you've come to my rescue. Just remember, you guys, that if you ever need us, we're there for you."

"As a matter of fact, Tyrone, I do need your help with something," Terry said.

"Shoot," Tyrone said.

"Bye, Tyrone. I'm going to leave you two to discuss this," Eric said.

"Goodbye, Eric. And thanks again, man."

"Okay. Sit back and settle in, because this may take some time," Terry said before she began to fill Tyrone in.

# Twenty-eight

$T$erry sat back and closed her eyes. She had dressed comfortably for the trip, but her clothes were not casual. It was, after all, a business trip. She wore a stylish black pantsuit, and had brought a loose-fitting jacket to put on once they were out of the car. She had on black leather shoes with enough of a heel for business, but not so much as to be uncomfortable if she had to do some walking. She had packed similar clothing that she could mix and match, as well as an evening outfit.

Eric had come as close as Terry had ever seen to blowing his top. She told him that Bebe's proposal sounded like a good way to earn money to get her project off the ground, and it seemed a good cause to boot. After all, she reasoned, Bebe had done so much for Tyrone and Yolanda.

"Terry," Eric had answered. "Sure Bebe has done a good deed. But that does not put you under obligation to work for her. Besides, we've got a wedding to plan. Now if it would make you feel better, I'll donate some money to Bebe's scholarship fund."

"Eric, I've asked you this before, and I don't feel I've gotten a clear answer. Exactly what is your problem with Bebe?"

"Sweetheart, some things about her just don't add up. It's probably more of a gut feeling than fact, but I just don't want you caught up in something that turns out not to be as claimed."

She looked into Eric's eyes and saw only genuine concern for her. She knew he kept his clients' finances strictly confidential, so his hinting that things were not on the up-and-up with Bebe gave her pause.

"Okay," she said. "Let's compromise. Since I've already promised to go with Bebe to Wilmington, I have to keep my word. But I won't accept any job offer from her."

Terry went into deep thought for a moment. First a puzzled look, then one of clarity, came over her face.

"So that's why those vivid images came to me," she said.

"What?"

"The scenes that came so sharply into my mind. Do you remember that day I raced home to get them down on paper?"

Eric nodded.

"The story Mr. Benjamin told me. Do you remember? He told me about his family and many other black families' nights of terror at the hands of whites in Wilmington, North Carolina." She could tell Eric wasn't following her, but she continued.

"Eric, there's a connection between Mr. Benjamin's story and the stories that I've been writing. While I'm there, I'd like to do some research into the events of November 1898, and try to get a sense of the impact those events have had on the lives of the blacks left behind. I'd like to talk to some of the longtime residents, and some of the history teachers and professors. Events in my life seem to be nudging me in that direction. I feel that since the time I met Mr. Benjamin, things have come full circle."

Eric was appeased, since he knew Terry would be too busy with her own projects to get very involved with Bebe. He still made her promise that they would keep in close contact during her trip.

Terry had stayed in her own apartment the night before she and Bebe left, since she had some research and planning to do. Bebe picked her up promptly at eight o'clock for their four-hour drive to Wilmington. Terry had to admit that Bebe traveled in style. When she said they would be traveling by car, Terry thought that meant Bebe would be driving. Instead, they had a driver, so they could sit back and relax, or work, as Bebe was doing.

Terry opened her eyes and looked over at Bebe, who was studying files she had pulled out of the open briefcase next to her. Bebe saw Terry looking at her and smiled.

"It should only be two more hours. The first hour and a half of this trip is not that bad because there are several small towns with places to stop to get some quick food or drinks, and use the restrooms. But once you pass Hamlet, the trip is almost entirely rural, with cornfields, cotton fields, and gas stations that look like they're not in service." Bebe went back to studying her files.

They were traveling state highway 74 east all the way, and when Bebe looked up and saw the sign for Whiteville, and the exit to the business district, she said, "Good. We only have another hour or so. I always look for this sign as a marker for how much longer I have to travel." She went back to her work.

When they came to a sign that said *Leland*, Bebe told the driver to take that exit.

"When I first came across this area, I found it fascinating," she said to Terry. Terry looked around her and wondered what the fascination was about. She saw a hodgepodge of buildings—some roughhewn, others new and substantial—trailer parks on one side of the street and middle-class brick homes on the other, churches both modest and storefront, old gas stations overrun with junk cars, and new gas stations with expansive convenience stores attached.

They came to a stoplight. There was a gas station on the corner.

"Take a left here," Bebe instructed the driver. "Down here is a small community known as Navassa. She said this just as they neared a sign that said *Navassa City Limits*. "It is virtually all black and has been that way for as long as anyone seems to remember. One of the residents has written a history of it. I had a copy, but I don't know where it is now. Maybe I can get another one sometime during my stay."

They crossed a bridge over a waterway called Sturgeon Creek. Then Bebe instructed the driver to go left at a fork.

"I was invited to a few civic meetings at the town hall. There was such an outpouring of warmth and hospitality that is hard to find anywhere. In some ways, it is basically a poor neighborhood, but it is full of surprises. It seems like one of those places that Charles Kuralt would have discovered on the road."

The driver had taken them through most of the neighborhood in less than ten minutes. Some of the homes were nice, brick ranch styles with neat lawns. Others were ramshackle with junk-filled yards. There was a new-looking, well-cared-for fire station and, adjacent to it, a newer community with neat brick homes. When they turned onto the road that looped around the outskirts of the community, Terry saw large tracts of land that Bebe said belonged to local industries.

Bebe instructed the driver how to get back to the highway, and soon they were heading across one of the bridges that led to the seaport city of Wilmington.

# Twenty-nine

Jessie had been chasing prospects all day, trying to get commitments both for donations and for the scholarship seminars. His leads were still promising, but he wasn't having much luck finding people.

"Oh, what the heck," he thought, and called Colleen from his cell phone. He got her answering machine.

"Hi, Colleen. It's me, Jessie. Can you come over to my house right after work? I'm going to head home soon, so I can have dinner ready when you get there."

He hung up, hoping Colleen would be in the mood for some pre-dinner activities. He couldn't get enough of her. They were planning to marry and open a gym together, and Jessie could hardly wait. He was working extra hard to earn more money and hurry things along.

His phone rang. It was Bebe.

"Hi, Jessie. Do you have time to stop by my office? I have a small token of appreciation for you for the business you've brought in. I also want to introduce you to someone I've been trying, without luck, to recruit. Maybe your enthusiasm and charisma will win her over. Can you come?"

"Sure. I can be there in about fifteen minutes. I needed to talk to you anyway."

"Oh? What about? Is there a problem?"

"Oh, no. Just some financial stuff."

"Sure, then. See you in fifteen. Bye."

Jessie pulled into a nearby gas station and filled his tank. He needed a few extra minutes to think. When he paid for the gas, he also bought some orange juice and stood by his car until he had finished drinking it. He realized he was stalling, and asked himself why he had qualms about asking for his own money.

Jessie pulled back onto Oleander Drive, made a left onto South College Road, and drove past the university to the shopping center where Bebe's office was. He had no idea why she no longer had her office on the university campus. She simply announced to him one day that she was moving, and that was that. He knew so little about her.

Jessie drove to the rear of the shopping center. He parked in front of the office with a sign on the door that read

*BB & Co., Inc. Financial Services.* He didn't see Bebe's late-model Mercedes or any other car nearby.

When he walked in, he was in an outer office that was the waiting room. Jessie had been in these new quarters once before Bebe had left for Charlotte. The suite was impressive. Everything was art deco to appeal to the college crowd who generated most of Bebe's income. To the left of the waiting room was a spacious conference room, where Bebe hosted workshops when she couldn't book them at the schools.

Straight ahead was the inner office, where Bebe had her desk, computers, and files, and several chairs and tables. Bebe was sitting at her desk, and another attractive young woman was sitting in one of the chairs. They smiled at him as he walked in. Bebe stood and walked toward him.

"Jessie, how nice to see you. I'd like for you to meet Terry Weeks. Terry lives in Charlotte and she is engaged to a longtime friend of mine. I'm trying to recruit her for my Charlotte office, so I brought her here to meet my star salesman. Terry, Jessie Campbell."

Jessie shook hands with Terry and they exchanged pleasantries. He liked her right away and thought she was one of those people who inspire instant trust.

"Oh, before I forget, these are for you," Bebe said as she handed him two envelopes.

Jessie, still standing, opened the envelopes. Bebe was standing next to him, and she seemed to be paying close attention to his reaction to the contents. The first one he opened contained his bonus, and the amount pleased him. The second envelope contained a card that read *Congratulations on a job well done.* Inside the card was another check. This one was for twenty-five hundred dollars. Jessie could hardly believe it. In addition to his fat bonus, he was also getting two-and-a-half grand just as a token of appreciation! It looked like there was money to be had in the world and he had found the place to get some of it. He hoped Bebe had no inkling of the doubts he'd harbored about her.

"Oh, Jessie, I almost forgot. You said you needed to talk to me about something. Would you like some privacy?"

Jessie felt his stature diminishing to a mere two feet. How could he bring up his prior doubts now that Bebe had shown so much generosity?

"It was nothing, really. I just wondered when you would be sending out the statements on my investments. I have my eyes on some property, so I may be cashing out soon."

Bebe's answer was comforting and reassuring.

"Just as soon as I get the stock reports, Jessie, I'll plug in the numbers. These stocks are not traded on the big boards, so it takes a little more time, but I anticipate sending out your information by the end of this week, or early next week. Now, Terry and I are going out to dinner. Would you like to join us? You could help me fill her in on our operations, and you two can get to know each other."

"I'd like to ladies, but I may have a dinner date already. But I do have an idea, Terry. If you'd like, I can meet you for breakfast and go over some things with you. What do you say?"

"That sounds wonderful. Are you sure I'm not putting you out?"

"Of course not. Is eight thirty a good time for you?"

"Eight thirty is a perfect time for me."

Jessie made arrangements to pick Terry up at her hotel, and then he left. When he got home, Colleen was there, and she had started preparing dinner.

"Hey, I thought you were going to have dinner ready by the time I got here." Jessie knew it was good-natured ribbing, because Colleen was an excellent cook and she enjoyed surprising him with scrumptious dishes that he couldn't find anywhere else.

He stood at the kitchen entrance looking at her. She had on a pair of tight jeans and a top that draped her breasts in a very sexy way. Her hair was braided in a way that people sometimes braided their children's hair—parted in blocks with the braids falling where they would. One advantage to her working at a gym was that she used the facilities, and those jeans were showing off her firm, shapely butt. She smelled as if she had just showered.

"I had planned to, but since you have things started, I need to work up an appetite."

Jessie said no more, but when Colleen saw him again, he was in the kitchen wearing only his briefs, and he had a just-showered smell. He went up to her and encircled her waist, then slipped his hands down and unfastened the jeans. When his hands started to travel down to her soft, furry place, she reached out and turned off the stove. They found the closest piece of furniture and tore out of their clothing. Afterward, neither of them had an appetite, so they went to the bedroom to lie down.

"I went to Bebe's office this afternoon," Jessie began, but was interrupted by the phone.

"Hello," Jessie said.

"Hello. Is this Jessie Campbell?"

"Yes, it is."

"Hi Jessie. This is Jules, the owner of the warehouse you're interested in."

"Oh, yes. How are you?"

"Fine, thank you. I called to let you know that I'm prepared to accept the terms and conditions of that offer you submitted on the property at 1818 Market Street. I would, however, like to expedite things so I can get back to California. Before I have my attorney draw up the purchase and sale agreement, I wanted to make sure you have a reasonable amount of time to get your inspection done, finalize your financing, and have your attorney look things over. Would four weeks give you adequate time?"

"Four weeks would be pushing it, Jules. Let's shoot for five."

"Well, if that's the best you can do, I guess I can hang on for an extra week."

"Good. Thank you."

"As soon as I have a draft of the purchase and sale agreement, I'll fax it to you."

"Okay. I'll wait to hear from you."

Jessie hung up the phone and grabbed Colleen. He let out a big whoop.

"Let me guess. The owner of the warehouse property accepted your offer."

"Yes, he did. Colleen, things are starting to come together. We can start making plans, babe."

"I only wish I had enough to go half with you on this deal. Unfortunately, my contribution will be minimal."

"Don't worry about that. You'll be my wife and my cheerleader. Besides, you're going to be working there right alongside me without getting much of a salary initially. In addition, I'm counting on your expertise in running a gym."

"Honey, we'll make a fabulous team. Just keep me happy, and I'll work my butt off for you."

"No thanks, darling." He kissed her, but when Colleen saw furrows crease his forehead, she knew something was bothering him.

"Have you received your statement from Bebe yet showing your earnings and account balance?" she asked.

"No, not yet. When I went by today, she had someone with her, someone she was trying to hire for the Charlotte location, so we didn't get into a big discussion. She gave me my earnings from the Baird account, and she gave me a bonus of twenty-five hundred dollars. She said she should be getting the stock reports by early next week at the latest."

"But Jessie, I heard you say to that guy on the phone that you would shoot for five weeks. I'm assuming you meant that the deal could close in five weeks. If that's the case, you need to know right now how much money you have so that you can arrange financing for the rest. It's your money, and you have a right to know how much it is."

"Don't you think I know that?" Jessie snapped, but he was sorry immediately. He knew where the testiness was coming from. Colleen was voicing out loud the doubts and suspicions that he hadn't faced head-on.

"I'm sorry, sweetheart," he said to her. "Please forgive me for snapping at you like that, because you didn't deserve it. I will see Bebe tomorrow and force the issue. I might as well, since I'm going to have to take all my money out of the account anyway."

"Damn right, Jessie. And don't let her stall you. Insist on getting all of your money within the week."


Colleen hoped she hadn't made Jessie feel like a fool. She was just concerned for him. She couldn't stand by silently and let his dream go *poof*. If necessary, she would confront the bitch herself.. And Colleen would have no intentions of backing down.

# Thirty

---

"Eric, I miss you, and I'm ready to come back to Charlotte," said Terry. "Bebe told me we would be here for three days, but yesterday, from what she said to Jessie, she might be here until next week. I hadn't planned to stay that long, but I could use the extra time for research."

"I knew there was a reason I didn't want you running off with Bebe!" said Eric. "She's already changing the terms of the agreement. Here's what I'll do. Tomorrow, I will work in the office until noon. Then I'll drive there. We can spend the night and return the next day, or we can stick around through the weekend if you'd like. I can even help you do some research. How does that sound?"

"That sounds wonderful. I'll see you tomorrow around five then. Call me when you hit the road."

"Okay. Bye. I love you."

"Me too, Eric. See you soon."

Terry was not used to having a man who was so protective of her, but she had to admit it made her feel loved. She reached for her briefcase and took out a thick sheaf of papers. All of her work was on a hard drive and zip disk, but since she did not want to travel with her *iBook*, she brought the hard copies. She liked traveling unencumbered. Also, since she wouldn't leave her computer in a hotel room, she would have had to carry it with her everywhere. She looked over the latest copy, made some margin notes, and called Tyrone.

Yolanda picked up and Terry chatted with her. She seemed much happier now that she had the scholarship, and therefore would not have to drop out of school or kill herself with overwork. Also, her parents wanted to reconcile with her. She promised to keep Terry posted.

Tyrone picked up the phone.

"Terry, did you get the notes?"

"Yeah. I like your idea of adding a narrator, or chorus. I think a chorus would be better. That way we can have more music. Music is such a big part of our history; it's ingrained in us."

She listened to Tyrone for a minute.

"So, we need a songwriter. Okay, I'm making notes as we talk." Terry listened to Tyrone for a few more minutes, as he gave her the ideas he'd had since they last talked.

"Expanding the first scene in that way would take away the subtlety, although I don't want it so subtle as to be oblique. But I do want the audience to do some work by making the connection themselves. That gets them more involved and so they enjoy it more."

"Yeah, I see your point, Terry. Now I hope you don't mind, but I showed this to Ary Williams, my drama professor. She was so interested that she hooked me up with this super agent. In other words, we're almost guaranteed funding, so let's put on the finishing touches and get this show on the road."

"I'm so excited about this, Tyrone. I can't wait to see what my research here turns up, and if we'll be able to incorporate any of it."

Terry hung up, went back to her papers, and made more notes. She paused, put her pencil down, and thought about the day all of this started. She recalled the intense, vivid, colorful images that had played in her mind—stories and events she had not seen, but that were so clear. It was like they had been in her brain all along, and revealed themselves to her in a sudden flash of light.

She had rushed to her apartment to write it all down, and had written furiously because the words just seemed to pour out of her. Even when she'd gone to sleep, she remembered having to get up during the night and over the subsequent three nights to write down the thoughts because they were flowing as easily as water. Terry had kept on writing until finally she had it all.

She had typed and edited her pages, and sent a copy to Tyrone. Before she could call to find out what he thought, he called her, excited, saying that whatever it took, and however long it took, this story had to go into production. They decided it would be a joint effort, and Terry felt relieved. She knew she needed Tyrone's dramatic expertise to pull it off.

Jessie was already seated in the hotel dining room when Terry entered that morning. He was not wearing a suit this time, but he was still quite handsome in a white shirt and a thick, blue v-neck sweater and navy blue casual pants. The blue of the sweater went well with his color. He stood and smiled when he saw her.

"I wonder if he's a native of the city. If so, why not start my research with him?" Terry thought, but when she walked over to him and shook his hand, she felt that something was very wrong.

The waitress came over and took their orders.

"How was your dinner date last night?" Terry asked him.

"It was wonderful. My fiancée is an excellent cook. I was supposed to do the honors last night, but by the time I got home, she had things going."

Terry just looked at him and smiled. He did not seem at all centered.

"I was planning to take you along with me to follow up on some contacts, but I'm afraid I can't do that now. I have to see Bebe, and then I have personal business to take care of."

To Terry, he seemed more and more agitated. "No problem," she said with a smile. "Bebe's still trying to recruit me, and I applaud the work that she's doing. But as I've told her, I'm working on something else and I just won't have the time to do the quality work that she needs."

The waitress brought their beverages. They both sipped their juices quietly for a few minutes.

"Jessie, you've lived in this area all your life, haven't you?" Terry was not usually uncomfortable with silences, but this one was heavy and she had to break it.

"I sure have," he answered. "How well do you know Bebe?" he asked, so abruptly that it startled Terry.

"Not well at all. I met her through Eric, my fiancé. She was able to get scholarship money for the wife of a friend of mine. It was a *very* generous scholarship and it helped them out big time. Why do you ask?"

Jessie looked down at the table and was silent for a long time. Finally he looked up at Terry, and the expression on his face surprised Terry so much that she almost drew in her breath.

"I don't know. Bebe's been very good to me. She got me out of working twelve-hour shifts at a factory, that's for sure. I was dying of boredom and fatigue. But I had this dream—I have this dream, of owning a business. I want to open a gym. The only problem was that I wasn't making enough money to save adequately. I met Bebe and all of that changed. She gave me a position with her company and taught me a lot. She told me she had invested money for people and had earned bragging rights for the returns she got them. So I gave her my life's savings to invest for me."

Jessie paused and looked down again before continuing.

"The thing is, she doesn't send out regular statements, and I don't know how my investments are doing. I just hope they've done okay, because I found a building that I plan to renovate into a gym. The owner called me last night to accept my offer. So I have to go see Bebe today to get my money. I just hope it's enough."

Eric's words came to Terry's mind: *Terry, some things about her just don't add up.*

"She said the investments were what many people consider very risky, but she said that if you have access to certain information, they were not that risky. She, of course, has access to that information."

Terry could see the rawness of Jessie's desire for that gym. If his dreams were leveled, he would have a very hard time. She reached over and put her hand on his. The waitress brought their food, but by this time they had both lost their appetites. Terry suspected that Jessie's appetite had been lost before he got here. They nibbled at the food.

"Jessie, maybe things have turned out better than you think," said Terry. "You may be in for a pleasant surprise." At that point, Terry thought the most important thing was to try to make Jessie feel better. "I'd love to see the building you're going to purchase. Would you take me there when we leave Bebe's office?"

That put him in a better mood, and he smiled.

"Sure. There's nothing I like better than showing the place and planning the work I'm going to do. Colleen, my fiancée, is going to manage it. She manages a gym now."

"Congratulations on your engagement. You're fortunate to have someone you know and trust to run things for you."

"Thank you. Yep, Colleen is a gem. She's so unusual. She's the type who will get in there and hustle with me. I can hardly wait for this all to become reality."

"Jessie, with the amount of passion and commitment you have, it's bound to work out. And remember, a big part of the pleasure is in the journey. Now, let's get over to Bebe's office and straighten things out."

Jessie paid the bill and they left the restaurant. Outside, Terry looked around. The day, although crisp, was beautiful. She was wearing a black cashmere pantsuit, and with the layers she had on underneath, she didn't need a coat.

She was having no problem with the milder climate here. The hotel parking lot was nearly empty, so it was just a short walk to Jessie's car, a Volkswagen *Jetta* that looked brand new. Jessie opened the door for her and when Terry got in, she noticed how clean the interior was. The only visible item was a briefcase on the back seat behind the driver.

Terry barely had her seat belt on before the Jetta was in motion. She looked over at Jessie and it was like he was unaware of her presence. Things were not going to be okay. She was nervous and wanted to talk to Eric. He would just be arriving at his office, so he wouldn't be getting on the road for another four to five hours. She would call him when they arrived at Bebe's office. She could stand outside and use her cell phone so she could have some privacy.

The hotel where Terry was staying was only five minutes away from Bebe's office. It was only a few minutes past nine thirty when Jessie pulled into the shopping center area and drove around back to where Bebe's office was located. "If Bebe's not here, that will buy some time," Terry had been thinking. That hope was snatched away and Terry got a sinking feeling in her abdomen when she saw Bebe's driver pulling away and heading out of the complex, minus Bebe. When Jessie pulled to the curb and shut the engine off, he jumped out of the car and rushed inside, saying nothing to Terry. He didn't even look her way.

Instead of following him inside, Terry took out her phone and dialed the number to Eric's office. Sylvia answered

"Sylvia, it's Terry. Is Eric there yet?"

"Hi, Terry. Yes he is. Just a minute, and I'll put you through."

"Hi, honey. Is everything okay?"

"I don't think so, Eric. I'm here at Bebe's office, and Jessie, her assistant, you know the one she mentioned the day we had lunch, well, I just had breakfast with him. He seems very upset. He told me that he gave Bebe his life's savings to invest for him. Now he needs his money to buy some property. The problem is, he doesn't know how much the money has grown, or shrunk. It seems that Bebe does not send regular statements. As a matter of fact, he mentioned something like that to her the day I met him. She told him then that he would be getting the statement within the week, or early next week. Things may be okay, but I have the feeling that if Bebe can't give him what he wants, he will implode."

"What? You're saying the guy is there at Bebe's office with you? Well, where the hell is Bebe?"

"They're inside, Eric. And I'm standing outside. Jessie picked me up at the hotel this morning. I was supposed to go with him to see a couple of clients, but he got a call last night about his offer for this property, so he needs his money from Bebe. I'm going in." Terry started walking toward the office door.

"No. Let me call Bebe. Stay where you are. I have three-way calling, so I'll keep you on. It may take a few minutes, because I'm going to have Sylvia get her number for me."

After a few minutes, Eric clicked her back in.

"Is Bebe on the line?"

"No. No one picked up. Can you see what's going on inside?"

"No. The window shades are pulled down, so I can't see inside at all."

"Terry, just stay on the line, and if you see anything alarming, hang up and call the police. Better yet, is there a place nearby where you can wait?"

"Sure. Bebe's office is at the back of a mall, and there's an entrance to the mall stores a few feet away."

"Then I want you to do that. Hang up and go inside the mall. I'll keep trying Bebe's number."

"But Eric, what if there's real trouble inside?"

"If I can't reach anyone, I'll call you back. In the meantime, look for mall security so you can at least have a location on them if you need to send someone in. But do not go in yourself."

"Okay." Terry ended the connection, all the time watching the office door. She stood in her tracks, wrestling with whether or not to follow Eric's directive.

"I can't do this. I can't just walk away. I've got to go in," she decided.

She took a deep breath, then walked up to the door, opened it, and went inside.

# Thirty-one

---

Jessie had become more and more enraged as he drove toward Bebe's office. He heard Terry talking to him, but somehow it was in the background, and pretty soon he stopped trying to make out what she was saying. He let the rage take over. He welcomed it, because the rage would make him do what he needed to do.

"That bitch! I have plans and dreams, and she thinks she is going to take them away from me, just like that? Just who does she think she is? What if Colleen is right and Bebe hasn't invested the money for me at all, but has simply stolen it? Well, she is going to pay up now, one way or the other." These thoughts and worse, much worse, were going through Jessie's mind.

As soon as he whipped around the corner and parked, he was out of the car. He didn't take the gun from his briefcase. There was no need for that yet. He was just going inside to talk to her reasonably, and see if they could do business. But if he had to use the gun, he would. He wondered how classy she would look while staring down the barrel of a .45.

Bebe looked up from her desk when he walked inside. Her face registered surprise.

Jessie's mean inner dialogue had ratcheted up a notch. "Not expecting me, were you? You probably thought the bonus and thank-you checks would keep me at bay for at least two more weeks. Cunning little snake. It was my goddamn money to begin with. If this weren't so serious, it would be laughable. There you were, handing me a fraction of my own money, and presenting it in such a way that I practically genuflect before you. Well, today's a new day, baby, and Jessie's got a new attitude."

"Jessie, I didn't expect to see you today. Where's Terry? Did you pick her up as planned?"

Jessie kept his voice soft and deliberate.

"Yes, I picked her up as planned. But I made an unplanned detour here to pick up my money. All of it."

"Jessie, if you mean the money I've invested for you, I told you yesterday . . ."

"Oh, no, no, no, no. Today's a new day, and today, I want my money. All of it."

"Jessie, what's gotten into you?" Bebe's eyes were large O's. "You can have all of your money if you want it, but I told you that I won't have the full amount until I get a few more statements."

"I'll tell you what, Bebe. Why don't you just check the ol' computer, there, and see how much I had on the last statement date. I'll take that amount. Then, when you get those statements you're waiting for, if the amount is more, you can give me the difference. If I owe you, I'll give you the difference. Fair?"

The phone started ringing, but Jessie and Bebe kept their eyes locked.

"I believe that's fair, Jessie. The problem is, I don't keep those records on my office computer. Those are special investments for special clients, and I keep those records on my home computer for security reasons."

Oh, that was a good one. Jessie had to give it to her. She was remaining calm under pressure. But he was about to turn up the heat.

"And what are those special investments and security reasons, Bebe?" he continued in the same measured tone.

"For a limited number of my clients, including you, Jessie, I have an arrangement with an advisor who is a financial genius, and he deals in some complicated trading. Believe me, there are people out there who would go to great lengths to get at that information."

"Oh, then it's just a matter of taking a little trip to your house, then, isn't it? That would be fine with me. I'll even drive you."

"Now talk your way out of that one," he thought. He could see the mental work she was doing. "I've got her now. I've got the thieving, lying bitch now."

Bebe's eyes averted to the door, and Jessie heard it open tentatively as someone walked in.

Bebe turned to look at Terry as she walked in. To Terry, Bebe's expression looked almost normal, just a little off kilter. Terry started to relax a little. Jessie did not look at her or acknowledge her presence. He just stood staring at

Bebe. Terry's relaxation vanished. She knew that she couldn't just record what was going on. She had to act.

"Bebe, Jessie told me he has money invested with you. He's also found this warehouse that he's going to renovate into a health club. I don't know if he's told you, but that's been a longtime dream of his, to own a commercial gym. As a matter of fact, as soon as we leave here, he's going to take me by to see it. Anyway, is there a problem with cashing out on his investments with you so that he can buy the property?"

"No, not at all. As I've explained to Jessie, this could take a little . . ."

"Cut the bullshit, Bebe!" Jessie thundered. His eyes were bulging, his nostrils flaring. Terry could not stand to look at him. She looked away, and the next thing she heard were Jessie's footsteps heading out the door. She turned to watch him as he headed toward his car. Something inside of her told her to go after him. This time she didn't second-guess herself. She just turned and followed him. She could hear the phone ringing as she walked out, and Bebe saying *hello*.

By the time Terry caught up to him, Jessie had opened the rear door to the *Jetta* and was reaching for his briefcase. Another car had pulled up—a gold Acura with a round-faced white man wearing gold-rimmed glasses in the driver's seat. He looked over at them as if something had piqued his interest.

When Jessie opened the briefcase, Terry groaned. Lying on top of his papers was a handgun, looking designer sleek. Terry almost expected to see an insignia on it from a major fashion house. She hated the look of that gun. It was a deadly weapon, and it should look ugly, not like a fashion accessory.

She found her voice.

"Jessie, you don't want to do this. Listen to me Jessie. Once you go down that road, you can never come back. There are some things in this world you can never take back, never undo or make better."

His movements, which were previously hurried and deliberate, slowed down and became less certain. She took this as a sign of hope and pushed forward.

"Jessie, this is a mental world we live in. You have to use your mind." She pointed to her head for emphasis.

"I guarantee that if you think things through, you can find a far better way than what you're contemplating. The action that you're about to take does not make sense, and I'll tell you why. First of all, there are strict laws against murder. You'll go to prison. In addition to the ignominy and the humiliation of being handcuffed and shackled and taken to prison, and enduring the other unmentionables of prison life, you still will not have what you want. The health club, your life with Colleen, all of those things will be lost to you forever." Terry didn't know where these words were coming from. All she knew was that she had the inspiration and she had to keep talking.

" On the other hand, if you drive away now, you have an excellent chance of still getting what you want. Eric and I know someone, his name is Guy, and he's a millionaire many times over. He earned his millions by doing exactly what you want to do. But he did some other things as well, such as marketing energy bars and videos, and setting up a personal training program. He's very good at what he does, and we can hook you up with him. In addition, you can sue Bebe to get back any money that she owes you, and get a hefty damage award as well. Think about how rewarding that would be. But if you take the other road, if you take that gun and go in there now, you'll never know what you could have done."

Jessie took his hands away from the briefcase and stood there, his hands now at his sides. Terry never took her eyes off him. The demons that had taken possession of his mind seemed to be leaving; nevertheless, Terry knew she couldn't stop just yet.

"What if she has a gun, Jessie? What if you walk in there now and she shoots you? It would be self-defense. Are you sure you haven't underestimated her? After all, she talked you out of your money. She must have great survival skills. And she was calm when I walked in there on the two of you. You were enraged. In these types of situations, the calm person always has the advantage."

She paused, studying his face. She had succeeded. He was Jessie again.

"Get in your car and drive away now. I promise I will help you in any way I can to get your money back."

Slowly, Jessie turned his head to look at her. Then he did something she had never seen a man do before: He broke down and started crying. She put her arms around him and just held him, telling him it was okay. After a few moments, he moved away from her, closed his briefcase and the back door of his car, opened the driver's door, and climbed in. Without hesitation, he turned the key in the ignition, backed up, and drove off.

Terry stood trembling after what she had just witnessed. She walked the few feet to the mall entrance, went inside, and sat on one of the benches. She fought the urge to cry. Instead, she took out her phone and called Eric.

"Hi, Sylvia. It's Terry. May I speak to Eric?"

"Hi, Terry. Eric left about ten minutes ago. He told me that if you called to let you know that he is on his way to Wilmington."

Terry hung up and closed her eyes. Her lips mouthed these words:

"Please hurry, Eric. If ever I've needed you, I need you now."

# *Thirty-two*

---

It was two thirty when Eric pulled into the parking lot of the hotel. He parked and ran inside. Terry was in the lobby. When she saw Eric, she ran to him and held on to him as if for dear life. He took her to a quiet corner and they sat down.

"Oh baby, are you okay. I was so worried about you."

"Eric, you were right. Coming here with Bebe was not a good idea. But you know what? If I hadn't been there today, we might be at a hospital now, or worse, a morgue. It was so awful!"

"Terry, I want you to tell me, as best as you can remember, what happened."

348

"Okay. Well, I told you over the phone about Jessie investing money with Bebe, and how he told me at breakfast he'd found this warehouse he wanted to buy to convert into a health club. Well, it seems he had reason to believe that Bebe either lost all of his money in bad investments, or she simply had scammed him."

"Surprise, surprise," Eric said, shaking his head.

"Anyway, when I went inside . . .."

"Terry, you went in there? I didn't want you going in there, and I told you specifically not to."

"Eric, I know. But I had to. I was acting on pure instinct, and I had to go inside."

Eric pulled her close and held her for a long time. He finally let her go and asked her to finish her story. When she told him about Jessie and the gun, she could see the pain on his face for what might have happened to her. She touched his arm.

"Eric, it was okay. Everything turned out okay. I know you think I was careless, but Jessie was not going to hurt me. He wasn't trying to commit a murder and cover his tracks. He was just enraged because he thought Bebe had taken his dream away."

"But how could you know that. You met him yesterday for the first time."

"What can I say? You're right. When you look at this in a cold, rational light, you are right. But I was thrust into a situation where I could either walk away, or take a chance and try to save a life. I made my choice, and I'm still here."

"Right, but if you were not still here, my life would have to go on without you. Please think about it from that perspective if you're ever faced with similar circumstances. Agreed?"

"Agreed," Terry answered.

"Now we need to get to the bottom of what's going on in Bebe's make-believe world. I'd like to talk to Jessie, and I'd like to talk to Bebe. I'm sure it's no surprise to you that I believe Jessie's on the right track. The reasons, though, I haven't given you. As Bebe's tax planner, I've seen some things that are shaky at best. I'd like to see some documentation from Jessie. She must have sent him statements. That would be a good place to start. Do you have a phone number for him?"

Terry found the business card that Jessie had given her. His home phone number was on it. Eric dialed and talked to Jessie. He recognized the vulnerable, emotional state Jessie was in, so he was very tactful. In addition, Eric realized that he was a perfect stranger to Jessie, so he would have to work to gain his trust. In the end, Jessie agreed to meet them at the hotel in a half-hour.

While they were waiting, Eric noticed how tense Terry was. He brought her a glass of wine from the bar and watched some of the tightness disappear as she drank. Soon, however, she tensed up again. Eric noticed it and followed Terry's eyes to a slightly tall man and a petite woman approaching them.

"That's Jessie," she said to Eric. "That must be his fiancée, Colleen, with him."

She and Eric stood. As Jessie got closer, they noticed the sorrowful look on his face. He extended his hand to Eric first and introduced himself and Colleen. Then he turned to Terry.

"Terry, please accept my sincerest apologies for what I did today. I am so sorry for putting you in that position. I saw my dreams going out the window, and I was in a rage, but that was no excuse for my behavior. Please forgive me."

Eric stepped forward.

"Listen, as I said on the phone, I'm going to try to get to the bottom of this. But man, what you did was wrong. Someone could have gotten hurt. If you felt that Bebe had stolen from you, you should have notified the proper authorities. But right now, we need to try to figure out exactly what's going on? Do you have all the papers?"

"Yes. I have them right here."

"Okay, then. There's a café down the hall, and there aren't many people in it. Let's go in there and take a look."

Eric looked over at Terry as he paced the floor of their Wilmington hotel room in. She was fast asleep. In the three days he had been in town, they had done some sightseeing, and seen a movie. They had also done a small investigation, and come up with a plan to get Jessie's money back from Bebe. Although neither Eric nor Terry wanted to, they were prepared to report her to law enforcement if she couldn't be persuaded any other way. But the plan that Eric, Guy, and a few other friends had come up with was a good one, and he thought Bebe would bite.

Eric crawled into bed next to Terry, but he didn't sleep much that night. They had a meeting with Bebe early the next morning, and a lot was hinging on the outcome.

# Thirty-three

Guy was filling his gas tank at a station a few blocks from his main gym. It was Sunday and he had spent almost a full day in his office, going over the books, looking around, trying to decide which capital improvements would give him the most bang for the buck. He had gotten some interesting perspectives from Eric. One good thing that had come out of his relationship with Neena was her introducing him to Eric. Theirs had become a good business, as well as personal, relationship.

This was the first time he had thought about Neena in a long time. When he called her after receiving the check for back dues, she was somehow different. He was feeling guilty for not responding to her messages that time when she seemed a little frantic. She never brought it up, though, and when he asked how she was, she said she had never been better.

He had been shocked when he got the check. It was so unlike Neena. She'd even sent a nice note with it.

Guy walked inside to pay for his gas. He couldn't believe all the time he was spending at his office these days. It wasn't like his business needed it. He was realizing more profits than ever before, but his business had been successful for years by anybody's standards.

The truth was, Guy was tired of the player scene. He had wanted to make Neena *the one,* but when he saw the relationship wasn't going anywhere, he tried to transmute those feelings to Andrea. And Andrea had thrown him.

Guy could spot a woman like Neena a mile away and know what he was getting into. After all, he had been a player too. But Andrea was different. She didn't have gold-digger genes. When he met her, he stopped playing, let down his guard, and so he didn't see it coming. There were no red flags, no gut feelings. And so he had missed the signs. He'd attributed Andrea's aloofness to her being British. But he had felt irritation that Judy was frequently invited to go out with them, even when Judy didn't have a date of her own.

He didn't mind so much at first. Two women? That's an ideal situation for most men. But he did question Andrea's wisdom in having an unattached woman with them so much. Why invite trouble? And besides, Judy's constant presence interfered with the intimacy Guy was trying to establish.

"Guy? I thought that was your car outside. How are you?"

Guy looked around to where the voice was coming from. He didn't recognize the woman, but she obviously knew him. Maybe she knew him from his gym.

"Guy, it's Neena."

"Neena? Oh hi, it is Neena. I didn't recognize you. You look so different."

The woman standing before him had her hair pulled back in a plain style, and she was wearing no makeup. On closer inspection, he saw that she was dressed in clothes that Neena would wear, except they weren't put together in the same way. The Neena he knew would have worn a tight-fitting sweater, but this Neena had on the tight sweater and another bulky sweater over it. And she had on sneakers with her jeans, rather than the platform shoes or stilettos, which was why she looked two inches shorter.

"Oh, yeah. I keep forgetting why people that I know don't seem to recognize me at first. So are you doing okay Guy?"

"Yeah. I've been working very hard lately, trying to stay at the top of my game."

"I'm sure you will do just that. You've done a fantastic job with your health clubs and you should be proud." She handed the attendant twenty dollars for her gas.

"Guy, I have to get going, but it was nice to see you again." She put her hand out and Guy shook it.

Guy stood in shock for a moment or two. He had to find out what was going on. He paid the attendant and hurried out after Neena.

"Neena, wait up." She was already in her car, but when he walked up she rolled the window down and looked up to hear what he had to say.

"I was wondering if you had plans for dinner, and if not, if you would have dinner with me."

"Guy, I'm sorry, I'm going to have to decline your invitation. I was actually on my way home to cook dinner for some neighbors of mine who've been sick and shut in. They aren't very old—the husband is in his mid sixties, and the wife in her late fifties, but they have some serious health issues. They take care of their nine-year old grandson. He's a sweet kid, but I'm afraid for him." Neena stopped talking for a few seconds.

"Guy, since I can't go to dinner with you, would you like to have dinner with me and the Craigs? I'd like for their grandson to meet you. I think that would be good for him."

"Sure. What time should I come?"

"Once I get home, it's going to take me about an hour to prepare everything. So, come in about ninety minutes. I'll see you then."

"What the hell is going on?" Guy was thinking. "Neena looking out for neighbors? Inviting me to dinner? And what's with the plain Jane look?"

Guy couldn't fool himself, though. True, he wanted to find out the reasons for Neena's transformation. But he had to admit he was still attracted to her. As a matter of fact, this Neena was more attractive to him than the old one. Maybe he had Andrea to thank for that, for his new appreciation for something other than the flashy and the glitzy.

He remembered the night that ended his relationship with Andrea. They had been at a bar—a threesome of course—when they ran into Seth. Seth was in his late twenties. He was a bartender and he tended bar at Andrea's restaurant. He greeted them all when they walked in, but he had a strange look on his face that Guy couldn't interpret.

Guy, Andrea, and Judy got a table and ordered some food. Then the two women got up and went to the ladies' room. Seth walked over to the table with a beer in his hand and sat down.

"Guy, my man. I've been meaning to talk to you ever since Andrea told me you own a couple of health clubs. I need a place to work out. You know I'm pushing thirty, so I've got to start taking better care of myself."

"Here, let me give you one of my cards." Guy reached into his pocket and then handed Seth a business card. "Give me a call and I'll set up a personalized tour for you. Yeah, come on in and I can set you up with a trainer, even, if you want. That's the best way to do it if you've never worked out, or if you haven't worked out in a long time."

"Okay. I'll do that. So, the girls are in the ladies' room, huh? You think they're getting it on in there, you know, like in one stall? What I'd like to know is, do they ever let you in on the action, or at least let you watch? I don't know, though. The type of relationship they have is not the kind to turn a man on, you know what I mean, with Judy playing the male role the way she does."

Guy stared at Seth for a full minute. When he spoke his voice was icy.

"Seth, what are you talking about? And whatever your explanation is, it had better be good."

Seth was nonplussed.

"You mean you didn't know?" He stood up and started backing away. "Look man, I didn't mean anything. Maybe I'm wrong. It's just that most people suspected. Hey, I'm sorry. I'm so sorry."

Seth went over to the bar, paid his tab, and left the bar. Guy always wondered whether that was Seth's way of telling him about Andrea's sexual orientation, or if he really didn't realize that Guy had been unaware.

When Andrea and Judy returned from the restroom, Guy looked at them in a new light. He looked at Andrea a long time.

"Seth came over to the table while you were in the restroom. Tell me, do you two like Seth?"

"Yeah. He seems like a nice person," Andrea said.

"I guess he's okay. I don't really know him that well," Judy said. "Why?"

"Well he made these accusations against the two of you. If he hadn't left the bar, we'd be fighting. Anyway, he said that I had it wrong, that you're not interested in me,

Andrea. Rather, you're interested in Judy here, and I'm just a front."

Guy kept his face very serious, and he kept his eyes on Andrea the whole time. She started to deny it, but her face told the truth. Judy reached over and put her hand over Andrea's.

"Don't," she said to Andrea. "Tell him the truth. He deserves to know the truth."

.

And that was how Guy found himself alone and brokenhearted again. Only this time, he couldn't find solace in being a player. Lord knows there were a lot of women at his gym who were willing. He wanted out of that life, though, so he started throwing himself into his work, so much so that he no longer took any days off, and most days were sixteen hours long. He contented himself with watching his bank account grow. He would find something to do with the money later.

Guy pulled up to his house and went inside. He thought about updating the place. Either that or buying a new house altogether. He could even do both. He certainly had enough money.

Guy's phone rang. It was Eric.

"Guy, I have a favor to ask of you. It's more like a business proposition. But it's going to take me some time to explain. Are you free right now?"

"Yes, I am. But I have to leave for dinner in an hour, so what we don't settle in that time, we can continue later."

"Fair enough."

Guy had no idea that Eric was indeed going to take the entire hour. But more than an hour had passed, and they were still going strong.

"What you've said sounds good to me, Eric. Count me in for two-hundred thou'. We can meet when you get back to work out the details. Now, I do have to run. My dinner is with Neena. When was the last time you saw her? You won't believe how she's changed. Good luck tomorrow."

Guy got off the phone, sat back, and closed his eyes. "What a difference a day makes," he thought. First he had a chance to become re-acquainted with a changed Neena, then Eric called and offered him an opportunity to buy into a company that would not only make him money, but also give him an opportunity to give back to the community. He got up, went out to his car, and headed to Neena's apartment.

"Life is good," he thought as he drove down the highway.

# Thirty-four

---

"Eric, how dare you come into my of fice asking me these questions about my business?" said Bebe. "Now, I don't know what Jessie told you, but he came in here like a crazy man demanding his money right away. I told him I would give it to him by the first of this week, which is a reasonable timeframe. But he stormed out of here. Well, I'm going to give him his money, but he no longer has a job with me. After all I've done for him, that's the gratitude I get."

"So then Bebe, am I hearing you say you're prepared to give Jessie his money today? "

"No, I can't get the check to him today, Eric. But I will get him his money."

"How much will the check be for, when you write it?"

"I don't have that information here in my office."

"But since you had a raving madman in your office last week asking for his money, didn't you start to process his request this weekend?"

"No, I didn't. I take most weekends off."

Eric looked at her. Bebe didn't flinch. Eric decided it was time to pull out the heavy artillery. He opened his briefcase.

"Bebe, Jessie gave me some papers to look at. Do you recognize these?" He held two up for her.

"Yes, of course I do. One is Jessie's statement of earnings, and the other is the sheet for donors to the scholarship fund to fill out." Now she seemed nervous.

"Uh-huh. And when I saw this, I thought these returns were incredible. I had my broker check them out so I could get in on the action. My broker sent me a report. The returns she found for the same period indicated on your statement, were not nearly as stellar. As a matter of fact, they were not at all stellar, but performed slightly above the major averages, which is not saying a lot in today's market."

He needed to take her a little further, and he needed to do it quickly before she could think of more stories. She had a sharp mind, and a keen ability to cover her tracks.

"I also studied your donor information sheet, Bebe. And I talked to two of the donors. It's very interesting how you've set that up. It would only take a government investigator about one hour to unravel what is going on, if you want to go that route. However, if you don't wish to go that route, I'm prepared to offer an alternative, and I don't think it's one you can afford to refuse."

Bebe took a deep breath. She knew he had her. She looked as if she started to offer an explanation, and then decided not to.

"Alright. Let's hear your proposal." Her voice was softer now, barely above a whisper.

"I convinced a group of investors to buy the scholarship service from you. We checked out similar companies and came up with a generous offer. We're prepared to offer you six-hundred thousand dollars, presuming you've paid Jessie back his initial investment plus interest amounting to a four percent annual return. If you cannot pay him back, the money will come out of the six-hundred thousand dollar figure."

Bebe seemed to be relieved. "Is that it?" she asked.

"Not quite. As a further condition of the deal, you will dissolve the investment part of your business. Now, we both know that you've been commingling money, and we're going to try to sort that out. But we're also going to insist that all of your clients' funds be liquidated, and they be given their honest returns. We're not going to require you to give them any amounts shown on a bogus statement, and these accounts don't have to be liquidated all at once. There will be a reasonable time period. But if you can't come up with the money, the six-hundred thousand dollars will have to go toward that. So you'd better start thinking, Bebe, if you need to sell a house or time share, or both."

"I'll have you know, Eric, that all of my clients will get paid."

"Well that's good. I hope it's true. Now I've drawn up the contract here. Look it over. Terry and I are going to wait in your conference room. Call me when you're done."

All this time, Terry had been sitting in the waiting room. She heard enough snatches of the conversation to know it had gone as planned. Eric came to her and they went into the conference room.

"She's going to sign it," Eric said once he and Terry were behind closed doors. "She knows it's a good deal. And the amount of money she has after it's done depends on how honest she's been. If she only started "borrowing" with Jessie's money, she'll be okay. Even if she misappropriated some of the donations intended for scholarships, she might do okay if she hid it well enough. But if she's been on a spending spree, then she's going to come out of this with nothing. I feel sorry for her, that she was so misguided, but she dug her own hole."

"Yeah. It's too bad. I keep thinking about how she helped Tyrone and Yolanda."

"I understand your sympathy, Terry. That took some skill to be able to locate those scholarships so quickly. So once everything is settled, if we see that Bebe is going to be destitute, we can always offer her a short-term position as consultant in the new company, just until she can get on her feet."

There was a knock on the door. Both Eric and Terry looked up, wondering if Bebe had changed her mind.

She stuck her head in the door. "I'm done," she said. "I've signed."

Eric got up and followed her out to the central office. "She must be utterly defeated," he thought. That was a good sign.

He sat down with Bebe, preparing to go over the documents. She surprised him by starting to talk, and before he left that day, he believed he had the whole story.

# EPILOGUE

*Two Years Later*

Tyrone drove up to the enclave of contemporary houses. He stopped before he reached Eric and Terry's house, pulled to the curb, and stopped. He checked the address he had written down.

"This is it," he said, and turned into Eric and Terry's driveway. He sat in the car for a moment, marveling at the path they had traveled.

Tyrone and Yolanda were planning to buy their own home here in Charlotte. Eric had put them in contact with his realtor neighbors. Once Tyrone got past their affectations, he found that they were more than competent. The Wallaces found a beautiful home in a nice neighborhood that he and Yolanda could afford.

Tyrone's brother Reginald was studying engineering at a college in Raleigh. Their mom refused to move south, saying she was in no frame of mind to learn a whole new way of life. With the boys on their own and doing well, she could now enjoy herself.

Tyrone walked to the front door and pressed one of the glass figures. He didn't puzzle over the doorbell as long as some of the other guests had, possibly because of his artistic genius.

"The maestro has arrived," Eric said with a big smile as he ushered Tyrone in and then hugged him. "Terry, honey, Tyrone's here," he said into the intercom. "She'll be down in a minute. She's been obsessing over that play all night and early this morning."

"It was her project—her brainchild. I'm grateful to be part of it."

"Come on into the family room. I have some people I want to introduce you to. Tyrone, this is Guy Pelham, a friend and business partner, along with his wife Neena. And as you can see, there is a little Guy or a Neenette in there incubating. Neena, Guy, this is Tyrone Brown, a friend of the family."

They all said their *nice to meet you's*, and made some small talk.

"Tyrone, sit down and make yourself at home. The restroom is down the hall. We're going to have lunch here around noon. Also, Bebe will be stopping by. I suggest you all hold on to your wallets as well as your common sense."

Everyone laughed except Neena. Eric noticed.

"I was just trying to make light of a serious situation. I hope no one was offended."

"I know you didn't mean any harm, Eric," said Neena. "It's just that I can identify with Bebe. Some people just get into a different mindset. I think most of them grow up with it. You think it's okay to take advantage of people. Unfortunately, it takes a tragedy for people to stop and examine what they do. I should know, because I was there, just not to the degree that Bebe was."

Guy put his arm around Neena's shoulder and kissed her.

"I was so shocked when I heard about that," Tyrone said. "I was sad because I will never forget the way she rescued Yolanda and me. Just how did her operation work?"

"In a nutshell, some of the donations that were made to the scholarship fund went into her personal business account. And on the investment side, when the overall market started to tank, she kept sending her clients good earnings statements

But she did do something that turned out to be quite smart. She took all of her investment money and put it in safe investments, like money market accounts and bonds backed by the government. That way, at least she wasn't losing any principal, and was earning some interest as well, just not as much as she claimed. I guess she was afraid that if she let her clients know their real returns, they would pull out."

Eric's pause here was dramatic, which was fitting, considering the reason for the assembly.

"And there were a few clients whose money she just used as a personal spending account. Those were the newer investors. She thought she would have time to make the money up before they were ready to pull out. Jessie was one of those clients."

"Wow. Well did she end up with nothing after she paid everybody back?"

"Actually, she didn't end up so badly. Most of her investors were small, from two thousand dollars to sixty thousand. Jessie was the biggest one. Anyway, because she hadn't been losing money in the market, she was able to pay everyone back and still have half of the money we'd paid her. She had to give up the Wilmington house, though."

"So it all ended fairly well," Guy said. "Eric introduced me to Jessie, and I've been able to help him get his health club established. It's starting to show some profit now."

"Tyrone, it's so good to see you," Terry said as she came down the stairs.

Tyrone looked up at her. She looked the same as when they lived next door to each other in Boston, except a little slimmer, and with much more confidence. As she came closer to embrace him, he saw that her eyes sparkled more brightly than ever.

"How are Yolanda and Kayla?"

"They're very well. Kayla is with her grandparents. We let them have her for a few weeks while we get settled here."

"Please let us know what we can do to help with the move," Eric said.

"Thanks, but you two have done too much already."

"Nonsense," Terry said. "Are you ready to get started?"

"I am. We've got a crew coming in to rehearse at three o'clock. You're going to love how it all comes together. And all of the shows have sold out."

"That's phenomenal. Now, since we have an audience right here, I say we use them. We can work right here and have them listen in and give feedback. Are you two willing?" Terry said to Guy and Neena.

"We're game."

Terry, Eric, and Tyrone sat together on the sofa. Terry placed the folders she was holding on the coffee table.

"I want to change what we've done with the letter," Terry began. "Oh, and let me explain to everyone about this letter. It is an eyewitness account from a black woman who was in Wilmington in1898 during the unrest and massacre. What I'd like to do is have a narrator read parts of it just before the second act. What do you think?"

"Let me take a look at the second act," Eric said. Terry handed him one of the folders. She and Tyrone looked on as he opened it:

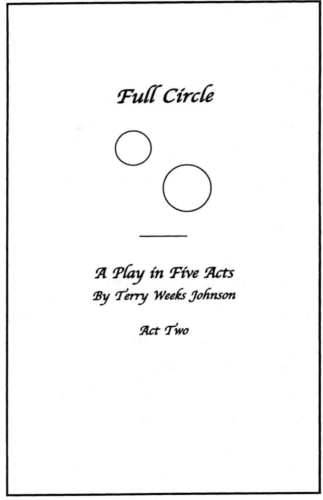

Both Terry and Eric nodded enthusiastically, so Tyrone began:

*Wilmington, North Carolina. November 13, 1898*

*William McKinley – president of the United States of America*

*Honorable Sir,*

*I a Negro woman of this city, appeal to you from the depths of my heart to do something in the Negro's behalf. The outside world only knows one side of the trouble here, there is no paper to tell the truth about the Negro here in this city or any other southern state. The Negro in this town had no arms (except pistols perhaps in some instances) to defend themselves from the attack of lawless whites. On the tenth, Thursday morning between eight and nine o'clock, when all Negro men had gone to their places of work, the white men .*[6]
*. .*

---

[6] <u>The National Archives</u>, Record Group No. 60.

Do you have comments about this book that you would like to share with the author?  Send correspondence to her at:

*Beatrice Joseph Publishing*
*Attn:  Sheila Kinston Dean*
*P. O. Box 191383*
*Boston, MA  02119*

# Know someone who would enjoy reading this book?  Please give us contact information:

**Name**_____
**Address:**
(Street Address)
_____

(City)_____(State)_____(Zip)_____

**Phone:**_____ Email:_____


**Name**_____
**Address:**
(Street Address)
_____

(City)_____(State)_____(Zip)_____

**Phone:**_____ Email:_____


**Your Name:**_____
**Your Address:**
(Street Address)
_____

(City)_____(State)_____(Zip)_____

**Your Phone:**_____Your email:_____

May we say that you recommended _Full Circle_?  ☐ Yes          ☐ No

Send this form to:   Beatrice Joseph Publishing
                     ▣  Fax  617 427-3165   or
                     ▣  P O Box 191383, Boston, MA  02119

# Order Form

**Fax orders**:  617-826-3400.  Complete this form.

**Telephone orders**:  Call 1 - 866 FUL-CRKL (1- 866 - 385-2755).
Have credit card ready.

**Postal Orders**:  Beatrice Joseph Publishing, P. O. Box 191383,
Boston, MA  02119  USA

*Please print:*
Your Name_____

Address_____

City_____State_____Zip_____

Telephone_____

Email_____

| Qty | Description | Price |
|-----|-------------|-------|
|  | *Full Circle*    $24.95 each | $ |
|  |  |  |
|  | MA residents add 5% sales tax → |  |
|  | Shipping* (*$4.95 for 1st book, $3 ea. additional book) → |  |
|  | **Order Total** → |  |

Payment enclosed:  ☐ Check      ☐ Money Order

Please charge my:  ☐ Visa   ☐ MasterCard   ☐ AMEX   ☐ Discover

Card number:_____

Name on card:_____Exp.Date:_____

Make checks payable to **Beatrice Joseph Publishing**.  Allow 4 weeks
for delivery.